ALSO BY

LAURA HARRINGTON

FICTION
Alice Bliss

THEATRE
The Perfect 36
N (Bonaparte)
Joan of Arc
Martin Guerre
Crossing Brooklyn
Resurrection
Hallowed Ground

A CATALOG
OF BIRDS

Laura Harrington

A CATALOG
OF BIRDS

Europa
editions

Europa Editions
214 West 29th Street
New York, N.Y. 10001
www.europaeditions.com
info@europaeditions.com

Library of Congress Cataloging in Publication Data is available
ISBN 978-1-60945-403-6

Harrington, Laura
A Catalog of Birds

Book design by Emanuele Ragnisco
www.mekkanografici.com

Cover photo © shaun/iStock

Prepress by Grafica Punto Print—Rome

Printed in the USA

Grateful acknowledgment is made to Matt Adrian
for permission to quote from his paintings and titles:
It Had Seemed Such Innocent Pleasure, copyright © 2011;
Had I But Hands to Put Around Your Throat, copyright © 2012; and
The Unsung Magnificence of Half-Remembered Songs, copyright © 2011.

CONTENTS

PROLOGUE - 13

FEBRUARY 1970 - 17

MARCH - 72

APRIL - 108

MAY - 160

JUNE - 217

ACKNOWLEDGMENTS - 261

ABOUT THE AUTHOR - 263

For my brothers, Kevin and Tim
And my nephew, Ted

A CATALOG
OF BIRDS

PROLOGUE

Nell claims the taller maple, scrambles up higher than her brother. Eight, she is fearless and fast, laughing, egging him on. In the upper branches that bend beneath their weight, they lean and push to make the trees sway, riding the supple limbs. Billy is a daredevil, swinging by his hands, legs churning the air. Nell imitates him and creates such a snap she loses her grip. A lower limb breaks her fall, knocking the wind out of her.

Billy is hollering before he reaches her. She wants to say: don't shout, it hurts me, but has no breath. Opens her eyes, he swims before her, the tree above quivering green. She tries to sit up, can't, blood drips from her nose. Shakes her head to try to clear it, more blood.

It is soft in the grass, the damp already seeping into her shirt. Billy, frantic, are you hurt, runs his hands over her arms and legs, looking for broken bones. Why does he keep asking her that? Didn't she answer him? She tries to think what happened. Was it an hour ago? Longer?

Billy swears under his breath, wipes the blood from her face, shhh, shhh, he says, as if she is crying, but she doesn't think she is. Why doesn't it hurt yet? She feels as if she is floating, that she could float away into the sky, and he is holding her to the earth. She would like to put her arms around him but her limbs won't do her bidding. She would like to listen to his heartbeat, rest there.

She moves her hand, finally, to her face, searching for her

glasses. Gone. There is a deep cut above her eye. Why can't she talk? She rolls to one side, vomits, coughs. Billy gets his hands under her, drags her away.

"Not a fair fight," he says. She tries to smile at him. There's blood all over his hands. "Mom's gonna kill me."

"We won't tell her," she manages to croak. Lifts a hand to her throat, "Why can't I . . . ?"

"Got the wind knocked out of you. Bruised your ribs maybe. Windpipe."

It seems ages before she can sit up, propped against the trunk. Billy goes to the stream for water, uses his T-shirt, works in circles swabbing her face and neck, the cuts and scrapes on both arms and legs.

Shuts her eyes, opens them, wants her hated glasses, knows she's in for it, having wrecked them. Are both eyes working, she needs to ask, but can't put words to that fear. Did she really feel broken glass? Longs for the comfort of their secret language, a magic circle that kept everyone else out, until she had to give it up to go to school. She had to wait three years to follow her big brother onto that yellow bus; she would have promised anything.

Maybe he'll sing to her. Her head droops, she topples again. He's not much of a singer. Not like Brendan or Sheila or their father. Still.

She puts her head in his lap.

"Sing," she commands.

He wipes his nose, tries to push the bloody hair off her face. The birds are making a racket.

"Can't compete with that," he says.

"Sing."

He sings until she sleeps. Lets her be. She's got to get her legs under her. It's a long way home. Canada warbler overhead. He imitates its call, then whistles back and forth with a blackbird.

The blood scares him. He keeps forgetting how little she is. He touches the wound. It's a nasty gash, pieces of glass above her eye, needs tweezers, a bandage, maybe stitches.

Nose seems to be intact. Her skin is cold. He cups his hands around her face.

He'll be beaten for this even though his father doesn't have the heart or the stomach to beat his kids. A trial and a cross.

She'll be teased at school for being clumsy even though she's anything but. Always a little apart, too serious for other children; too wild for other girls. Except for Megan Alsop who has no sense when it comes to danger and will do anything to impress him. Strip naked when other girls lift a skirt or pull down their shorts behind the barn. Turning slowly, that sweet little kid body, freckles all over her chest, until her father catches them, just about jerks her arm out of its socket as he hustles her inside. They can hear the strap he uses on her bare bottom. Counting the blows before they disappear into the woods. Not a sound out of her.

Nell moans, wakes, the sun low in the sky. The walk to the lake is long, how can it be so far, her feet, flap, flapping like clown's feet, they hardly seem to belong to her. Everything hurts. It's hard to take a deep breath, when she does something stabs her chest, grips and lets go. Her head aches; the wound above her eye is on fire.

She keeps lagging behind, not realizing, eyes on the ground, until she looks up, can't see him, tries to call out, her voice still not working right. Stops twice, woozy. Feels Billy's impatience, the dark falling fast.

He waits for her, takes her hand. "Almost there," he says. How can he find the way, she wonders. He always knows the way.

Tucker's Point, finally; the boat hidden in the weeds. She's swaying on her feet as he rights the rowboat, steadies her as she climbs in. She curls up on the lifejackets in the stern, watches him row. Sees for the first time that he's scared.

Stars glitter, smudged without her glasses. The lake is a mirror, the wooded shore black and unbroken. The oars grind and splash; he's working hard, breathing hard.

The pain fades in and out, she feels absolved and free, content to skim the water with her brother, the earth turning, sun gone, moon rising, the boat rocking, rocking. As if it doesn't matter which way is home or if they will ever get there.

FEBRUARY 1970

T he last thing he remembers: two grunts and a stretcher materializing through a covering shroud of white phosphorus, getting crammed into a chopper full of the dead and dying, the medic finally stabbing him with morphine. He doesn't regain consciousness until the sixth day on the hospital ship. A blessed blankness while his burned skin peels away from half his upper body, leaving pain in its wake no narcotic can touch.

Was it mercy or a mistake to have hauled him off that mountaintop? He woke fifty miles from shore in the South China Sea with the scent of his father in the bed beside him: cigarette smoke, Old Spice, the sensation of being held against Jack's chest.

Billy had been sure he would die on that ship. Prayed for it some days when the pain stripped him of hope and dignity, his spirit diving into the sea to escape; the lure of water, colder and colder as he descended, becoming a slow, silken creature of the deep; fins and gills and unblinking eyes.

The transfer to the Army hospital in Japan: the bruising landing, the shock of December cold. He'd passed out as he was moved from the stretcher to a bed, IVs taped back into place, his body like a side of beef, waiting for the next round of surgeons and the next as they set and reset bones in his forearm, elbow, shoulder, picking out shrapnel with each surgery, waiting, always waiting for the specialist to arrive and begin to reassemble what's left of his hand.

He'd survived long enough to be wheeled into this hallway, club-footed Sam dialing the phone, negotiating with the operator.

The second he hears Nell's voice he can see her: jeans and boots, almost eighteen, no longer a kid. Sunlight spilling across the beat-up linoleum in the kitchen, her schoolbooks piled on the table, an apple, an orange, Jack's red plaid scarf around her neck, Flanagan waiting on the porch to go out.

Maybe he should've held on to that Saint Christopher medal she'd given him. He'd worn it looped around his neck with his dog tags. His first sight of the sea in Vietnam, he'd waded in, pulled the medal over his head, touched it with his lips for luck, and dropped it into the water. The water flat calm, soupy, shimmering in the heat. Jets taking off from Tan Son Nhut, a radio wailing on the beach, barbecue and diesel washing over him. Somehow there was cold beer, USDA hamburger flown in from God knows where, soldiers dancing in their skivvies, running into the sea, sunburned and stoned, taking a break from the war before heading back into the jungle.

How often he thinks of Nell on the day she fell from the tree, falling asleep beside her, waking to find her staring at him, face drawn, the pain registering. No whining, not a word of complaint. Struggling to her feet, one sneaker missing. How calm she was, retreating deep inside herself like the soldiers do. In shock or stoic, they endure the running, jostling panic as they are loaded on stretchers, carried onto the medevac chopper or simply boosted or shoved aboard, the scream of its rotor blades the sound of salvation.

How many die on his ship; he promises himself not to count. Focus on the bird, getting in, getting out. He gets a reputation, doesn't want one. Don't call him lucky, don't call him anything, draw no attention to the bubble he flies within. Illusion, faith, skill, sooner or later it will shatter, like the glass they picked out of the skin around Nell's eye. Another millimeter, their mother kept saying, just a fraction of an inch and she would have lost that eye.

In the hospital hallway, he looks at his hands. His mind hits a snag every single time. Reaches to hang up the phone, drops the receiver. It swings on its black cord, banging against the wall.

He wants a cigarette, wonders if he'll ever roll a smoke again. Looks out at the lights dotting the parking lot, a dog sniffing the perimeter of the fence. From this vantage point the hospital looks like what it feels like: a prison compound.

He must've fallen asleep. The dial tone grows louder, or begins again, changes to a thin wail that wakes him. Out the window the shifts are changing, the able-bodied walking to their cars. Soldiers stir in the rooms behind him, waking to the news of their losses over and over.

It's time to piss off home.

The VA hospital in Syracuse is a sprawling, shabby redbrick building. Yesterday's snow still fills the parking lot; the walkways are rutted with ice. The facade appears to weep in the weak sun, snowmelt from the roof and broken gutters.

Nell pushes through the revolving door, her mother's fury trailing her. Billy insisting that she come alone, her mother relegated to the parking lot. Nell wonders how long she'll last. Waiting is not Marion's strong suit. Billy always puts her in the middle: the chosen one and the buffer, too.

The hospital is hot and airless. She unzips Billy's hunting jacket, waits at the information desk. It smells musty and damp; the hallways, half-lit, stretch forever. Catches a glimpse of a girl exiting through the door at the opposite end of the building, a boy's watch cap hiding her hair. Megan? It can't be Megan; how would she even know Billy is home?

The man who finally appears can't find Billy Flynn.

"Admitted last night," she tells him, "from Japan."

He shuffles folders.

"Burned. Where's the burn unit?"

He runs his finger down the list of floors and departments. Finally: "Floor 6. South Side."

Nell takes the elevator, follows the arrows to the South Side, walks through corridors with soldiers waiting everywhere: in wheelchairs, on gurneys. Those who are awake watch her pass. The doors to all the rooms are open. She's afraid to look inside, can't stop herself. Boys missing arms, legs. She stops looking, looks at the floor instead.

The smell is overpowering: bleach, urine, vomit.

Two soldiers in wheelchairs, arms and hands intact, chase each other down the corridor, shouting. A radio, something about a radio. They will not be stopped, no matter who yells at them.

Nell flattens herself against the wall as they flash past. The soldier on the gurney beside her reaches for her hand. His bandage covers the top of his head, one eye, his jaw. The gauze is pink with blood, frothy, the sheet soaked. She lets him grip her hand, then turns to him.

"What's your name?"

He licks his lips. "Scotty."

"Are you waiting for surgery?"

"Just waiting." His voice is scratchy.

"I have to go. My brother is here."

"Come back. Come see me."

The burn unit is through a set of double doors. First impression: it's so much quieter than the ward she just walked through. She takes a breath, tries to calm the panic she feels. Intermittent moans, cries. The crash of a metal pan.

A wife visiting in high heels and lipstick, purse held tight against her belly, stops next to Nell, coat over one arm, eyes darting. Wearing her best dress, the one for church or maybe

Friday nights, slim gold band on her left hand, hair flipped and lacquered. How'd she get through all that snow in those heels? Where's her mother? What made her think she could face this alone?

Nell finds Billy's room, crowded with six beds. She takes shallow breaths against the smells, tries to reconcile the thin, bandaged man pinned to the bed with the exuberant animal Billy has been all his life. Thinks, then, of building wings together; their stubborn belief that if they could just solve the practical problems, they'd be able to fly.

The side of his face, his neck and ear are bandaged in gauze and an elaborate dressing covers his hand, arm, shoulder, and torso. It's his right hand. No, she thinks. *No.* She slips between two beds to reach him, careful not to jostle the other soldiers. Registers that one of them is dead, eyes staring, mouth open.

Billy is asleep. She rests her hand on his chest, afraid to hurt him, needing to touch him, to reassure herself that he is breathing.

His heartbeat is slow. There's an IV in his good arm, delivering fluids, morphine? The bag is nearly empty. She hears water spilling to the floor, turns to see urine pooling beneath the bed by the window, the collection bag overflowing.

He opens his eyes. "Nell."

He is so pale he seems to come from another world.

"I want to hug you, but I don't want to hurt you . . . " she says.

"Plenty of time for that."

He looks at her, assessing the changes, she knows, noticing everything.

"Your hair like that," he says. "I wish I could draw you."

"Quit it."

"It's your neck."

"What's wrong with my neck?"

"You're like a fucking swan."

"A freak of nature, then."

"Just don't tell me how *I* look."

"You look good to me."

"At least I'm not in a box," he says, which makes them both laugh. "How'd you manage Mom?"

"She's in the parking lot."

"How's Megan?"

"She's good."

"Did you tell her I'm back?"

"Not yet. I thought . . . "

"Boyfriend?"

"He's a jerk. It's . . . "

"It can't be serious."

"No." He doesn't need to know it's been going on since September.

"There's something you're not telling me."

"She's running with a different crowd."

"Megan?" He tries to sit up, can't. "Tell her I want to see her."

"Okay."

"Water over the dam, Nell, you tell her."

"I will."

He shuts his eyes against the pain. He is whiter than the sheets he lies on, as though his blood has turned to water, losing color and the power to heal. It about kills her that she can't take the hurt away.

As darkness begins to fall, Nell thinks about standing in that kitchen in East Syracuse more than a year ago: the same watery half-light; the same sense of being suspended in time; something begun, but not yet finished.

Nell and Megan walk the length of Dorset Street, the end

of summer air hot and heavy. Tended yards give way to broken toys, discarded machine parts, busted streetlights. Cars spill their guts in rutted driveways. A woman hisses at them from her porch as if she knows their business.

"You sure this is the right street?" Nell asks. "It's further than you said."

A massive dog stands, head heavy, feet splayed, the chain around its neck rusted and rattling.

"You scared?"

Megan doesn't respond. The dog growls, tests the length of his chain.

"Did Helen Palmer tell you anything?" Nell asks.

The roll of cash falls out of Megan's bra again. An impossible sum. Nell snatches it up and shoves it into her pocket. Megan starts to laugh, then quits.

"It would be nice to know something," Nell says.

"Nice? You gonna write a lab report?"

"What if something goes wrong? What if . . . ?"

"Shut up."

"How long does it take? Does it hurt?"

"Of course it hurts."

"Billy . . . "

"Is a million miles away."

"You need to tell him."

"I'm not discussing this with you."

"Did you use protection?"

Megan lets the question hang in the air.

There are no lights on outside the house as they make their way to the back door. They wait on the porch for long minutes before the woman lets them into the kitchen.

She is older than Nell expected, older than her mother, wire thin, wiping her hands on a towel. She pours a drink, sits at the table, unlocks a moneybox. Looks at Megan expectantly. No greeting, no small talk. There are dirty dishes piled in the sink, a congealed pan on the stove. The house smells of cigarettes and cat.

Nell watches the woman's hands, counting Megan's money, and wants to bolt.

"It's all there," Megan says.

"That's what all you girls say."

She stands, moneybox under her arm, says to Nell: "You wait here. Don't touch anything."

Megan follows her out of the room, won't let herself look back.

Nell stands in the dirty kitchen, thinking about blood and tissue, a collection of cells, her brother's cells, the lab at school, dissecting a pregnant cat, then the embryos, each sac heavy with possibility. Sweet sixteen, what a joke, this is the worst year of her life.

She walks down the dark hall, moving silently as Billy has taught her, places her hands on the doorframe. She needs to be here for Megan, for Billy. She wants and does not want to be inside that room.

Megan takes off her skirt and underpants as instructed while the woman washes her hands. Smells ammonia, blood, her own sweat. Looks for a sheet. Sees the instruments on top of a chest of drawers, jumbled in a glass baking dish; the alcohol bath sharp in the air.

She climbs on to the improvised operating table, wishing for something to look at: a picture, a window; wishes for Nell, wishes for her mother when the procedure begins. The cold speculum, the woman's rough hands; the lamp she brings close.

"This is going to hurt."

Gripping the edge of the table, she whispers to herself: I don't care, over and over.

"Be still, now!"

She feels sick. How could any of this: the rusted lamp, the metal bucket on the floor, the warm gush of blood, have anything to do with Billy and what they'd done every chance they got?

Why isn't there a sheet, something, a towel to cover herself? Is this part of the anger she feels radiating from this woman, who did not ask her name or share her own, yet here she is scraping out—

"Is everything okay?" Megan asks.

"Think I can see the future, lookin' up here between your legs? Start using what's between your ears or you'll be pregnant again before I can spit. And just so you know: Ain't nothin' going up there for six weeks. You hear me? Nothin'."

Megan cranes her neck to look at the woman as she pulls out the wand, removes the speculum.

"You're gonna ache and you're gonna flow, like you've got a real bad period. Three days, four, that's normal. You get fever, you start vomiting, losing more blood; you go to the doctor. If the doctor's closed, you don't wait til morning, you go straight to the hospital. They ask you what happened, you had a miscarriage: cramps, clots. You don't know my name; you already forgot my address. You got that?"

"You have kids?" Megan asks.

"That's none of your business."

"A daughter?"

"Your friend out there, she's gonna stay with you tonight." It was not a question. "Tomorrow you stay in bed. Make up some lie. Looks like you're good at that."

She opens the door, brushes past Nell. Nell sees the slop bucket, a vivid swipe of blood on the floor, the mess of being a girl.

Walking to the bus station Megan is giddy with relief. She wants to run, pretend, forget; cuts her eyes away every time she feels Nell watching her. She does not want to talk, to make this moment real by naming it. She's craving something, anything to bury this night. *When's Billy's next leave? She'll never tell him; they'll never tell him, right, Nell? It's over. It never happened.*

The dark of Dorset Street gives way to the lights of lower Main, the bars and pool halls, soldiers spilling onto the street. So many boys, and every mother's son of them wants Megan. They crowd around her, offer drinks, a ride, a burger, propose marriage, a weekend, a dance. Bring your friend, they say, uninterested in the awkward, too tall Nell, but willing to do just about anything to get their hands on Megan. She laughs and says no. You can't blame them for thinking she means yes. That killer smile.

Megan walks through the door at the bus station and pauses.

"Are you okay?" Nell asks.

"I want a beer."

"You can't. You're . . . "

"Watch me."

She is thin, pale, her skin chalky, but even in the fluorescent light her red hair sparks. She wades into a new group of soldiers; they eddy around her like a school of fish. Megan does the choosing: this one, not that one, changes her mind, chooses again. Leaves the station.

Nell tries to stop her. Megan dances away, arm in arm with her soldier, laughing, nearly running, like a kid let out of school. Angry, Nell waits in the doorway, watches the clock. The last bus home is already idling in its bay.

A soldier approaches: stiff new fatigues, shiny boots, razor burns and acne, hair so short, so badly cut, he looks like a shorn sheep. Did they do this to her brothers? Is it any better in the Army? What does better mean?

He starts talking. Southern accent. Skinny as he is, his voice is rich. If he sang he'd be a baritone.

"Where you from?"

"Geneva."

"Where's that?"

"About forty minutes from here."

"You waitin' on your friend?"

"I am."

"Could be awhile."

"I know."

This boy wants to touch her, the way Billy touches Megan, the way she wishes Harlow would touch her and never has. But even that isn't true. He wants to touch a girl, any girl, and she just happens to be in front of him.

He buys two sodas; they lean against a dirty wall. His unit is headed for Vietnam. He's a radio operator, says he wants to open a shop when he gets home: radios and television, sales and service. Says he has a girlfriend. Only sixteen. Isn't sure she'll wait for him. Two years. Anything could happen. It's a lot to ask a girl.

"You love her?" Nell asks.

"Since first grade."

"You think you'll make it?"

He looks at her, surprised. "Mostly we don't talk about that."

"But you think about it."

"Try not to."

He asks if he can hold her hand. So polite it's hard to say no. Asks, then, if he can kiss her.

"It's not me you want to kiss," she says.

"You'd be surprised," he says, leaning in to her.

His lips are sticky with Coca-Cola, his breath sugary. She pulls away.

He shoves her, hard, hisses: *You little bitch!* And walks away.

Megan appears, extricates herself from the soldier, sloppy now, he doesn't want to let her go. She grabs Nell by the hand, runs up the steps to the bus, a cold beer hidden inside her shirt. Chooses a seat in back where the driver can't see them.

"What'd you do with that soldier?" Nell asks.

"Went to the liquor store."

"And?"

"Bought a few beers."

"And?"

"And nothing."

"He's just a nice guy?" Those sudden spots of color on Megan's cheeks. "I don't understand you."

"C'mon. A couple kisses. What's the big deal?"

"Billy . . ."

"Is never gonna know anything about this night."

"Megan . . ."

Megan looks at Nell for a long moment, eyes swimming. She leans against her, rests her head on Nell's shoulder, "Don't be mad at me, Nellie," and falls asleep before Nell can answer.

Nell digs Billy's latest letter from her pocket. He's heading for flight school. Hours and hours in the sky. A full year of training after he completes Basic. Four hundred helicopter pilots graduating every month. To replace four hundred helicopter pilots who . . . ? Nell can't complete the thought. Billy's excitement. The language: birds, choppers, airborne. Her brother will be airborne.

On the back of the letter, a sketch of a scarlet tanager with the caption:

It Had Seemed Such Innocent Pleasure.

The bus is half empty. They'll head to the boathouse, see if they can sneak inside to sleep, to complete the lie of the slumber party at Janet Sims's house, the last hurrah before school begins on Monday.

Nell's stomach grumbles. If only they had a few bucks for breakfast. The bus pulls in, doors wheeze open. She wakes Megan for the long trek to the boathouse.

Standing next to Billy's hospital bed, Nell knows it's too easy to blame Megan, but she can't let it go; wonders if she'll ever let it go. She shakes off the memory, crosses to the window where an American Redstart huddles in the cold. Coal black with vivid orange patches on its sides, wings, and tail. Much too soon to be this far north.

She feels a shadow pass over her, dark and cold. She doesn't believe in luck, in signs or omens. Or does she?

Marion Flynn follows the surgeon to a pair of chairs in a busy hallway, so alarmed by his youth it's hard to concentrate on what he's saying. Good lord, she thinks, he's still having trouble with his skin.

"Are you an intern?" She asks.

"No, I'm not."

"You look like an intern."

"I get that a lot."

"Are you in charge of my son's care?"

"I am."

"Do I call you Don or Doctor Dienst?"

"Doctor Dienst will be fine."

"You can call me Mrs. Flynn."

"I was intending to."

He opens Billy's file. Thick. Dark green. Marion looks for an ashtray. In a pinch, a metal wastebasket will do. Pulls out a pack of cigarettes.

"Do you mind if I . . . " she asks while striking a match.

"I'm afraid I do. Mind."

She narrows her eyes at him, but he misses the intended effect, having already gone back to the file. Son of a bitch, she thinks, blowing out the match. How is she supposed to cope without her husband or one of her daughters? It's too much. Anyone with a shred of sense would know that. Is he stupid? They'll need to replace him if he's stupid.

"What did they teach you in medical school?" she asks.

"Excuse me?"

"About how to deal with distraught parents of wounded or damaged children?"

"I don't . . . " He tries to retreat to the file again, she holds his gaze.

"There's not a unit on making eye contact, touching a shoulder, offering a cup of tea or a glass of water? Though why would there be? Your own mother would have taught you these things."

"Mrs. . . . " He looks at the file again. "Flynn . . . "

Oh, God, he's going to tell me he's shy or has a speech impediment of some kind.

"Let's talk about your son."

Nell is waiting in the hall when Marion appears. She braces herself before going into the room. Billy is asleep or just plain gone with the new morphine drip that finally arrived after repeated requests. Marion stands beside the bed, one hand wrapped around his good arm, the other resting lightly on his chest. She touches his hair, his lips. Nell sees her head snap up as she begins to register the smells, the crusted bandages, the dead soldier still lying in the room, waiting to be moved to the morgue.

"Let's go home," she says, joining Nell in the hall. "There's nothing we can do for him right now."

"I'm not leaving him alone."

"I don't want to argue with you."

"What's wrong with this place? It's not . . . It's like a warehouse. Is there another VA hospital? A better one? In Rochester, maybe. Can we move him there?"

"One thing at a time."

"When Dad sees this . . . "

"Can you drive? I don't think I can . . . "

"I'm staying, Mom."

"How will you get home?"

"The bus."

"School?"

"I'll be a little late."

Marion opens her wallet, hands Nell a five-dollar bill.

"Find something to eat." A quick hug. "Call your sister."

"Sheila's not home. I called her school. She took a few days off to go to the city. Protest march, I think."

"I hear that kind of thing, I feel like my head is going to explode."

"She might have a point, you know."

"Don't ask me to be reasonable. Not today."

Nell locates the cafeteria after getting lost twice in the warren of hallways that wind through the basement. Closed. Finds a few vending machines near the elevators. Searches her pockets for change, enough for a candy bar.

Back on Billy's wing a janitor is slowly washing the floor, hands twisted with arthritis. He makes his way into Billy's room, mops up the mess, then draws the sheet over the face of the dead soldier.

"Where are all the nurses?" Nell asks.

"Sixty-four-thousand-dollar question, kid. Two nurses quit yesterday. First job. Right out of school. Scared to death. Happens all the time."

She carries a chair into the room and sits beside her brother. Tries to comfort him when he thrashes in his sleep. Wonders just how bad it is under all those bandages.

Leaving the hospital the next morning, Nell, groggy, gets

turned around. Ends up walking past the neurosurgical inten-
sive care unit where soldiers are paralyzed from the neck
down. Meets a guy coming off shift, lighting a cigarette as soon
as he gets outside. His face is empty, eyes worst of all.

He searches his pockets, unearths a pill bottle. Reads the
label, offers it to her. She shakes her head. He pops the top off
the bottle, fumbles, pills go flying, scattered in the snow and
slush.

"Shit," he scrapes up a handful of snow, crams it in his mouth.

"What are you doing?"

He counts the pills that are left, swallows three, four, five.

"Hey! What is that?" she asks.

"Slow me down, help me sleep. And then I've got these,"
he produces another bottle, "to keep me up all night. Up,
down, round and round."

"Where'd you get those?"

"Where do you think?"

"It's crazy in there."

"Boyfriend?"

"Brother."

"Where is he?"

"The burn unit."

"Get him out of there. They've got a lousy mortality rate.
Almost as bad as ours." He laughs. Catches himself. Tries to
stop, can't.

"Sorry," he says.

"Who are you?"

"Orderly. Flunked out of med school. Actually got booted
out. A little drug problem as you can see. Medical leave, they
call it. That's funny, right? VA had no problem with my record.
Nobody wants this job. They die at night. Wait all day and then
die on my shift. I can't take it anymore."

He lights another cigarette, eyes getting dreamy, face going
soft.

"The mothers come, the teenage wives, the sisters. They're a complete mess. The kid in the bed's gotta endure all that: the tears, the touch he can't feel. The fathers come in and it's worse. They can't look at their sons. Big men. Working men.

"Kid goes through all that. And dies on my shift. It's fucked. You wanna come home with me?"

"No, thanks."

He orients toward the parking lot, puts himself in gear.

"You okay to drive?" she asks.

"Oh, yeah. Do it all the time. " He gives her a woozy smile. "What's your name?"

"Nell."

"Allie. Alistair. But that's a stupid name."

He has a nice smile. Straight teeth. Braces, maybe, with a name like that.

"Get your brother out of here," he says, suddenly serious. "Whatever it takes."

The bus to Geneva is full and so overheated she feels carsick. She can't face school. The long walk home calms her stomach at least. She wishes Harlow Murphy would drive by, give her a ride, stop ignoring her, stop treating her like a kid, tell her everything's gonna be all right, even though it's a lie.

At home she climbs the stairs, pinches the bridge of her nose, eyes prickling. She feels that old thudding ache in her chest, hears crows rasping outside. *Cry it out*, her mother's oft-heard advice, but whatever is grappling around inside of her feels too big. Her brother in that hospital bed, a fist in her throat, tears threatening to ambush her.

She opens the door to Billy's room; lies down on his too-neat bed, the walls alive with his paintings and drawings. Her gaze sweeps the room, the jars full of colored pencils, paintbrushes, feathers of all kinds. Nests, lichen-starred branches, reindeer moss on the windowsills, eggs of every size and shape and color, the *Encyclopedia Britannica*, borrowed from downstairs, never returned. Sketches of birds large and small, in piles on his desk. She reaches to touch the bird beside the bed, follows the gaze of the great blue heron, poised, ready to strike.

Megan hesitates before boarding the bus to a place she's never been before, hesitates before accepting a ride with a stranger. Thinking of Billy, that horrible hospital, all those wrecked young men and boys. She's in flight, in flight from it all.

Remembers Billy's last leave. A year of training under his belt. Three days at home before shipping out to Vietnam. Both of them in the grip of something: anticipation, fear, the unknown.

And she is walking down that rutted drive again in the failing light, biology textbook under her arm; a prop to the lie of studying for a test with Nell. The ponies call to her from the pasture, skittish, dancing in the dark, keyed up by her unexpected nearness. She sends the dog back to the barn twice.

Waiting beneath the purple beech tree, the Indian summer warmth leaching from the day, cool air rushing in from the lake, exhaling from the woods. She should have brought a jacket. Billy will warm her up.

She feels exceptionally awake, the anticipation of touch and taste singing inside her. She is breathless and sad. Wanting him an ache so loud, so persistent, how is it possible no one else can see it or hear it? Every feeling amplified by the fact of his leaving, by the fact of a year away, all that has happened that they do not talk about. Part of her wants to peel away the secrets, confess, be comforted and forgiven. Maybe one day.

She sees the truck headlights threading up the lane, down

the service road, across the railroad tracks. Billy opens his door, she climbs up and into his lap, discards her textbook, it falls to the floor, forgotten. His arms around her, he pulls back onto the road.

All the wanting in the world can't keep him here, she thinks.

"Where do you want to go?" He asks.

"Someplace close. I have to be back by 10."

She can feel the anger in him; a sharp bolt of tension runs up her own spine.

"How about right here, then?" He makes as if to turn into a driveway.

"Funny."

"Side of the road?"

"Don't be thick," she says, then, "Turn here."

The dirt track leads them up a hill to a boarded up farmhouse. The headlights sweep neglected fields, broken fences, come to rest on a sagging porch.

"How come you know about this place?"

"Nell and I like to ride up here. You skirt the woods above our farm, cross Mill Creek, and after another mile or so, come down through that stand of poplars. We'd let the ponies graze and sit on the railing. Pretend like it belonged to us."

Stepping onto the porch they hear small animals scurrying away. The red-orange moon tilts into view above the hills opposite. It's cold. Maybe too cold. Billy pulls her against him, wraps his jacket around her, suddenly tender, surprising her, as he always does, that sweetness just below the surface.

"We could buy this place."

"Sure we could," she laughs.

"I've got some money saved up. I'll be getting hazard pay with nothing to spend it on but cigarettes and beer. We could have a down payment, maybe."

"I'll be in college, Billy. And so will you."

"After, then. But we could get started, that's all I'm saying. Get a stake."

"Share the house with Nell and Harlow. Split the costs. And the work."

"One of us would need a real job, income to pay expenses while we got up and running. I could get my commercial pilot's license."

"I'm gonna want horses, you know. Great big draft horses. They've still got the old plows and harrows in that barn. Harnesses, too."

"Whatever you want."

"Promise me," she says, suddenly serious.

"Anything."

He kisses her, pulling at her clothes; whatever separates them. Unzips her pants, eases her down on the rough boards, their clothes jumbled beneath them. He unbuttons her shirt, impatient, tears the buttons.

She tries to grab her jeans, there's a condom in the pocket, and he's inside her, his mouth on her neck. She wants to give in, let go. He looks at her, says her name: Megan, Megan, wonder in his voice, in his touch, what passes between them overwhelms her, like ice, like electricity. "Billy. Stop. The condom." He pins her arms over her head, watching her. There is a recklessness she almost wants to surrender to. He'll pull out before he climaxes; she reassures herself, fear gripping her. The sounds he makes when he comes, choked, sad somehow, like a wounded animal.

She's angry then, confused, terrified of getting pregnant. Does he know? flashes through her mind, does he want me to be pregnant again? The hell with that, she thinks, as he pulls her against his chest. Soothing her, caressing her.

"You didn't use a condom, you . . . "

"Shhh . . . Shhh . . . It'll be okay." His lips move down her body, fingers inside her, gentle, stroking her. Now his mouth where his hands were. She grabs his hair, alarmed. He's never done this before.

"What are you doing?" His hands move to her breasts, his mouth is hot, the air cold; she has never felt so exposed. She's resisting this orgasm, her mind stuck on what just happened, until she can resist no longer and falls over the waterfall with him, the ride down a revelation. The further revelation, she wants him again, more, again and again, she wants this wildness, wants to match his wildness with her own.

When he enters her now there is no thought of the future, or the past. He's looking at her; he's seeing her, seeing through her. Those eyes. A gentleness now. The words last time, last time, rise up in her. She pulls him to her, wraps her arms and legs around him. Just one more year. They can make it through one more year.

Megan hesitates one more time before deciding she can handle the guy who offers her a ride. Toys in the backseat, dog tags hanging from the mirror, a roach on the dash, Crosby, Stills and Nash on the radio. Shy smile, working man's hands. She'll be all right.

Megan Alsop disappears the day after Billy Flynn gets home from Vietnam.

When Nell walks up the hill to do her chores at the farm after school, no one knows yet that Megan is missing. Or that the Alsops' dog has also vanished.

It's easy to lose track of a girl who lives in two places: her father's farm, her mother's apartment in town; easy to lose track of a girl like Megan, sleeping with a boy who doesn't love her, running with a crowd she doesn't really know, her status so provisional there's no one to notice when she's not there, no one to pick up the phone, sound the alarm, give a damn.

Maeve Alsop drives up to the farm, tires spinning in the snow, talking at Asa as she hurries across the ice-crusted yard to where he stands at the woodblock. He has spent the last hours splitting logs, each bite of the axe ringing in his arms and shoulders. He knows it's madness to have an axe in his hands. He sets it down as Maeve approaches, the handle slick with sweat, his breath rasping. Nothing she can accuse him of can be worse than the blame he heaps on himself. He has been mute with fury since storming the police station demanding that something be done and done now. Nothing he said or shouted cut through their calmly infuriating reassurance: Kids wander off; she'll show up, probably a fight with a boyfriend.

Asa reaches for Maeve when she slips on the ice. She jerks away from him.

"The police aren't doing anything. Why haven't you organized a search? This would never have happened if you could have kept your family together."

He reaches for her again, thinks, but doesn't dare say: Maeve, sweetheart, won't you come home? She resists; then lets herself be pulled into his arms.

Later that night, Nell, Jack, and Marion Flynn gather in the Alsops' kitchen with Billy's best friend, Harlow Murphy, his father Ely, and Asa's closest neighbors, the Morgans and the Donovans, eldest sons in tow. Panic is spreading. Concerned citizens have set up a phone chain to organize volunteers. There are dozens of quickly assembled search parties all over town. People feel the police are moving too slowly, no matter that these amateur efforts might destroy evidence. They want to do something.

With flashlights and lanterns they move into the numbing

cold, heading for the dense woods above the Alsops' farm, a wall of white. They spread out, keeping within an arm's length of each other as much as the trees will allow. Nell walks between Harlow and her father, welcoming the shelter of the woods after the relentless wind, but soon finds the forest terrifying. Every unexpected sound, every clatter of branches lashing over their heads, every pile of leaves makes Megan's disappearance more real. Nell keeps imagining that she sees a skein of Megan's hair, or the outline of a boot or a body, buried in the snow. She looks to her father for reassurance; he is fully concentrated on the ground in front of him, holding himself together through force of will. Harlow reaches out and takes her hand, briefly, then returns to methodically raking the ground with his torch. Like a brother, she thinks, his cool reserve just about killing her. She flashes on Megan's blood on the floor of that awful room, imagines blood in the snow.

Billy, floating in and out of consciousness those first days and nights, isn't sure if he dreamed his father sitting beside him reciting his rosary, or his older sister Sheila, drinking coffee and gossiping with the night nurse. He turns his head once to find Nell working through a set of math problems. Has Marion been here, fighting with the staff? Rosie, beautiful Rosie? He can't remember.

Where's Megan and why hasn't she come to see him?

Harlow Murphy. That booming laugh. Flirting with the nurse. Yes. Harlow bending to whisper in his ear: We've gotta get you out of here, buddy.

And Brendan, no, it isn't possible his brother Brendan could fly in from Texas.

Bits and pieces of conversation. Is he dreaming or are they real? His father telling him he's in one piece, over and over, like he's trying to convince himself: You've got your mind, your body, your family. You hang on to that, you hang on.

The rosary, his father's voice again, slipping away. Holy Mary, mother of God . . .

Nell stands by the window while Billy sleeps and looks through his wallet. Finds a picture taken when she was four or five, hair in braids, bangs uneven, no doubt cut at home. She hadn't been a pretty kid, and she'll never be as pretty as her sister Rosie, at least that's what everyone tells her. She's not vain, but it sticks in her guts sometimes.

Another photograph, taken in the Alsops' orchard. Megan on a ladder, Billy's arm around her waist; baskets of apples at their feet; Nell looking away from Harlow, his last leave before shipping out to Vietnam, lean and muscled, hair too short, sideburns too long.

She'd gathered her courage for weeks and finally reached for him, pure longing propelling her past fear. He'd taken her hands, then pushed her away. She couldn't see how hard he worked to do the right thing, to let her grow up and make a real choice. All she could see was the way he moved away from her, head down, eyes averted, waiting for the moment to pass.

She looks at Billy now, his face closed against the pain. Dreads telling him about Megan, not sure if it's kindness or cowardice that's keeping her mouth shut.

The search for Megan Alsop, with local policemen, firemen, volunteers, and dogs, ends after seventy-two hours. They comb through Geneva, fanning out over the surrounding hills, torches winking on and off as they advance through fields and woods. The heaviest snowfall of the year had obliterated any hope of finding tracks.

Neighboring towns organize volunteers to search their own areas. The news of a missing eighteen-year-old girl flashes around the lake like a forest fire. Nothing like this has ever happened here. Kids wander their neighborhoods, range far and wide, and no one blinks an eye. There's a lot of talk about last year's unsolved Alphabet Murders up in Rochester. Three preteen girls sexually assaulted and murdered within a span of six months. Carmen in Chili, Wanda in Webster, Michelle in Macedon. No suspects. No arrests.

Two policemen stamp snow off their boots at the back door and sit down at the kitchen table, accepting Marion's offer of coffee.

"We're just here to ask a few questions," the tall one says, stirring sugar into his cup, smiling as he introduces himself: Detective Jim Johnson. The sandy-haired dimpled one, former high school running back, former fourth grader in Marion's classroom, is Dale Pope. His father owns the funeral parlor in town. You can understand why Dale might choose another line of work.

Marion ushers them into the front room so she can make dinner. Jack, visiting Billy, is expected home soon.

Nell glances up from her lab report when the two men enter the room. She stands suddenly, knocking her chair over. Looks to her mother for help or an explanation, but Marion has already returned to the kitchen.

Dale Pope rights the chair as Johnson opens his notebook, flips through several pages, and asks:

"Did you see Megan Alsop the day she disappeared, Thursday, February 3rd?"

"I saw her at school."

"Did you notice anything out of the ordinary?"

"She may have had a fight with her boyfriend."

"Did she talk to you about this?"

"No."

"How did you form this impression?"

She could see Megan in the restroom, smoking, pale, her hands too busy, hiding something, her mascara a mess. Her new friends had brushed past Nell, leaving Megan behind. Nell hadn't known what to say. Don't say anything, Megan said. I don't want to hear it.

You can't be pregnant again.

Leave me alone.

Do you need help?

I'll deal with it.

"She seemed . . . I don't know what the right word is. Preoccupied. Sad."

"Do you know her boyfriend?"

"I know him to say hello to."

"You're not friends."

"There's not a problem between me and Rob Chandler."

"Someone saw you getting into Mr. Alsop's pickup truck that afternoon."

"That's not true. He stopped to say hello. He was heading into town."

"Does he often offer you a ride?"

"If he sees me walking."

"Are you ever uncomfortable with Mr. Alsop?"

"No more uncomfortable than I am with any other adult."

"Would you describe him as a loner?"

"I'm not going to help you paint some awful picture of Mr. Alsop. Is he a suspect?"

Johnson looks up from his notes. "Did you see Rob Chandler at school that day?"

"I'm not sure."

"Was he in your English class?"

"I can't remember."

"Did you see him at lunch?"

She shakes her head.

"After school?" he prompts.

Why are these questions so upsetting?

"No. Wait. He drove by me that day," she says.

"Was Megan in the car?"

"I don't know. I assumed she was."

"Could you see if there was someone else in the car?"

"He was driving really fast. They honked. I about jumped out of my skin."

"Have you talked to him since Megan disappeared?"

"No."

"Has he approached you in any way?" he asks.

"Why would he?" As the words leave her mouth she can see Rob Chandler lounging in the hallway outside Mr. Ware's calculus class, staring at her. She had been so surprised she'd turned around to see who was behind her. What day was that?

"That's all for now," he says. "Thank you for your time."

"Mrs. Flynn, thanks for the coffee," Dale calls out.

"One more thing," Johnson says. "Did Megan have any reason to run away?"

"Not that I know of."

"Could she have been pregnant?" He stands up, straightening his tie.

She gives him a long look. "Theoretically possible, I suppose."

"If she confided in you . . . "

"She didn't."

Detective Johnson hands Nell his card.

"We may need to question you again. Here's my number if you remember a detail, a conversation. And you can always call Sergeant Pope."

Nell grabs her coat and heads out to feed the Alsops' ponies. Late. Damn it. All of the detective's insinuations . . . But if Megan has run away then she can be found. If she's pregnant or in trouble of some kind then it can all get straightened out.

She remembers walking the long blocks of Dorset Street, feeling as though the night had eyes and ears. She'd lagged behind, frightened, upset, with no words to corral the turmoil inside her, the dog barking at the limits of his chain grating inside her skull, the dark closing in, each step bringing them closer to this unredeemable act, when Megan unexpectedly stopped, turned back, and took her hand.

Did Nell love her or hate her in that moment? Was it Megan's capacity for friendship or seduction which was on display? Nell isn't sure. She may never be sure. But she will remember the gesture for the rest of her life.

Who was that?" Marion asks as Jack pulls on his pants in the dark.

"AmVets. Watkins Glen."

"At this hour?"

Finds his boots.

"Trevor?" she asks, knowing the answer. "You're driving halfway around the lake at midnight."

"I'll be back in time for work."

"Jesus Christ, Jack. You can't keep doing this."

Kisses her. "See you in the morning."

Jack drives the hills too fast, the truck rattling like a son of a bitch, his window cracked open to help him stay awake. The February air is cold enough to sting. He's got the heater going full blast, trying to warm the ache in his feet and legs. Crap circulation ever since the war. Coldest winter on record across Europe. And they lived in frigging tents.

He turns on the radio. As usual the reception is terrible. Until: *American fighter-bomber and a rescue helicopter have been shot down inside North Vietnam. All crewmen aboard both aircraft are listed as missing in action* bursts through the static.

"God help us," he flips it off.

Movement along the shoulder catches his eye. He takes his foot off the gas, sees a coyote top the berm, dark against the snow, and disappear into the trees. His first impulse: it could have been a girl; it could have been Megan. Thinks of her somewhere on the side of some road. Feels sick to his stomach.

At least Billy is home. In pieces, but home.

He pulls up in front of the American Legion to find Trevor sitting on a bench outside, asleep. Place locked up tight. They couldn't have waited? Called a cab?

Jack touches his brother's shoulder.

"Jesus, Jack! You trying to scare the piss out of me?"

"Thought I'd take you home."

"Took you long enough."

"Where's your truck?" Jack asks.

"Repo man."

"No cabs tonight?"

"No cab fare."

In the light from the streetlamp Jack can see cuts and bruises on Trevor's face. His knuckles look like hamburger.

"Fight?"

"What's it look like?"

Jack opens the passenger door, tries not to watch as his once athletic brother wrestles himself into the truck.

"What's all this?" Trevor knocks a can of soup off the seat.

"Grabbed a few things from the pantry."

"I don't need your charity."

The cabin is dark when they pull into the drive.

"Where's Ida?" Jack asks.

"Wichita. Visiting her sister."

"For how long?"

"Awhile."

Trevor lets himself into the house and lights a lantern. It's colder inside than out, Jack notes as he walks through the door.

"What's with the lantern?"

"They cut the electric."

"Heat?"

"I've got the woodstove."

"What's going on, Trevor?"

"You've done your duty, boy scout. You can head on home."

"I'll call the electric company in the morning."

"You gonna pay my bill, too?"

"You working?"

"Too cold for roofing."

"Nobody's working inside?"

"Nobody who hasn't fired me at least once," Trevor laughs. A bitter sound.

"I thought Ida was working at the cafeteria at the grade school."

"Maybe she got tired of my sorry ass."

The lantern hisses in the quiet.

"Peter? Tommy?" Jack asks.

"I'm not calling my kids for help."

"You should get that hand cleaned up."

Jack rinses out a dirty pan in the sink, fills it with water. The gas for the stove is still on, he sees with relief.

"If I could get my truck back, I could look for work in Syracuse, maybe."

"How much you owe?"

"More than I've got."

"Let me see what I can do. Who's got it?"

"McBride's, up in Geneva, that son of a bitch."

Jack buttons his coat. If he leaves now and doesn't get nabbed for speeding, he might be able to climb back into bed for an hour.

"How's that boy of yours doing?" Trevor asks.

"Coming along."

"I never liked Marion much."

"You've said."

"But that woman stuck by you. All those years after the war."

"She did."

"You were in rough shape."

"True."

"She pulled you through."

"That's right."

"I respect that. Still don't like her much. But I respect that."

"You tend to that hand now, Trevor."

"You worried about a little infection? It'll take more'n that to bring me down."

"I'll call the electric and McBride's. We'll get this sorted out."

"You got a bottle of whiskey in that truck of yours?" Trevor calls to his retreating back.

"Fresh out," Jack replies.

Another gurney, a thick medical file crammed beside him, no X-rays, lost, apparently, wheeled down the stinking hallways, into the grumbling elevator, the slow descent, through the basement to a rear exit, for the morgue, maybe. Another ambulance, a nurse seated at his head, orderly at his feet, no lights, no siren, thank God, it hurts his head, an hour-long ride to Strong Memorial in Rochester and the best hand surgeon in the area. His parents are suddenly paying for private care; he can't imagine what this is costing them. Light splashes through the window, bouncing off the snow. He squints in the unaccustomed glare; then closes his eyes, basking in its warmth.

The nurse touches his head and neck, feeling for fever, then rests one hand on his forehead, the other on his good shoulder.

Remarkable how soothing it is. She's young, skinny like Nell, almost pretty. No wedding ring. Her coat is shabby; cuffs frayed. Maybe she has a boyfriend in country. Maybe she'll come with him into the hospital, keep her healing hands on him.

Billy's field journal arrives home inside the trunk with all his other gear, courtesy of the U.S. Army. Marion runs the washing machine all day trying to wash away the sand and the smell of smoke.

Nell sorts through the pages, organizing them by date, if Billy had even bothered to date them. Then she reassembles their combined journal, his pages interleafed with her own. Better than letters, Billy used to say. They'd done fairly well sending entries back and forth while he was training in Texas, and even through the first months of his tour.

The early pages from Vietnam alternate between scenes on the base: insects, common birds, sketches of his crew; and pages where he was off the base: acres of green, rice paddies, water buffalo. There are birds Nell has never seen before, drawn as only Billy can; each of them so individual, so full of personality you expect them to sing.

Black crowned night heron

Glossy ibis

Pacific swift

There are fewer entries as the months drag on: a lone man crouched in tall burning grass, the shadow of a gunship passing over him, mountaintops ringed with clouds, ravines dark as the far side of the moon. These give way to drawings of the dead, downed helicopters, the last pages full of fire. Page after page: birds, trees, fields, burning.

Her own observations seem insignificant in comparison:

Clover leaf—found in schoolyard

Norway maple seed

October 5: Sunrise: 6:40 A.M. Sunset: 4:38 P.M.

Billy stopped taking notes, words increasingly inadequate to what he was seeing. Nell's pages continue:

American beech tree

Close view of male and female mergansers

In the bottom of the box, beneath a rusty rag, a stack of letters from Megan, held together with a rubber band. Childish, loopy handwriting, little hearts on the envelopes. SWAK.

Had she ever told him? Megan had been inconsolable after the abortion. For weeks, her family thought she was sick. Nell avoided her, too confused and upset to offer comfort and understanding, or even simple acceptance. Nell only realized how angry she was as the weight of the secret and her acquiescence grew heavier. It could never be spoken of; she would never be able to set it down.

She went to confession and sat mute, Father O'Rourke gently prompting her. She longed to be absolved, but it was not her secret to tell. She was an accomplice, drawn inside this sin against her will, by accident, out of love and loyalty. And then she watched as love and loyalty frayed beyond recognition.

Inside one of the letters, there's a series of photos Megan took of herself in her bedroom. A ninety-five-pound seventeen-year-old's idea of sultry. On the back of one:

I want you to imagine what I'm going to do to you when you're home on leave.

Marion appears in the doorway.

"I came up to see if you wanted to come to the hospital with me."

Nell hands Marion a stack of unopened envelopes. "He saved our letters. But didn't open all of them."

Marion flips through. "Not that many, considering all we sent."

"It just seems . . . "

"What?"

"Sad, I guess."

"You coming?"

"Not today," Nell surprises herself by saying.

She picks up the scrap of cloth to rewrap the journal. Fine red-brown dust falls to the floor and she realizes it's a bloody rag, a piece of a shirt. She drops it back in the box and shoves it under Billy's bed.

In the bathroom she scrubs her hands under water as hot as she can stand it, then bolts down the stairs to join her mother in the car.

Strong Memorial is another world after the VA Hospital: clean, quiet, a private room, adequate nursing staff. Marion won't let herself think about the expense. Not yet. They're making progress. The burns on Billy's face, neck, shoulder, torso and arm are nearly healed. A second surgery to repair tendons and ligaments is scheduled for later in the week. The nurses tell her that they don't know yet how extensive the nerve damage is but suspect shrapnel has done a great deal of harm.

When Marion leaves to consult with Billy's hand surgeon, Nell opens the book she's brought, Audubon's *Birds of America*. Billy traces the image of the Arctic Tern with his good hand.

"Four ounces powered by instinct and desire. The longest migration of any species: 25,000 miles, half the globe."

"Listen, Billy, I need to tell you something and it's never a good time."

"Megan." Not a question.

"She's missing."

"Off on a joyride with the new boyfriend?"

"No. She . . . She disappeared the day after you got home. There's been a search."

"What are you talking about?"

"The investigation is ongoing."

"Wait a minute. You're serious." He looks at her now, the book forgotten. "They can't find her? That's ridiculous."

"I know."

"Did she talk to you?"

"Ever since she moved into town with her mother . . . "

"Her parents separated?"

"Mrs. Alsop took a job at the bank. And then she left the farm, got an apartment."

"Why didn't you tell me?"

"It was probably in one of my letters you didn't open."

Billy is silent.

"Megan's part of a different crowd at school. I didn't . . . I don't see much of her anymore."

"You've been friends your whole lives."

"Not lately."

"That doesn't sound like Megan."

"Did you stop writing to her, too?"

Marion appears with coffee and a sandwich, stops in the doorway.

"Megan Alsop," he accuses his mother. "Is anyone doing anything?"

"Nell, did you have to . . . ?" Marion asks.

"It would be better if he heard it from someone else?"

Billy begins pulling at the needles in his arm.

A nurse pushes past Marion; speaks quietly to Billy, one hand on his shoulder.

Marion moves toward the bed. He turns his face away from her.

"I'm on night duty," the nurse says. "I'll keep my eye on him."

"Billy . . . " Nell tries.

"Just go."

What the hell are they talking about: Megan Alsop missing. What does that even mean. A runaway? Kidnapped, or murdered? In sleepy little Geneva, New York. Impossible. Girls don't just disappear. He tries to reason it out, push through the panic and think: what might have happened, where she could be. But he can't think about Megan without sensing her in his arms, on his tongue. The whores in Saigon taste of cheap bourbon and cigarette smoke, their skin smells of sandalwood and other men. Megan tastes like apples and smells like new mown hay and good clean dirt. She'd wrap her legs around his waist. He's losing . . . what's that sound? Why is it so hard to think this through? Someone is weeping. He just needs to concentrate. His face is wet; his chest aches. He turns to see the nurse injecting something into his arm and then he's sinking into the South China Sea: deeper, colder. Gone.

At home Nell sits down to work on her biology project, still wearing her coat. The front room, as usual, is freezing. The piano is closed, all her music put away. She plays so rarely now.

She'd rather be outside, gathering materials for her work in the field, checking nets, finding her notebook, the blood collection slides and sleeves. Wishes for spring and the freedom of the woods. Turns back to the cell diagram, knows instantly she's too physically wound up for the detailed concentration this project requires. Tries closing her eyes, breathing deeply. Puts her palm on Billy's painting propped on the piano, her touchstone. A juniper titmouse in profile, its black tufted head somehow looking tired and unkempt and sad, titled: *The Unsung Magnificence of Half-Remembered Songs.*

Yesterday her favorite math teacher asked who was helping her with her work. Not exactly an accusation of cheating but close. She completed a more difficult problem in front of him and he was still skeptical. He doesn't believe girls are capable of higher-level mathematics. When she protests, his parting shot is: Time will tell.

Lately she's been wondering if she has what it takes to claim a place in the inhospitable, competitive world of science. With Billy in the hospital it suddenly feels nearly impossible, like she's lost her compass. She sometimes wishes she were a child again, climbing into the boat with her brother, the day theirs to explore. Coming home in the dark, filthy, exhausted, a pool of light on the end of the dock, the lantern their father lights for them.

She pushes out the back door, ignoring Marion's protests as she climbs the path to the railroad tracks, shining thinly in the moonlight. Her breath puffs around her, snow crunches under her boots in the stinging cold. She kneels, puts her hand on a rail, feels the distant vibration of a train, thinks of Billy's accusations, all he doesn't know, might never know. Hears the buoyant wingbeats of a barn owl and looks up in time to see its pale shape pass close overhead. The long drawn-out hiss of its call sends shivers down her back. It feels as though she could reach up and touch its white underwings, its downy breast.

Nell is at her locker on Monday digging out a notebook when Rob Chandler stops beside her. Much too close for comfort.

"What did you tell the police about me and Megan? I know they questioned you."

"They're questioning everybody. Back off, would you?" She tries to duck under his arm. He slams her against the locker. "Get off of me!"

One or two students look up, see it's Rob Chandler, and walk on. Jamey Conley, her lab partner, starts toward them, but is stopped by Miss Rosenthal ushering him into class.

"They have some idea we had a fight. Like I might have been a little rough with her. Where are they getting that idea?"

"How should I know?"

His face is inches from hers. "Because of you, they think I'm a suspect."

"Did you treat her like this? What a tough guy, pushing Megan Alsop around."

She shoves him with both hands, to no effect. "I told them she seemed sad that day. That's all. But if they question me again, how should I describe this, Rob?"

He moves one hand from her shoulder to her throat. "Maybe whatever happened to Megan was her own damned fault."

"How could any of this be her fault?"

"I broke up with her because she was messing around with one of my friends."

"That's ridiculous."

"Maybe you didn't know your little friend all that well."

"Just who was she supposed to be flirting with?"

"Tom Clifton."

"That's crap. She thinks he's an idiot."

"I know what I saw."

"You made that up. An excuse to break up with her."

"Best theory I've heard is that her father kidnapped her and has her hidden away somewhere. To get back at his wife," Rob says. "It's somebody we know. That's what the police say."

"I heard they found a hair ribbon in your car."

"Big deal."

"And blood."

"She was always tearing at her fingers."

"Are the police buying that explanation?" Nell asks.

The bell rings, the last scramble to class. Students steer around them.

"Her mother found a packed suitcase under her bed," Rob says.

"So?"

"Who and what was that all about? It wasn't about me. We didn't have any plans."

"Why are you telling me this?"

"It could happen to anybody. Anytime."

"Are you threatening me?"

A teacher walks by, fast, late: "Is there a problem here?"

"Not at all, Mrs. Lawrence," Rob says, remembering her name.

"Get to class, you two. Now," she says, smiling at Rob, ignoring Nell.

Nell feels a jolt of fear so sharp it takes her breath away. She has never allowed these thoughts to surface. How easy it would be for Rob to hurt Megan, to erase her. She can still feel his hand on her throat.

The following day, Nell leaves school after calculus and rides her bike through the slushy streets to Harlow's garage. He comes out from the service bay, cap pulled low, unshaven, looks up with that *when you gonna grow up, girl* look.

Harlow is part Seneca. Blue-black hair, tawny skin, snappy, almost ebony eyes. He has the height and grace of the legendary Iroquois riveters who built most of Manhattan, walking skyscraper girders like they were standing on solid ground.

The Murphys live directly across the lake from the Flynns'. Harlow and Billy, in spite of being two years apart, have been best friends since they met and misbehaved in church school. As kids, they rowed, paddled, and drove Harlow's motorboat back and forth across the lake. Ran in and out of each other's houses, if you could ever get them to come indoors.

He throws her bike into the back of his truck, flips over the CLOSED sign, and drives to the Flynns' to pick up Flanagan. Nell has things to say, or thought she did, all fantasy when it comes right down to it. Sitting in his truck, the floor a mess of newspapers, Coke bottles, beer cans, duct tape holding the leatherette seat together, more or less, and oh, God, the smell of him, enough to tongue-tie any girl. She does know how to talk, she reminds herself. Still. The physical fact of him. Next to her. Doors and windows closed. She could just reach out and put a hand on him.

He pulls up to the house. She sits silent, embarrassed by her own thoughts.

"The dog . . . ?" he prompts.

She whistles up Flanagan, who leaps into the truck and settles between them. "You didn't really need my help, did you?" Harlow asks, as he accelerates on to the highway.

"You're the decoy," she manages to say, shoving her hands under her thighs to keep them out of trouble.

"Right," he laughs. She meets his gaze. Those black eyes. Lashes longer than her sister Rosie's. Sweat runs down her back, she feels loose and liable to say anything. Presses her lips together.

How is it that everyone else moves, acts, does things, while she remains behind, good girl, good student, good sport. Is she going to end up like her sister Sheila? She couldn't bear it.

She is not going to end up like Megan. There is no sex in sight, no sex even on the horizon, but she's been to Planned Parenthood. A dodgy neighborhood in Syracuse, crumbling building, fat counselor falsely friendly. Chose a diaphragm; getting fitted for it was her first internal exam. Hates the way that everything to do with sex and being a girl is humiliating. Sanitary napkins: the discomfort of wearing them, trying to hide their bulk under pants or skirts, the unpleasant task of disposing of them. The smell. Seems strange to hate your own body like this, but how else is she supposed to feel. And now the saucerlike diaphragm in its little blue case, hidden in the back of her sock drawer, smelling of plastic. The tube of spermicide, with its alarming applicator; she's not sure she'll ever be able to use the stuff.

She doesn't think of herself as squeamish, but in this instance she is. The church would condemn her both for pre-marital sex—is thinking about it a sin?—and using birth control. She wishes she could laugh off the church's contradictions; even better, shake them off entirely.

Right now, if she could just slide across the seat to be next to him. Just that. Knows she's lying to herself. She wants more. The next moment and the next, and the one after that.

Harlow flips on the radio, finds the Rochester R&B station; cranks up the volume. Sam Cooke: *Bring It On Home To Me*. The same song they were playing the night he told Billy he was going to enlist and Billy got pissed as hell, tried to talk him out of it. Told him Nell was too young for the hundredth time. Like Megan wasn't. Wound too tight. Looking for a fight. Like if they could just draw blood or break a bone, Harlow would come to his senses.

Two years later, spring of his senior year, some asshole recruiter promised Billy he'd fly and all bets were off.

Some men are made for war. He never thought Billy Flynn was one of them.

He looks at Nell. She reddens, turns away. She has no idea how the graces have smiled on her. It's good not to know. He doesn't like girls who do know.

Nell's plan is for Harlow to charm the nurses while she brings Flanagan up the service stairs. The riskiest moment will be leaving the stairwell and walking the entire length of the corridor to Billy's room.

There's an emergency on the opposite side of the nurses' station; they make the dash to Billy's room undetected. She and Flanagan slide across the slick linoleum and almost crash into the bed. Nell's still not used to the spit and polish of Strong Memorial. "Nice job cleaning up for your visit," Billy says, taking in Harlow's filthy coveralls.

"Wouldn't want to excite the nurses."

Flanagan licks Billy's hand trying to get the taste of him, or trying to wash those last years away.

"Help her get up here."

"Your nurse will kill me," Nell says.

"Do we care?" Billy laughs.

There's hardly enough room. Flanagan lies on her belly, stretched against him. Nell stands beside the bed, leaning against Flanagan, feels the dog trembling. Billy buries his wrecked hand in her fur. His defenses fall away, and she sees how alone he's been, how hard he works to hold himself together, how punishing that effort is.

She pulls up the side railing, heads to the cafeteria for coffee. When she returns Harlow is sitting in a chair by the window, head resting against the glass, sound asleep.

She sips the coffee, shudders, thinks who is she kidding, she should've gotten hot chocolate. Picks up yesterday's newspaper, searches for a mention of Megan, the ongoing investigation. Nothing. Reads the lists of the dead, the body counts. It's been a bad week.

She pours the coffee out in the sink, rinses her mouth. Sits on the floor beside Harlow, leans against his leg. Flanagan yawns and settles again with a sigh.

Nell wakes to find Harlow resting his hand on her head, full dark outside the window. She holds her breath.

"Time to go," he says, leaving the room.

She has some trouble convincing Flanagan to come with her. Billy grabs her hand, says thank you. She wishes he wouldn't. It makes her stomach ache to have Billy quiet and grateful, she'd rather his usual uproar, running down stairs, slamming doors, embarrassing her.

She looks up to see Harlow chatting with the nurse, her protests about the dog silenced by his explanation. Or the simple fact that he is standing too close, his hand on her shoulder, making her blush.

Driving home Harlow asks Nell about her plans for college, where she's applied, when she'll hear. She deflects, wants to know what happened at SUNY Binghamton.

He has no idea where to begin. How to talk about the oblivious privilege of spoiled, draft-dodging eighteen-year-olds. How lost he felt. The waste. Was he too old? Had he missed his chance? He could never quite manage to play the game, take his professors' authority seriously. He'd had men's lives in his hands for too long to be able to settle down and acquiesce in the classroom. He's not stupid; he knows that. He'd done well in school and he's still interested in engineering. Or the Merchant Marine. Or the Coast Guard. Working with his hands, having a crew, living on the water.

How he'd chafed to get out of Geneva, to escape. But then you come back to the world. Home was all they ever talked about in country, their waking dream: ice cream, whiskey, girls. Nice, clean, soft, getting over.

"Harlow?"

"I asked you first," he turns the question back to her.

She tells him about the new science teacher, Miss Rosenthal, her independent study project, working on a team at the Ornithology Lab.

"There are hardly any girls. Maybe there will be more in college. A lot of them won't make it, that's what Miss Rosenthal says. I've already had math teachers who accuse me of cheating, of having someone else do my work, because they don't believe I can do higher-level math."

"Sons of bitches."

"Maybe you could teach me how to get mad so I don't keep getting blindsided."

She steals a glance at him, his face lighting up and falling into shadow as other cars sweep past. She tucks her hands beneath her thighs. Again. Pulls her glasses off, cleans them with the tail of her shirt. Shoves them back on her face. Right. The boring, bookish, plain kid sister.

Friday afternoon, Esme Tinker walks into Billy's room carrying a portable cassette player. She is forty-five, handsome, not pretty, an ornithologist at Cornell and one of Billy's closest friends. She blanches when she sees the scars on his face and neck, stoops to find a plug to hide her reaction. Stands, taking in the extensive bandaging on his arm, torso, hand. Right hand.

Looks into his face; he has seen her reaction. She holds his gaze: "How you doing?"

"Can you sit on my left? Still some trouble hearing."

"Eardrum?"

"Concussion. You name it."

"Your dad told me you've got burns and broken bones."

"And shrapnel. It's gonna be a while."

"How's the pain?"

"They're generous with the meds."

She picks up the cassette recorder. "One of my grad students, Danny McNeil, came to your sit spot with me and recorded the dawn chorus." She presses play.

"Can you make it louder?"

Adjusts the volume.

"Even more?"

Pushes it to maximum.

"Bring it closer." Billy listens with his ear pressed against the speaker, then: "American robin . . . indigo bunting . . . " He smiles at her. "Wood peewee . . . song sparrow . . . gray catbird . . . great crested flycatcher?" He guesses.

Esme nods.

"Northern cardinal . . . wood thrush . . . eastern meadowlark . . . God, those sweet, lazy whistles . . . warbling vireo . . . "

"Danny is convinced soundscapes will help us understand ecosystem health."

"He's right. Play it again."

When Billy was twelve, Esme had walked into one of his preferred sit spots near dusk. She sat down nearby, recording observations every ten minutes or so in a pocket-sized notebook.

A fox had crossed within ten feet of them, screened by chokecherry bushes. Billy caught her eye, directed her gaze, or she would have missed it entirely.

"Can we talk?" she asked.

"Not here." He led the way to a small spit of land, overhung by willow and oak.

She introduced herself as though he were another grown up, shaking his hand. "Where do you live?"

"On the lake. What were you writing?" He scanned her notes. "You didn't hear the junco, the house wren . . . ?"

"No."

"You only listen to their songs? What about warning sounds? That's how I knew the fox was coming."

"The birds knew?"

"They knew it was a fox. I only knew it was a ground predator."

"Did I miss an alarm call, too?" she asked.

"No. A fox is a different kind of predator than a hawk. Just the usual chat. And body language."

"You do this every day?"

"I'd like to be a bird, if you want to know the truth," he said. "And I like to draw. I draw the birds."

A few days later, on a Sunday morning just before dawn, she showed up again. When she began to take notes, he stopped her. Her typical field methods, the pen scratching across paper, the sound of a page turning, were all interruptions.

Later, by the water, Billy introduced Esme to Nell.

"How old are you?" Esme asked.

"Nine," Nell answered.

"Why don't you talk in the woods, but you'll talk here?"

"If we keep interrupting we won't see or hear as much," Billy said.

"You're noisy even when you're not talking," Nell chimed in.

"I've been studying birds my whole life and never realized how loud my basic movements are," Esme said.

The sun was full up, struggling through clouds, shading the surface of the lake from silver to pink.

"You're kind of a bird plow," Nell said.

"A what?"

"You're scaring the birds. They fly up in the shape of a 'V,'" Billy said. "And then the hawks know where they are. You have to quit being a hunter."

"I've never shot a bird in my life."

"You're hunting your next find. That's why you miss so much."

Over the years Billy taught Esme a new way to listen, showed her how the birds organize their communication, how to read body language between pairs, the meaning of their back-and-forth chat, how they check in on each other, the various classifications of warning sounds.

Esme refocused her research on birdsong and communication. Billy had already observed in the field what Thorpe, in England, was discovering and documenting in the lab as he raised and recorded chaffinches. She made contact with

Thorpe's protégé, Marler, at UC Davis, and with Marler's famed student Luis Obispo, who rivaled Billy in his ability to identify individual birds, their songs, and their provenance.

The cassette recorder and the spectrograph were revolutionizing their research methods. The spectrographs make songs visible, recording and displaying frequency changes over time, the essence of a musical score. Recently revealed: the two voice boxes a wood thrush uses to harmonize and sing duets with himself.

Esme continues to feel a sense of urgency as she captures and maps birdsong. The woods are quieter than when she was a child. She does not want the next generation or the next to be born into silence.

The first time Billy visited her lab he was sickened by the drawers full of preserved and dissected specimens. But he'd been drawn to the birds, to be able to handle them, see the shape of wings and beaks, the patterns of color, though faded, even more subtle and exquisite than he knew. This study allowed him to make corrections to his drawings and paintings. He argued with Esme that observation in the field was enough, that the true colors were gone from the birds shortly after death. She countered that she'd never had another student like Billy, and that these were valuable study aids.

"Your students aren't worthy of these birds."

"If I teach thousands of students to appreciate and respect birds and the natural world, that has value. Unforeseen value. People need to be educated. Average people. Not everyone likes to sit in the woods all day like you do."

No one she has ever worked with has hearing or sight as acute as Billy's. She used to tease him about it, called him an extraterrestrial being. He took it entirely for granted. He watched and listened his way inside the birds, merging into the sky with them.

She looks at him now, his ear pressed against the speaker, and feels a bitter sorrow.

Billy shifts to try to find a more comfortable position. Futile. Presses play again, shuts his eyes against the pain; lets the birds fill his mind, a white-throated sparrow: *Oh, canada-canada-canada.*

On Wednesday, Jack waits for Nell outside of school. Realizes this is the third time in two weeks he's picked her up and tries to push thoughts of Megan Alsop out of his mind.

"We need to bail out Trevor's truck and drive it down to Dresden."

He writes a check at McBride's and hopes it won't bounce. Climbs into Trevor's truck and follows Nell down County Road 2. He left a message at the coffee shop in town now that Trevor no longer has a phone, but has no idea if he will be there to meet them. They'll cruise through town looking for him if he isn't home.

Trevor comes outside when the two pickups pull into the yard. Jack tells Nell to wait while he takes care of things with his brother.

"Hi, Uncle Trevor," Nell calls out.

"You don't want her coming in here."

"Didn't know what we'd find," Jack says.

But Jack is surprised. Trevor is sober, the cabin swept clean, dishes washed and put away. The fridge stands open and empty. A duffel bag sits by the door beside a few boxes tied with twine.

Trevor's face has been scraped raw by a razor. His shoulders, slumped as though he is a tall man trying to fit into a low-ceilinged room, straighten up when he's near Jack.

"About the truck. I'll pay you back," Trevor says.

"I'm not worried."

"Sure you are. You're just too much of a gentleman to say so."

"Where you headed?"

"I hear there's steady winter work in Maryland. Maybe the Carolinas."

"Home for the summer?"

"We'll see how it goes."

"Place looks good."

"I drained the pipes. Can you keep an eye on it for me?"

"I will."

"Any news about that girl?" Trevor asks.

"Not a word."

"It's an awful thing. How's Billy doing?"

"Few more weeks, he should be home. The right arm. It's a mess."

"He's young. He's got you."

"I sold Gram's highboy. Marion wasn't pleased, but I figured you could use the cash."

He hands Trevor the bills, then pulls his brother toward him, a quick, awkward embrace.

"Marion wasn't glad to get rid of that old thing?" Trevor asks.

"She'll come around."

"Good thing you got Billy out of that VA hospital. They're a rat-infested disgrace."

"Private hospital's bleeding us."

Trevor folds the bills, gives them back.

"No, we'll be okay. You keep it."

Trevor peels off a hundred. Gives the rest back, insists. Walks out to the truck. Nell hops down, hands him the keys; throws her arms around him. Thinks of all the times she'd ridden in the back of her uncle's truck with her brothers and cousins. Summer nights, Trevor at the wheel, flying over bumps and railroad crossings. Skylarking, he called it.

"I'm gonna miss you," she whispers.

He hands her a china cup. "Thought you'd like to have this."

She takes it, puzzled. "Thank you."

"You and your friend came here one summer. She loved those yellow cups. Your aunt gave her one. I thought you might like to have the other one."

Nell pictures the cup on the drain board at the Alsops' farm, the breadbox gaping open and empty, crumbs scattered in front of it.

"You don't remember?"

"No, I do. I do remember." She hugs him again. "I wish you didn't have to go."

Jack climbs into his truck. "You write and let me know where you land. An address. A phone number. Holler if you need me."

"I will."

"Don't just disappear on us."

"Wouldn't that be doing everyone a favor?"

"I'm not a good worrier," Jack says.

"I'll be fine."

"I know you will. Better times ahead."

"Sunshine, at least."

"We filled the truck up in Geneva. You'll have a good start."

Trevor stands in the yard watching them. Jack looks back at his brother, waves out the window before pulling onto the road.

They ride in silence, Nell turning the yellow cup in her hands.

"It's hard to accept help from your younger brother. Makes a man feel small."

"Where's Aunt Ida?" Nell asks.

"Wichita. Her mother's."

"For good?"

"Looks like it."

"That could never happen to you and Mom?"

"Never."

"Even though you fight."

"Differ."

She looks at him.

"Wrangle," he says.

"You fight."

"No one on earth is agreeable one hundred percent of the time."

"Mr. and Mrs. Alsop split up."

"They're not us."

"Will Uncle Trevor come back?"

"Time-tested advice: don't marry a drinker."

"He's always been a drinker."

"A woman gets fed up. All the money goes. Jobs get scarce."

"He never changed?"

"After the war . . . " He can't continue.

"Dad?"

"He tried. God, how he tried."

He glances at her, turns his attention back to the road.

"You want to save them," he says. "And you can't."

Late Monday afternoon Rob Chandler skids to a stop beside Nell as she's walking home, rolls down his window, the funk of dope spilling into the cold air, and shouts:

"You want a ride?"

"No thanks," Nell says, and keeps walking, head down. The wind coming off the snow-covered fields is sharp as a razor.

Ever since Megan's disappearance she has hurried through here, the woods to one side, the abandoned orchard on the other. Wrens call alarms deep in the ice-crusted weeds and brambles.

It starts to snow; heavy flakes coming down fast, melting on her hat and red mittens, making the road slick.

He inches along beside her. "C'mon. I'll give you a ride."

"What are you doing on this side of the lake?"

She hears a hoot of laughter and then a beer bottle is thrown from the car; it smashes against a tree. Rob's ridiculous friends: drinking, dropping acid, making themselves stupid. A fluke of birth allows them this indulgence while other eighteen-year-olds are coming home in body bags.

He pulls the car onto the shoulder, cutting her off, sliding on ice and snowpack. John Gibbs jumps out of the passenger side as Rob gets out of the car.

"Get in."

Chandler grabs her arm; she slips in the snow. She looks over her shoulder to see the road empty in both directions. He pushes her toward the car.

She tries to twist free as Asa Alsop's truck crests the rise. He flips on his bright lights as he gets closer. Chandler releases his hold on Nell, shields his eyes.

Asa rolls down his window. "What's going on here?"

"Nothing."

"What's Nell Flynn got to do with you?" Asa asks.

"Friends is all."

Nell stands, brushes snow off.

"Looks like you're stuck," Asa says, then, to Nell: "You okay to get home?" She crosses the road, stopping on the other side of the railroad tracks to watch.

"Can you give us a hand?" Chandler asks.

"Sure thing," Asa backs his truck up and then swings around, carefully inching closer to the back of Chandler's car.

"What are you doing?"

"Tell your friends to get out of the car."

Two more boys scramble out of the car, stand beside Gibbs. Asa pushes the Mustang further into the ditch.

"Son of a bitch!" Chandler says.

"You got a beef with me, kid?" Asa asks, inching closer again. "I'd suggest you start walking. You're gonna need a tow."

"And you're gonna pay for it."

"You slid off the road while you were threatening Nell Flynn. I had nothing to do with it."

"Hey, don't you live near here?" Gibbs asks. "Can we use your phone?"

"Any of you set foot on my property, I'm calling the police."

Asa never raises his voice. Waits until the boys disappear over the rise, heading for town. Sits for another twenty minutes to be sure none of them double back to trouble Nell. He puts the truck in gear and heads for home only when he sees Marion turn up the drive.

Nell shucks off her wet things in the laundry room, stuffs her boots with newspaper, sets them by the radiator. Upstairs, she pulls the Messiaen from its sleeve, sets it on the turntable; lowers the needle. The Oriole fills the room. Billy's gift: leaving his records and record player when he deployed.

Still cold, she climbs under the covers, wondering if she will ever get warm. The music washes over her. Sunrise, mist, dappled light on birch and fir, the oriole's fluted song.

She doesn't want to think about what could have happened if Asa hadn't driven up, or if Megan had been forced into a car some other dark afternoon.

But Megan, trusting Chandler, would have gone willingly.

She begins to tremble. Stupid. She shouldn't have let them frighten her. What did they want with her? Hears her mother's car pull up. Home from the hospital.

Nell finds Marion at the kitchen sink, her purse and a bag of groceries discarded on the table, still in her blue coat, looking out the window to the lake and the darkening sky. Nell stands beside her, reaches an arm around her waist.

"Is Billy okay?"

"He's fine. Well, that's not true. Sometimes it just hits me so hard. What a long road his recovery will be." She takes a breath. "It's such a shock to see the burns. His face . . . "

"It'll get better."

"Oh, honey. Burns like that . . . "

"It's just one side, Mom."

"My beautiful boy . . . "

She has the rare, unsettling sensation of holding her mother up. She knows now that she can't tell her mother about what happened on the road. It was just a prank, Nell tells herself. Nothing to be afraid of.

"Can I help with dinner?"

"Not much to do, but I'd love the company." Marion turns the kettle on. "First some tea. Warm us both up."

Nell unpacks the groceries. Pork chops, frozen green beans, potatoes, and a pack of cigarettes.

"Mashed or Potatoes Anna?" Nell asks.

"Potatoes Anna. Make your dad happy."

In the hospital, there's too much time to ask questions that can never be answered. When you're inside the mountains with their clouds and fire and treacherous winds there's no time to think.

They'd circled back a third time to try to get all the men out. You never do that. They've got your coordinates. They're going to hit you. Plenty of time to prepare.

But the wounded are waiting.

Every crewmember saying: *Yeah, yeah, go back in. We can do it.* One more time.

The smells of blood and smoke and waste fill the air, the staccato bursts of covering fire, the *whup whup whup* of the blades overhead.

The boys who can still walk help each other aboard; infantrymen carry stretchers, medics run beside them. They are taking fire to the ship, to the wounded. You can hear the *thunk* every time a round connects. One kid has lost his shirt, his bare torso burned, vivid as a flame. A corporal, his shoulder flayed open, lips so swollen with mosquito bites he can't cry out. Red dust rises with each rotation of the blades, coating their teeth, their tongues with grit.

We've gotta go.

Lifting off. Struggling to lift off.

Slow climb, overloaded, rotors howling. Billy angles the ship to tip right over the edge of the mountain, drop below the mortars, gain some speed, and hope like hell he can stabilize and get some control.

Tracers cross overhead; the first RPG takes out the tail, the second ploughs through the midsection. The ship splinters under his hands. Metal and men screaming.

The crash is heavy and hard and fast.

On fire.

MARCH

N ell sits beside Billy's bed, waiting for him to wake after the latest surgery. She pictures the intricate structure of a hand, a wrist, Billy's artful renderings of bird skeletons and wings. Thinks, then, about the birds' eggs she's studying: too thin to contain the growing embryo, the birds that do hatch, too fragile to survive. Invisible poisons in the air, in the water, in the bodies and blood of the insects and fish that sustain them, so potent they alter the chain of DNA itself. What has always seemed immutable—the body and its boundaries— is changing more quickly than anyone could have predicted.

She looks at her brother, realizes she has yet to see him on his feet. Recalls his pride when he surpassed first Jack and then his older brother Brendan in height.

Remembers standing on the sleeping porch looking down the hill to her two brothers on the dock, smoking and talking. They were leaving the next day for Basic. The occasional word floated up to her.

She'd come up the hill to change out of her bathing suit. Water dripped down her shirt. Billy, earlier, had run his hands through her hair, forced her to face him, breaking the Megan tension, the Megan secrets, sex.

Megan had always been jealous of the way Billy was affectionate with her. *He's my brother. It's just his way.* But Megan pushed and pushed until Nell wanted to smack her.

Billy called up to her, then, insisting on the yearly challenge, seeing who could hold their breath longest, weightless in the sun-filtered water, rocking in the current. He gripped her hand when Brendan gave up, kicking for the surface, watched her: You can't beat me. A gray sturgeon floated up from below, too big to be believed. A trick of the light, maybe, or her own shadow falling deep.

She closed her eyes, concentrating, the ache in her chest, at the base of her skull, wished she had a bird's hollow bones to fill with air. As kids they'd imagined that their ears would split open, that the pain was their bodies transforming into gills or wings or fins.

His kiss, so unexpected, still watching when she opened her eyes, that look she knew so well—I'll deny it later—this never happened—was missing now, something sober and haunting in its place.

He swam for the surface, she resisted, broke his grip. He burst through the water, laughing. She had beaten him for the first time in their lives.

More likely he'd let her win.

That first breath, dizzy, hair wrapped around her throat. Flanagan barking on the dock, Billy shouting, the bells pealing out from Saint Joe's in town. She wanted time to stop, wanted to float there forever, her brother laughing beside her, the dog, the smell of her father's fire, the bells ringing.

Billy struggles to wake, senses Nell nearby, the drugs pulling him under. He counts helicopters, why, he doesn't know, imagines birds in flight: they fill his mind, beating wings, turning rotors. Begins to surface, that familiar fight to come back, over and over, whether he feels like it or not. Thinks of the birds in Japan, so many strange visitors outside his hospital window.

He knows birds too numerous to count, he knows the lake like it's an extension of his own body, its impossible depths, currents, inlets and outlets, fish and fowl. He knows everything there is to know about wolves except how to be one.

He feels Nell's hand on his shoulder, hears her singing, so softly it's almost a dream. *If I were a blackbird, I'd whistle and sing* . . . Her voice pulls him up through the layers of pain and narcotics, all that weighs on him, gauze, sheets, memory. He nearly surfaces, is sucked under, another wave.

Friday morning half a dozen police cruisers pull up in front of the high school. The principal comes on the loudspeaker to announce that every locker will be searched. Class by class. Seniors first. Beginning now.

Students are instructed to stand in front of their lockers with the doors closed. Teachers patrol the hallways, shutting up the chitchat and the gossip. A policeman stands at each end of the corridor. Detective Johnson leans against a wall, watching.

Nell has a clear view of Rob Chandler's locker. He tries to pocket something when he opens the door for Dale Pope.

"What have you got, kid?"

Chandler shows Pope a pack of Trojans.

"Everything on the floor," Pope says.

Books, notebooks, a hockey stick, filthy gym socks, a windbreaker, girlie magazines, and buried beneath all the crap, Megan's favorite camisole and a pair of panties.

"Does this belong to you?" Pope asks.

"My girlfriend."

"Megan Alsop?"

"That's right."

"What's it doing in your locker?"

"She left stuff in here all the time."

"Why didn't you report this?"

Chandler shrugs his shoulders.

Dale Pope seals the camisole and underpants in a clear plastic bag. As Chandler starts to shove everything back inside, Pope stops him, calls to a cop nearby.

"Pack it all up, would you?"

"Yes, sir."

Chandler protests. Pope writes him out a receipt.

"Leave the schoolbooks. Nothing else."

Nell looks up to see Detective Johnson watching her. He shifts his gaze back to Chandler.

What will they find today? Anything? And if it's not Chandler, then who is it?

Billy is waiting for the miracle when the surgeries are done and the casts come off, for the burns to be healed, for his arm and hand to be restored to him, scarred and ugly, but functioning.

The days slip by, a parade of frustration. All the things he still can't do: button a shirt, pull on pants, zip his fly, for chrissake. Shoes and shoelaces, the list goes on and on. The occupational therapist won't leave him alone. Every day. Every fucking day. Galling to find he needs someone to teach him how to put his socks on.

He thought he was prepared for the cast to come off. He'd already been through the disappointment following the first surgery to repair his shattered elbow. The Army surgeon in Japan, happy to be dealing with a living soldier, sawed through the cast, looked at the X-rays, pronounced it: Great job. Healing well. Billy was confronted with an emaciated arm, a painful, if functioning elbow, and an almost useless hand.

Second surgery, stateside, to repair ligaments, also went well, or so he was told. Through the haze of painkillers, he heard the words healing well as your hand will be healed.

The shock when the second cast comes off is hard to measure. His wrist, forearm, palm, are crisscrossed with scars. The muscles in his arm have atrophied, his fingers unable to open fully, his hand crablike.

The surgeon's explanation of nerve damage, the function of ligaments holding bone together, what fine motor control he will and will not have, scarcely registers as static through the storm of Billy's reaction: panic fueled by pain and confusion and a sense of terrible betrayal.

"You son of a bitch, what have you done to my hand?"

"What we were able to do? Cutting edge. This kind of damage . . . "

"What about my hand?"

"You'll get a lot of your mobility back."

"You told me I'd be healed."

"You will heal. You are healing."

"Fully healed?"

"It takes time."

"How much time?"

"Depends on the patient, the extent of the damage. You have a lot of physical therapy ahead of you. There's significant nerve damage."

"Can you fix it?"

"Nerves? No."

"Can nerves heal?"

"Sometimes they regenerate. To a degree. But not when they've been shredded by shrapnel."

"And the pain?"

"Should improve over time."

Billy looks at him, panic rising.

"We've seen amazing results with young soldiers."

"You're not giving me much."

"You're in one piece, soldier."

"More or less," Billy says, thinking: You fucking coward.

"You'll start physical therapy next week. Rebuilding muscle and increasing your range of motion. By the time you're discharged you should see real improvement."

The surgeon writes a script for Billy's PT while Billy tries again to open his hand.

"It's numb." His voice breaks.

"That should get better."

He tries to make a fist, can barely curl his fingers. Gets his voice under control.

"How much range of motion is possible?"

"We'll see."

"That's the best you can do?"

"For now. I'll see you again in a month —"

"When can I go home?" Billy asks.

"I'll send the burn specialist up to see you."

He writes another note.

"You right-handed?"

"Yes."

"You should make the adjustment to writing left-handed quite quickly."

"What about drawing?"

"You draw?"

"Since I was a kid."

"A lot of it depends on motivation. I'd say you'll do well."

"But you don't really know."

"It's a hunch."

"What about flying?"

The surgeon gives him a blank look.

"I'm a pilot. That's not in your chart?"

"We'll reassess after some physical therapy."

"You're stalling."

"I don't have a crystal ball. And patients have surprised me plenty of times."

Billy walks to the lounge, shaky and weak. Stands by the

window. Rests his forehead against the cold glass, feels sleet ticking against the pane.

There are times he thinks he'd be better dead than to live like this, as though something else had been taken from him in the crash, in those days lying near death, some part of himself he isn't sure he can live without, faith or hope or just plain dumb animal determination. He looks around him, it all seems so simple to everyone else, this business of living, one foot in front of the other.

Maybe when he can get outside where the air blows stronger than memory and guilt, maybe then it will all come right, fall back into place, the hollowness will ease or fill. Seems to be no sense asking God about it, as if he ever would.

Against his better judgment, Asa Alsop pulls into the high school parking lot late Wednesday afternoon, looking for Rob Chandler's car. Finds it tucked near the maintenance shed, carefully backed into a spot. Asa pulls the truck up behind the shed to wait. A tire iron rests on the seat beside him.

The wind blasts out of freezing Canada, a mean snow squalling in circles, winter still hanging on.

Chandler crosses the parking lot alone. Just as well, Asa thinks, though he'd like to put the fear of God into Chandler and his friends, too.

He gets out of the pickup.

Chandler hears the truck door slam, looks over his shoulder, fumbles, drops his keys. Asa walks slowly toward him as he scrambles in the slush for his keys.

"Stand up."

Chandler backs up to his car, eyes frantic.

"You know anything about the whereabouts of my daughter?"

"No, sir."

"You lie about as easy as you breathe, don't you? Why were you bothering Nell Flynn?"

"Just wanted to offer her a ride home."

"That's another lie, isn't it?"

"I wanted to talk to her."

"About my daughter?"

"I don't know anything about your daughter."

"How is that possible when that girl thought she loved you?"

Chandler's eyes shift.

"Never had an enemy," Asa continues. "No reason to be afraid of anyone. Until you show up. And she disappears."

"I had nothing to do with that."

"Who did?"

"I don't know."

"Why don't I believe you?"

"Believe what you like."

"You don't belong on our side of the lake, do you?"

"It's a free country."

"You stay away from Nell Flynn."

"Are you threatening me?"

"I'm not a violent man," Asa says, revealing the tire iron in his hand.

"My father's a lawyer."

"Hiding behind your father, now."

"He'll press charges."

Asa grabs Chandler by the throat, nearly lifts him off his feet.

"You stay away from Nell Flynn or I will mess up your face so bad your own mother won't recognize you."

"You'll be sorry you ever spoke to me, old man."

Asa releases his hold on the boy, clenching the tire iron in his fist, thinks how good it would feel to wreck that sonofabitch car.

"You've been warned."

Billy is dressed and waiting when Nell arrives at the hospital, his clothes too big, belt needing extra notches. She gives back his hunting jacket reluctantly and stuffs his few belongings into a duffel.

He accepts a wheelchair for the first and last time in his life.

They are quiet on the drive to Geneva as the light thickens into dusk. The closeness to home washes over him, too intense; everything is too intense, threatening to drown him. Dazzled to be out of the hospital, in motion, the next phase, whatever it is, beginning.

He asks Nell to shut the car off before turning down the drive. He reaches across his body to roll down the window with his left hand. The pines lining the road shade from blue to black, soft yellow light falls from the kitchen windows; still he doesn't want to go inside.

"I can smell the white pines, I think . . . " He shuts his eyes and imagines the dark, billowing like a sheet, covering the lake and filling the valley.

They hear the late train's long whistle as it climbs the grade out of town. He hasn't heard a train whistle in a long time.

"I thought I'd get out of the Army, hitchhike across the country, figure out what's next. I never thought I'd be moving back home."

"It won't be that bad."

"Right."

"They've mellowed."

"Sure they have." He smiles at her. "You got pretty," he touches her face.

"Did not."

"I know a little something about good-looking girls."

"I bet you do."

"I should be living in some dumpy apartment, raising Cain and working hard."

"I could help you find a place."

"As soon as I get my feet on the ground." He pulls several pills from his pocket, swallows them dry. "Where's Megan?"

"The police searched the high school on Monday."

"You know something."

She lets the accusation hang in the air.

"Nell?"

"I don't."

"Really?"

"Really."

Why isn't Megan here, now, waiting on the porch for him, sensing the car nearby, those small hands reaching for him, that fierceness she has, that knowing look: yeah, yeah, set your duffel down, say hello to your parents, and then come to me, find me, just us, Billy, just us.

He isn't sure he can walk back into this house, this life, without her.

They'd written back and forth, full of plans and ideas. Talked about ag school for Megan. She was drawn to big animals, cows and horses; maybe she'd become a vet. Though what she really wanted was to raise them and work them.

Billy knew Esme expected him to come to Cornell, get his degree, work in the ornithology lab. But he'd realized he could never survive there, his time outdoors limited to research, his job—or what he imagined his job would be—in the classroom, like Esme. Leave that to his brother Brendan, a born teacher. Billy wanted as much physical freedom and time outdoors as he could get. He wanted to get his commercial license, fly for one of the big airlines for a few years while Megan was in college. He'd save up for a down payment on his own plane, or find a partner, Harlow maybe, go into business for himself, flying hunters, skiers, fishermen in and out of remote areas. He'd get to know the swath of woods, rivers, lakes that stretch north through the Adirondacks into Canada. In the slow seasons he'd work with Megan on their own place or they'd help Asa breathe some life back into the family farm.

This lake, this land is in their blood.

Billy looks at Nell for a long moment, thinks of the oceans that separated them for almost two years, how much he doesn't know, can't know. How much they've all changed.

"Why can't they find her?" he asks.

"The longer she's gone, the less likely she'll be found."

"Don't tell me that."

"It's just the truth."

"I don't know how to live with that."

"Neither do I."

Nell dreads going up to the farm at night alone but she promised Mr. Alsop she'd feed the animals. He'd phoned from the police station, said he'd been called in for questioning.

The mute darkness envelops her, the grief-struck strangeness of this place without Megan. Her throat aches, eyes too, head. Hurts enough to change her breathing.

The barn smells of hay and oats and manure, grease and old leather, as it always does, but the crows in the yard appear larger than usual, more numerous, threatening.

She turns on all the barn lights, none of which are very bright, feeds the chickens, brings the goats into the barn to be fed and watered. Both ponies put their noses in her palm, looking for treats, then nip at her when she disappoints them and walks on. They'll have to wait their turn.

There's one goat—Mike—a devil, who will never come in with the others, no matter how much grain you rattle in the pail. She chases him out behind the barn, cursing as she slips on melting snow and ice. She suddenly smells blood, hears whimpering.

Dash, the Alsops' border collie, is on her side next to the manure pile, shaking, skin and bones. Nell picks her up as gently as she can, carries her into the barn, and puts her down on fresh straw. Mike follows behind, nudging her with his nose. She herds him into his pen and brings water to the dog, covering her with one of the horse blankets, and then runs into the house to call her father.

"Slow down, I can't understand you," Jack says on the phone.

"The Alsops' dog has shown up, hurt. I need you to pick me up and drive us to the vet's."

"Where's Asa?"

"I'll tell you when you get here. Hurry, Dad."

"What about Evan?"

"He's not here. He must be at his mom's place."

She returns to the barn, feeds the ponies, and then sits with Dash. When she hears her father's truck she carries the dog out to meet him.

"Put her on the seat. You can kneel on the floor."

Nell closes up the barn. No lock on the door, of course, nor was the house locked. She isn't sure if that's trusting or foolish. Either way, tonight it scares her.

Dash has a broken pelvis. Will Haney, the vet, figures the dog got hit by a car. Lucky she hadn't broken a leg or her spine. How she'd survived five weeks of winter weather, avoided predators, found water, and got herself home is a mystery. They can't set the bone, but will try to keep her quiet enough to let it heal.

"Where's Asa?" Haney asks.

"He's at the police station talking to Detective Johnson," Nell says.

"Any news about Megan?"

"Rumors," Nell says. "We'll stop by the station and let Asa know Dash found her way home."

"He always said that dog was so smart she could run the farm."

When they pull up to the police station, Jack tells Nell to wait in the truck. She ignores him.

The sergeant on desk duty directs them to the interview room where Asa paces the perimeter. He's surprised to see them and then embarrassed. His lined, weather-beaten face is crumpled and weary. His big hands, capable with tools, machinery, animals, seem lost here, without purpose or purchase.

"Is everything all right?" he asks. "Is it Megan?"

"I found Dash out behind the barn. Hurt, but alive. She's at the vet's now."

Asa sits, as if struck by a blow.

"Mr. Alsop?" Nell says. "She's gonna be okay."

"I told myself they were together. And that Dash would find a way to bring Megan home." His voice breaks when he says his daughter's name.

"What happened, Asa?" Jack asks. "Why are you here?"

"Rob Chandler has accused me of harassing him. They're holding me while his father decides whether he's going to press charges."

"What do you mean?"

"I had a few words with him. Lost my temper."

"Did you hit him?" Jack asks.

"Wanted to."

"I bet."

"He'd been threatening Nell. Thought I'd straighten him out."

Jack turns to Nell. "Rob Chandler threatened you?"

"Not in so many words."

"Why didn't you tell me?"

"I didn't want to worry you."

"What does that mean, he threatened you?" Jack asks.

"He thinks it's my fault the police are questioning him."

"Why would he think that?"

"I knew what he was like with her. He knows something, Dad. Maybe everything. Otherwise why would he be trying to scare me?"

"I said if he came near you again I'd rearrange his face for him," Asa says.

"Have you called your lawyer?" Jack asks.

"He said they can't hold me or charge me based on a conversation."

Detective Johnson appears at the door.

"Sorry to keep you waiting, Mr. Alsop." Then, taking in Nell and Jack: "I'm going to have to ask you to leave."

"She found her way home, did she?" Asa stands, reaches out to Nell, cups the back of her head in his palm.

"That's a lucky dog," Jack says.

"I bet she's got stories to tell."

When Nell gets home from school the next day, Billy is dressed and sitting at the kitchen table.

"Can you drive me to the Y?" he asks. "They want me to start physical therapy in the pool."

"Already?"

"Maybe this is just an evaluation. C'mon. I'm gonna be late."

"Do you have your bathing suit?"

"Yeah, but it's too big. Can you find some safety pins? I don't want to flash the therapist."

"Not on the first day, at least."

Billy walks slowly to the back door. She tries to resist the impulse to help him, but can't stop herself. He jerks his gym bag away from her, nearly loses his balance, swears.

She should know better, she tells herself as she slides into the car.

Billy puts his bag in the backseat, slams the door. It pops open.

"What the hell!"

"The handle's busted. You have to press down . . . "

He wrenches the lever into place, climbs into the front seat, and struggles to close the door with his left hand. The radio blares when Nell starts the car. Peggy Lee singing "Is That All There Is?"

Billy snaps it off. "I don't know how Mom can listen to that crap."

They ride in silence, Nell tongue-tied by the wall of Billy's anger.

She drops him at the Y, promising to pick him up in an hour, then drives past Harlow's and down to the lake. Everything is white, the melting snow, the mist rising off the water, the lowering sky white with rain.

There are harlequin ducks near the shore. And a lone ring-necked duck, a bit early to be migrating. She rolls down the window. It almost smells like spring.

She opens *All Quiet on the Western Front*, but can't concentrate. Picks up her calculus homework. The problems swim in front of her eyes. Mr. Alsop called that morning to let them know Rob Chandler's father had not pressed charges.

She thinks of being found alone and taken away, up into the woods or down into the gullies and shale-bedded streams, tied up and left to rot. The cold closing in. Megan's hazel eyes, green in certain lights. So confident, so fierce, who would dare . . . ?

She rolls up the window as the rain begins again in earnest.

Billy's physical therapist invites him into a cluttered office and introduces himself: Kyle Walsh. He has a copy of Billy's evaluation from the hospital.

"What are your goals?" he asks, without preamble.

"In life?"

"Physically. What do you want to be able to do?"

"All the things I used to be able to do."

"Let's get specific. I find that working toward clear-cut goals is helpful."

"Complete use of my hand."

Kyle looks at the chart. "You're a pilot?"

"Army. Helicopters."

"Do you want to fly as a civilian?"

"Dream job. Since I was a kid."

"What else?"

"I used to draw."

"Have you tried writing or drawing left-handed?"

"No."

"Some people can make the switch. It's challenging but possible."

"Do you know something I don't?" Billy asks.

"It's a long haul with this kind of injury."

"How long?"

"We'll work hard. I can be relentless. Some days you're gonna wish I'd never been born. What else do you want to be able to do?"

"Drive. Paddle a boat. Swim. Fish. Work on a car. Hell, have a car. Hold a girl."

"Okay. Let's get started. I'll meet you in the pool."

In the locker room Billy realizes there's no way to safety-pin his trunks with one hand. Idiot. Should have asked Nell. Now he'll have to ask . . . what did he say his name was?

"Kyle? Can you give me a hand with this?"

"They feeding you at home?"

"Pain meds. Not much appetite."

"Try to eat. You'll need your strength for what we'll be doing here."

On the pool deck, two little boys stop and stare. As he walks past, one calls out to his mother: What's wrong with that man? She hushes him, her eyes glancing off Billy's burns. She tries and fails to rearrange the expression on her face.

Get used to it, he thinks, or wear a shirt.

He follows Kyle to the geriatric steps with handrails, feels another flare of anger. Steadies himself: he has work to do.

"We're just going to walk today. Waist deep. Rebuild your strength. We'll start with fifteen minutes, add five minutes each day. In a week, your surgeon says we can go shoulder deep and start working your upper body."

Billy eases into the pool. He'd forgotten about the water, the way it holds you and forgives your anger, the weight of guilt and self-pity that eats at you.

The water doesn't care.

"Once you get acclimated, we'll go backward and sideways, as well as forward. Waking up those muscles, okay?"

At least he's moving. Within seconds he's breathing hard; he can't believe how much effort this requires. He pushes himself on as Kyle leads him up and down, in figure eights. His face pours sweat.

"Five minutes," Kyle says.

Five minutes? You have to be fucking kidding me.

"Nice job. Let's take a break. Ninety seconds, then we'll go for another five."

The water is not feeling friendly or forgiving now, it feels like a wall he's asking his muscles to push through.

"Maybe that's enough for your first day," Kyle says.

"You said fifteen minutes."

"You've done eight. It's a great start."

"Fifteen," Billy says, pushing on.

Leaving school after a late session in the lab, Nell walks down Seneca Street to Exchange, the streetlights glowing softly in the rain, heading for Saint Joseph's and the Wednesday night supper in the parish hall.

The night before she'd found her parents in the kitchen, short-tempered, and for once not trying to protect her from their financial woes. The files full of bills were overflowing: Due, Past Due, Threatening.

Marion had been on the phone again with the hospital, demanding itemized bills, arguing over the crushing cost of a bed in the burn unit. The bills are recalculated, the terms extended; still they are drowning. Jack has been looking into remortgaging the house as a last resort.

Nell's college money is gone. She's on her own—scholarship, work-study if she can find it. She'll have to patch something together. Delay possibly, work for a year or two. Brendan has promised to help, but so far no checks have arrived. A drop in the bucket anyway, Marion says.

Nell needs a job; she needs to do what she can to help her parents. Maybe college will just have to wait. That thought nearly flattens her. She wants to fly through college in three years if possible, then graduate school, working in a lab, in the field. If only she could start right now.

In the parish hall, Sheila, who drives up from Syracuse after work on Wednesdays, is already serving up plates of lasagna and garlic bread. Mary Beth Farley and her mother make the main dish each week and leave it in the oven. Sheila makes the salad and dessert and handles serving. She and Nell take care of the cleanup.

Father O'Rourke carries plates to the tables, serving the guests, as he likes to call them. He smiles at Nell as she slips in and sits down at the piano.

More young men than usual are present, many wearing fatigues. Saint Joe's has no hard and fast rules about who can partake. Nell is glad there's no proselytizing, no sanctimonious quid pro quo for a meal, just a simple grace.

Father O'Rourke clears his throat. Those who had started to eat put their forks down.

"Would you please join me in offering prayers for Dorothea Clancy who passed on Tuesday, for John Jordan who moved to Rochester to enter a rehab program, and for all who are suffering in mind, body or spirit."

He bows his head. "Bless us, oh Lord, for these Thy gifts which we are about to receive from Thy bounty, through Jesus Christ our Lord. Amen."

"Amen," they chorus, some more heartily than others.

"Bless this food and fellowship and music. Bless you all."

Hal Lynch, who with his twin brother is trying to hang on to their family's farm, asks for "It Had to Be You". Mrs. Benson, who sits alone in a chair against the wall, sings along. She always knows all the words.

Sheila requests "Shenandoah" and gets almost everyone singing. She moves among the tables serving lemon squares. Nell watches how at ease she is, touching shoulders, sharing a joke.

When Father O'Rourke stands, Nell begins clearing tables.

"A few announcements: we've been putting together some information about local services that are available for veterans and the homeless," he begins. "It's not much yet, but we're working on it.

"Volunteers have set up a closet with some basic clothing and necessities. Toiletries and the like. I've left the doors open. You'll see it in the hall on your way out. Please help yourselves. There's a clipboard for suggestions. Let us know what you really need. At this point, we're just guessing.

"As many of you know, we've been holding a peace vigil

every Thursday in front of the church. We began in 1965 after Roger Allen LaPorte set himself on fire at the U.N. to protest the war. Some of you may have known Roger. He was born and raised here. I baptized him in this church. He was twenty-two years old and a member of the Catholic Worker Movement at the time of his death."

O'Rourke pauses to collect himself.

"The bishops have ordered me to stop these peace vigils and have forbidden me to distribute pamphlets informing people of our government's actions.

"As a Catholic, I apologize for their cowardice.

"We will continue. Please join us if you are so inclined."

Nell washes and dries dishes while Sheila scrubs the tables and sweeps the floor. Father O'Rourke comes into the kitchen to say good night. He looks exhausted and Nell's not sure she actually saw him eat.

She wraps up a lemon square for him.

"Say hello to your parents."

"I will. See you next week, Father."

They're surprised to find Harlow Murphy leaning against Sheila's beat-up Nova. He embraces Sheila, puts a hand on Nell's shoulder, making her blush. She's grateful for the darkness.

"What's up with Billy? He's not returning my calls."

"He was never any good with the phone," Nell says, trying not to stare at the rain beading on his hair and lashes.

"Lousy excuse."

"He's not really talking to anyone," Nell adds.

"You should stop by," Sheila says.

"Tell him he can run but he can't hide." Harlow walks off.

"You're blushing," Sheila teases.

"Shhh!"

"Look at you!"

"I can't believe he still does that to me. Ever since I was nine years old. It's nuts."

"Those long legs . . . "

"Those dark eyes . . . "

"Too bad I'm not gonna get involved with anybody," Sheila says.

"Too bad I'm too young."

"Closing the gap, girl."

Nell can't sleep. For all the weeks Megan has been missing, any girl anywhere near her age wakes up with Megan on her mind, walks to school, goes to bed, lies awake, all while wondering about Megan and where she might be and what could be happening to her. Or what has already happened to her. Halfway through Sunday dinner, going to confession, or attending Mass, Megan is more a part of her friends' and classmates' lives these weeks than she ever was before she disappeared.

Nell gets up, stops outside Billy's door; hears him thrashing in a dream. Hesitates, her hand on the knob.

Billy gathers her ardent body in his arms, the touch of her burning him. He holds her ribs, the sweep of her spine. She is speaking to him, he can't quite hear her whisper, promising him . . . When he wakes, the house silent, a sliver of moon floats in the black sky, thin as the edge of a knife. He hears the floorboards creak outside his door, then someone descending the stairs.

Nell pulls on a coat and heads out the back door. Climbs the drive, walks up the rise to the railroad tracks. Winter's grip is melting away. Streams are running high down to the lake, sap rising, a new season blowing in.

She can hear her mother forbidding them to play anywhere

near the tracks. Between the lake and the railroad, you had to scare the bejesus out of your kids and then pray they had enough sense to keep body and soul together.

She and Billy spent days walking the rails, in every season, in all kinds of weather. The trains go forever, Billy told her, all over the world. She loves those words. In her mind the rails are electric with knowledge, places, people. Someday she'll ride them right into tomorrow.

Dogs get to howling down the way, call and response, a brief frenzy, then quiet. Somewhere else there's a war on. In Texas, her brother Brendan is teaching new recruits how to identify and catalogue basic words and phrases in overheard military communications, how to look for patterns, who talked to whom, when, how often. Not unlike how she and Billy identified and tried to understand the interactions between birds. Or used to.

Brendan hasn't written Nell in months. Too busy, too distracted, too far from home to care anymore, maybe. At least he remembered her birthday. He'd sent her a microscope. Used, but in good condition. She finds something to slip onto a slide and look at every day. Her own blood sometimes.

She smells smoke, turns, and looks up. A man is walking along the tracks toward her. Tall, smoking a cigarette, wearing an army jacket. Harlow? Is that possible? How many times has she seen Harlow walking these tracks, Blue at his heels, rifle over one shoulder, a fox or a brace of pheasant lashed across his back. The blood-warm smell of the animals mingling with their musk, the cold night air; the pines along the tracks.

She waits. Neither of them speaks. How odd, she thinks, as she watches the moment unfold.

He stubs out his cigarette with the toe of his boot and reaches for her, twining his hand in her hair. His face is in shadow, eyes unreadable. The rails vibrate beneath her feet. Is it 4 A.M. already; is that the Albany train? One part of her asks these questions, while another registers the smell of tobacco and whiskey, sweat and shaving soap.

She could pull away. His touch is easy enough; he would let her go. What happens next is up to her. A shocking realization: the power to give or withhold. Like Megan.

She moves away, testing. He loosens his grip. The dogs begin again. She steps toward him. His kiss is hard and deep. It takes her breath and her mind away. His arms are crushing her. Here, she thinks, here is all she doesn't know, doesn't understand; here is the terror of Megan's disappearance.

The whistle from the Albany train startles her as it speeds through the crossing in town. She starts to say his name. He puts his hand over her mouth, pushes her toward home. She crashes down the path.

Did it happen? Was it real? She touches her lips. The rush of the train, the rush of his kiss, barrel right through her.

Billy hitchhikes to town late Saturday afternoon. He walks up Castle Street to Exchange, fighting a bitter March wind, timing his arrival at Saint Joe's for the last few minutes of confession. He sits waiting for old Mr. McNulty to limp to a pew near the front where he kneels down with his rosary, reciting the Hail Marys and Our Fathers of his penance.

Billy slips inside the confessional at 5:29; hears Father O'Rourke sigh; says, *Bless me, Father, for I have sinned*; and falls silent.

He hears the priest shift on the hard bench. Tries to quiet his breathing. Find the words.

"Son . . . ?"

"Billy Flynn, Father."

"You don't need to tell me . . . "

"I figured you should know who's wasting . . . "

"You're not wasting my time, but it's getting on toward . . . "

"Time for a drink."

"I was going to say suppertime."

"Saturday afternoon, everybody I know is thinking about a drink," Billy says.

"Still a devil."

"Yes, sir."

"I remember your father and mother—maybe they took turns—marching you in here that whole year you were stealing whatever wasn't nailed down."

"I didn't have much to say then either, did I, Father?"

"You were enjoying it too much was the conclusion I came to."

"That's the truth of it."

"Your father, now, he'd come in to talk about it, a real trial for him. Not a man to beat his kids, that about did him in."

"We're both stubborn."

"You are."

A silence.

"There's nothing you've done or could have done I haven't heard before."

"Oh, Father, there is."

"Is it a sin of commission or omission that's weighing on you?"

"Both."

Another silence.

"Any chance you'll be able to talk about this today?" O'Rourke asks.

"No, sir."

"Then have a drop with me. I've been sitting in this box too long."

Billy follows the priest into his office behind the altar. Tucked to the side is the room where Billy had changed into his robes the years he'd served as an acolyte. He hadn't had the right demeanor for that, either, but it was a requirement of his father's that he learn all the roads to God, even the ones he didn't want to go down.

O'Rourke pulls a bottle of whiskey from his desk drawer; rubs two glasses clean with the underside of his stole. They both take long draughts, more than pure thirst might dictate.

"I'd invite you to dinner except I've decided to spare you. Margaret is reheating yesterday's fish and I have come to the conclusion that Margaret harbors a secret loathing for fish. She buries it with the mustard and the breadcrumbs and some sort of topping besides. I have no idea what it is. Could be corn-flakes. Could be saltines. Could be the parings from a pony's hooves. Then she bakes it beyond recognition; so dry it requires a second sauce to help it slide down your gullet. She varies the sauce a bit week to week. Sometimes it's green. Sometimes it's tan. Could be spring onions. Could be parsley. Anybody's guess."

"We could escape to the pub, Father, have a burger."

"Does your mother cook fish on Fridays, Billy?"

"If I catch it."

"Trout, you mean?"

"Perch, too."

"And if you don't catch a fish?"

"Spaghetti."

"No meatballs?"

"No, sir."

"What's the point?"

"You could ask the Vatican, sir."

O'Rourke laughs so hard his face turns bright red.

"Smart aleck! Invite me over sometime. Free Margaret and me from our penance."

Billy stands.

"You come back, son. I'm here to listen."

Nell can't stop thinking about Harlow. The sensible side of her brain tells her it was an experiment, an anomaly, not an indicator of future events. The rest of her can still taste his mouth, feel his body, and the rails rumbling beneath her feet.

Arriving home from school on Monday, she flips through the mail on the back porch. Still nothing from the schools she's applied to. If she gets in she could delay. Work for a year, save. Who is she kidding? How will she ever earn that much money? She'd had a few hundred dollars saved from summer jobs. Gave it to Megan that panicked August.

It was Miss Rosenthal who'd pushed her to apply to Cornell, told her she was a good candidate for a scholarship. Brought her to the campus, introduced her to professors, toured the extensive labs.

She always thought she'd go to a state school. But even that might be out of reach now.

Walking through the house, she drops the mail on the counter and finds Billy at the kitchen table, paging through one of his field journals.

"Hi." She pours a glass of milk. "You want some?" Pours a second glass, puts some of Sheila's cookies on a plate.

"I got a job," she says.

"No kidding."

"At Bob and Dave's. Stocking shelves, bagging groceries. Saturdays, plus two afternoons."

"Fun."

"Pays better than babysitting."

"Uniform?"

"Apron. Cap. White shirt. Khakis."

"How's school?" he asks.

"Counting down the days. You remember."

"I do."

"I heard fox pups on my walk home," she says. "Near that stand of sumac by the Nielsons'. That faint high yapping."

"How many?"

"Three, I think."

"Not bad." Billy takes a tentative bite. "What are these, exactly?"

"Cowboy cookies."

"What's in 'em?"

"Chocolate chips, raisins, walnuts, oatmeal. Maybe coconut."

"Can you taste the coconut?"

"Not really."

"Me, neither."

He opens his journal to a page dated October 10, 1961, where he'd drawn flocks of migrating ducks near the crumbling stone pier in town. Buffleheads and goldeneyes among the canvasbacks and redheads.

"I was twelve years old when I did that." He pushes a pad of paper across the table. Labored block printing, not quite legible, wavers between the lines. "Now I can't even print my own name."

Nell looks at the page, looks at her brother, follows his gaze down to the lake and the freshwater light of the late winter thaw. Starlings drift past like smoke.

"You just got out of the hospital . . . "

"Don't be like the rest of them, Nell."

He slides another page in front of her.

"This is what it looks like left-handed."

"Not bad for a kindergartner," she tries teasing him.

"So it will take me seven years to go from barely printing to drawing like a twelve-year-old?"

"If anybody can . . . "

"Nell, please."

"What do you want me to say?"

"You don't have to say a word."

Silence falls between them and Nell has no idea how to breach it. Billy's journals are the thread of their childhood; his coming into his own as a naturalist, as an artist, developing his eye, his hand, his deepening identification with birds. From sketching in the field to detailed study, to painting the portraits he began to make the year before he shipped out.

"Will you give me another painting?" she asks.

"I was just playing around. A silly idea: words and birds."

"I like them."

"You can have them all. I don't give a shit."

The dog lopes up from the lake where she's been digging under the dock. Bangs her shoulder against the back door to be let in, greets Billy with nose and tongue and muddy paws.

"Did you see this?" He pushes the Geneva *Star* across the table. A fourteen-year-old girl named Pamela Moss from Penfield, up near Rochester, has been missing since Sunday. There's a photo from school. Pigtails. Soft, childish features. Nell pushes the paper away.

"There's been nothing about Megan," Billy says. "Not for days and days."

"I think Rob Chandler knows what happened to her."

"What would be the point of hiding information?"

"If he's responsible . . . "

"For what?"

"Her death."

"C'mon, Nell, this isn't *Peyton Place.*"

"Then where is she?"

"I wish I knew," he says, running his scarred fingers over the birds on the page.

There's an ache in her throat: Billy's hand on those pages, the birds so alive. Megan missing. She wants to touch him. Doesn't dare. She secs him register her thought, his uncanny ability to read her, and pull away.

Nell says yes to the four-hour drive south to Altoona, Pennsylvania, because she's glad Billy asked her. Marion lends them her car without any fuss. But Billy's silence is ticking her off until she sees him take more pain pills and fold his jacket to cushion his hand and arm.

When she turns to point out a red-tailed hawk, he's asleep. Hawks are messengers, Billy used to tell her when they were kids. Pay attention.

Crowded into Frank Buckles's kitchen with his wife and two babies, Billy knows instantly they shouldn't have come.

Lila offers coffee to go with the donuts they brought. Nell holds the baby while Lila fusses with the percolator.

"Do they look like Frank?" Nell asks.

"As much as babies can look like a grown man."

Nell shuts her mouth on her smile.

"There's a picture of Frank in the living room," Lila says. "His mother says both boys are the spit of him at that age."

"I didn't mean . . . "

"Frank couldn't walk through that doorway without stooping. Just hard for me to see Frank in a baby, that's all."

"Hands the size of baseball mitts," Billy says.

Lila smiles at him. The toddler clings to her leg.

"Go play, Samuel," she says, but he just grips tighter. "I can't move, honey." They make a three-legged game of moving between the stove and table.

"Billy, grab some cups for me. To the right of the sink. And open up that bakery box, would you?"

"Want a donut, Sam?" Billy tries to lift Sam into his chair, can't.

"I do it," Sam says, climbing in himself.

"You still hurting?" she asks.

"It's nothing."

"Can you use that hand at all?"

"I'm working on it."

"And the arm?"

"It's coming along."

Lila pours coffee, breaks a donut in half for Samuel. The baby falls asleep in Nell's arms.

"What's the baby's name?" Nell asks.

"Marcus."

Billy reaches for his coffee with his right hand, a bright flash of pain. Switches hands, scoops sugar, stirs.

"Frank said you had a sweet tooth."

"He wrote about me?" Billy asks, surprised.

"Said you had some plans, maybe, for after the war. The two of you. Sounded like pie in the sky to me."

"Probably."

"But it kept him going."

"Ma'am . . . "

"Lila."

"Some of the guys . . . we took up a collection. It's not much, but I promised I'd . . . " He places an envelope on the table, thick with small bills. "I know it doesn't make a damn bit of difference."

His hands are trembling. He hides them under the table. Lila reaches out and takes his right hand, smoothing the crabbed fingers straight.

Billy can't bring himself to speak the words he's come to say, how Frank sang at night in their tent, spirituals and raucous working songs, no matter how much they teased him. How they'd toss an old football back and forth in the twilight that seemed to last forever. How Billy tried to drag Frank from the burning ship, how he's got the burns and the scars to prove it; how he failed, his hands on fire, fusing to Frank's flak jacket where he grabbed hold. He'd be there still if a secondary explosion hadn't blown him clear, breaking his shoulder and his elbow and six ribs but saving his life. There was never any question of letting Frank go, was there? No question of leaving the big man behind.

"I don't know if Frank was even still . . . "

"Don't you bring that war into my house," Lila says. "These boys need their father. Can you give them back their father?

"Not you, not Nixon, not McNamara, not Rusk, not the joint chiefs of staff, can raise the dead. Every single one of those sons of bitches sending men and boys to die. For what?"

Billy looks out the window. A Cooper's hawk glides over the corn stubble, hunting. What's the message? What's the fucking message?

"They sent me a report, no doubt full of lies. They sent me his remains, but he was so badly burned . . . I couldn't see him. Not one last time."

She picks Sam up, wrapping her arms around him.

"Lila . . . " Billy says, her name soft on his lips.

"I think it's time for you to go."

Billy stands, his chair scrapes across the floor. He pulls himself erect, an act of will, looks directly at her.

"I'm so sorry."

She looks at him for a long moment.

"You let that go, you hear me, Billy Flynn? Don't let this war wreck your life, too. Nothing you can do will bring Frank back. You understand me?"

Getting into the car, they hear the low whicker and blowing of the mares in the field next door. Billy rests his head against the seat. He looks at the horses, grazing hock-deep in thistle, squints in the sun.

"My first tour . . . God, there were so many birds, Nell, fantastic things I'd never seen before. The Mekong River Delta where it meets the China Sea,

"The Red River, in late afternoon, when the sun fills the river, is really red. And the Black River is really black, full of shadows from the steep banks and overhanging trees.

"You watch the jets drop napalm from the safety of three thousand feet. You see the forest catch. If there are villages, and you know we target villages, every living thing is burned.

"The first time I saw napalm I thought—you'll laugh at me—I thought about the birds. The ibis and Himalayan swiftlets, Oriental skylarks. Birds, when below me people are burning."

He tries to stretch his hand open, feels the mutinous burst of pain.

"Napalm is a jelly," he says. "It adheres to what it burns."

Nell looks at him, then down at her hands, playing with the keys.

He knows he should stop. "Your mind plays tricks on you, but inside you know."

"It's not . . . "

"My fault? My responsibility? If we don't 'know' or are too naive to ask or protest, then you can't blame us, we can't be guilty, is that the bullshit you believe?"

"Billy . . . "

"Don't kid yourself."

She reaches out to him. He smacks her hand away; it bangs into the gearshift.

"Jesus!" She shrinks away from him.

"Let me see it."

"It's fine." She massages her wrist.

He reaches for her hand again.

"Let it be."

"I didn't mean . . . Damn, Nell, I don't know what gets into me."

He looks back at the house, the missing shingles, the peeling paint; all the things that need to get done that Frank will never do.

"I promised to bring him home," he says.

No one can promise that, she thinks.

"One minute I'm holding on to him, the next . . . There was nothing left, nothing at all in that box they sent Lila."

He touches his thumb to the scar over her eye. "You shouldn't be hearing this."

"It's okay."

"I keep trying to lock it away."

"I'm not eight anymore."

He tries smiling at her, wonders how long he can keep taking her forgiveness for granted. Looks up to see horses running in the field.

He sleeps through most of Pennsylvania. Wakes thinking of Frank Buckles and the whores in Saigon. You held them, used them, alert to every sound in the alleyway—cocks crowing at the oddest hours, water dripping, the slap of sandals on a porch step, a rickshaw creaking past—other soldiers, other rooms, drugs, booze; a debauchery of the spirit. A thin mattress on a dirt floor, filthy sheets, a bucket in the corner, and beneath you a girl, a country you drill yourself into, leave your poison behind.

Frank Buckles refused these exploits and was teased mercilessly. The big man didn't give a damn. He knew what he knew, wanted what he wanted: his wife and family at home. As though walking the straight and narrow would protect him. He prayed every night in their tent, on his knees, prayed before every mission; a man of belief, of ritual. Billy loved him.

And still he went to the whores.

He can't quite see himself talking about this with Father O'Rourke, not that he thinks the old man is a puritan, but no one wants to hear the truth about this war. Like we can all just leave our money on the table, leave that girl giggling and crying on the bed, filled with fear and hatred, reaching for a pipe to smoke, pull the veil, dull the pain, as her brother, uncle, father follows you out the door, down the street, as silent as the Seneca or Iroquois, as invisible to us there as here, murder and money on their mind. Her high thin voice following you, crying for the Coca-Cola she'd been promised before the next soldier pushes through the beaded curtain, unbuckling his pants, eyes wide: Christ, she's no bigger than a kid, he could pick her up in one hand.

Her first day at the grocery, Nell loses count of how many boxes opened, cans stacked, bottles of milk, cream, buttermilk slotted into the humming cooler.

The butcher, a wiry man with a walleye and a cleaver, intimidates her. He tells her she can call him Walt but she knows she never will. Megan started calling adults by their first names in grade school. Began with Marion and Jack, called her own mother Maeve. Asa would have none of it. Most adults overlooked the impertinence, thinking, mistakenly, that Megan was cute and sweet. Truth be told, she was an impudent devil, egged on by Billy, who reveled in what she could get away with.

Nell adopted her brother's approach: shake their hands, call them Mr. or Mrs. So-and-so, look them straight in the eye. No chumminess. Respect given. Boundaries drawn. She might need a fence with Walt.

He keeps sending her to the walk-in meat locker. The carcasses hanging from hooks terrify her. The smell of blood stuffs her nose. She wonders if she'll get used to it. Shakes off the nightmare thought of getting locked inside. Wants a shower.

Arriving home, she finds a letter from Cornell in the mailbox. Opening it, she allows herself to hope that the thickness of the envelope means good news.

She scans the letter as fast as she can . . . welcomes you to the class of 1974 . . . and skips to the last paragraph . . . We are pleased to offer you a scholarship in the amount of . . . which, in addition to your Regents Scholarship, will cover your tuition.

Maybe it's a mistake, maybe there will be a call and they'll take it back. She looks at the envelope again; yes, it's addressed to her.

Rereading the letter, she allows herself to feel a rush of excitement. She wants to tell someone. A year ago she would have picked up the phone and called Megan; she wonders if Megan's letters are sitting in the Alsop mailbox: acceptances, rejections, offers of financial aid.

She calls out to Billy, no answer, though Flanagan appears at the back door. She lets the dog out, then charges up the stairs to see if maybe, just maybe, Billy is home.

When she knocks the door falls open. The curtains are drawn, the bed unmade; there are beer bottles on the floor and under the bed, overflowing ashtrays. The desk is buried under a pile of clothes, his discarded duffel stuffed underneath it.

All of his paintings are gone and all of his drawings have been torn from the corkboard. In some places the board had been thick with paper, study after study, an individual bird emerging, finally, like magic, on the page.

Now the wall holds images torn from newspapers, from magazines, all of them, she realizes, a variation on a theme: the jungle on fire. Shot from above, helicopters caught inside the frame; shot from the ground, villagers or soldiers running, the fire pouring toward them. Fire and smoke rolling over fields and forest, the suggestive beauty and the scathing ruin.

Another group of photos: birds, impossibly on fire and in flight, some falling from the sky. Helicopters at the moment of crashing. A pelican's skeleton stretched over a huge rock. The first X-rays of Billy's hand and arm and torso. The shrapnel, even here, glinting like knives.

In a panic she searches the floor, under the bed, thinking something can be salvaged. Inventories the paintings she has in her possession: the great horned owl in her room, the Eastern Phoebe inside her closet door, the mourning doves in her locker at school, the small canvas at the piano downstairs. Turns to the wall beside Billy's bed: the heron is gone.

Looks to the bookshelf. At least his field journals are still here, she sees with relief, dozens of them, filling the shelves. Thinks of moving them to her room for safekeeping.

And then she smells smoke.

Pushing the curtains open, she looks out to the side yard. Billy stands with his back to her, a trash barrel burning in front of him, feeding his drawings and paintings into the fire.

She sees the grackle's shiny blue-black feathers, facing away from the viewer, looking over its shoulder, consumed in the flames. Feels the caption Billy had written rising up in her: *Had I But Hands to Put Around Your Throat.*

She lifts a hand to knock at the window, yell through the glass. Knows it's too late.

His hands are nearly empty, the fire blazing. He looks over his shoulder, up to the window, sensing her presence, unconsciously mimicking the bird. His eyes are blank.

APRIL

A month into rehab in the pool, Billy can feel that he's gaining ground. He buys a new pair of swim trunks when the old ones slide off, leading to a fair amount of embarrassment when Kyle has to find them in the deep end and help Billy put them back on without flashing the four-year-olds learning to swim two lanes over.

He still despises the water walking but has to admit he's growing stronger. Fighting his way through waist-high water never gets easier. He knows he should quit smoking, drinking, and showing up three times a week hungover, but knowing it and doing it are different things.

Swimming continues to be difficult, his right hand and arm weak and unresponsive. Even though Kyle and his surgeon explain that healing takes time, and healing nerves, if it can be done, takes longest of all, Billy is baffled by how an entire limb can feel not just dull, but nearly lifeless.

The nerves, tendons, ligaments, muscles, communicate, they tell him. The nerves send messages to the brain. When nerves are damaged, that fine-tuned communication system breaks down.

Understanding has not helped him live with it. Or be more patient. Or less angry.

So he fights through the water three times a week, correcting for the weakness on his right side with each stroke. His crawl is slow, his right arm like a beaver's tail, slapping the water. He still can't do the backstroke without running into the lane lines; the imbalance side to side is too great. And the breaststroke devils him.

When he tells Kyle he wants to quit fooling around in the pool and work out in the weight room, Kyle puts him through an upper body workout in the water that leaves his muscles like jelly.

On Tuesdays and Thursdays, he has additional therapy with a hand specialist. Cindy McAdams is just out of school: blonde, vaguely pretty, and very serious about her work. He has to take pain meds just to get through his sessions with her.

She has him hold a hockey stick horizontally. A rope is wound around it and she asks him to wind and unwind the rope between his hands. She does not allow him to cheat and rely on his left hand. This simple task is so difficult sweat drips from his face.

She asks him to turn his palm over and back while holding a short length of bamboo. When he keeps dropping it, she tapes his fingers around it. It takes every ounce of concentration he has to turn his wrist over. And back. She pushes him to do ten reps; at six he can no longer make his hand move.

Every exercise sounds Mickey Mouse until he tries to do it. Sitting at a table, putting his palm on a tennis ball and rolling it away from him and then back again. Trying to touch each finger to his thumb.

Cindy pushes him on. "We're trying to reestablish the neural pathways and connections."

She presents him with a fat crayon, asks him to print his name with his right hand. He can't grip it in his fingers; he can't even fist it. She tells him to take it home and practice. He'd like to take a hammer to it.

He leaves these appointments exhausted and demoralized. When Cindy jumps up to help him with his jacket, he has to restrain himself from striking her.

The fact that his mother dropped him off on her way to

work because he still can't drive adds to his fury. He emerges from the therapist's office not to his own car and independence, but to an eight-block walk to the bus stop.

The morning is still and rain-hushed, if he cared to notice. Instead of waiting for the bus, he walks the half mile to the Tap Room, the only bar open at 10 A.M. At this hour, drinking is serious business, unmitigated by girls, music, conversation. Even Billy can smell the bitter, sweat-stained air, the reek of piss and ammonia.

Cheap beer and cheap bourbon and a methodical approach get the job done. He waits for the anger that builds in him each day to explode or expire. He is not alone in this endeavor. Of the six men at the bar, half are Billy's age, survivors of the same war.

Harlow Murphy looks up from pumping gas as Billy Flynn walks by the station. He makes change for the college kid in the driver's seat while craning his neck to see where Billy's headed.

The Tap Room. Jesus Christ. So fucking predictable.

Harlow closes the open bay where he's grinding the valves on an old Ford truck, locks up the office, and follows Billy down to the boggy bottom of Exchange Street. Tucked into the corner of an old warehouse, the Tap Room is dark and dingy even at high noon.

He pulls Billy off a barstool and strong-arms him out the door.

"Not a word until I get some coffee and food into you. Though you can think up some good excuse for why you haven't bothered to return my calls, you son of a bitch."

He steers Billy up the hill to Luke's. Shoves him into a booth and calls out to the waitress behind the counter:

"Linda! Three cups of coffee, please. Strong, lots of cream. Line 'em up in front of my friend here."

Linda serves coffee, Harlow pours in sugar, stirs, presses the first cup on Billy. Watches him drink.

"What's the blue plate, Linda?"

"Macaroni and cheese."

"Two of those. And bring some bread right now, please."

He pushes the second cup of coffee in front of Billy. Linda delivers a plate with four slices of bread. Harlow butters them, hands one to Billy.

Billy takes a bite. "I can't," he drops the bread back on the plate.

"I didn't close the station to waste my time talking to a drunk."

Billy takes another bite.

"Keep drinking coffee, and get that bread in your stomach to soak up the alcohol."

Billy picks up the coffee cup again, his hands shaking. Their eyes meet.

"It doesn't work, y'know," Harlow says. "It's a waste of time."

"You're the expert."

"I've been there."

"Got out without a scratch."

"You and I both know it's what you can't see that'll kill ya."

The macaroni and cheese arrives. Billy groans at the sight of it.

"You're gonna eat, my friend."

"Enough, already." Billy pushes the plate away.

"Nope." Harlow slides it back.

"I don't think Linda will like it if we have a food fight in here."

"So eat. Or Linda will think you don't like her food."

"It's not personal. I can't taste much."

"Yup."

"You believe me?"

"Of course I believe you," Harlow says. "It's common. Should get better."

"Should?"

"What? I look like a prophet to you? Eat."

"You sound like my mother."

"I'm offering you a job."

"Get outta here."

"You can start this afternoon."

"No way."

"Why not?"

"There are some things I can't do."

"We'll focus on what you can do."

"You're relentless."

"This? What you're doing? Is bullshit."

"Maybe I don't want your shitty job."

"Don't be an idiot. We'll have some fun."

"Grease monkey? Fun?"

"Earn some money. Get your own place. Girls. You get the idea."

Billy bursts out laughing.

"That's better. And you can learn to pick up the fucking phone."

Harlow is miraculously unscathed considering he spent twelve months humping a pack through everything the jungle could throw at him and then survived Hamburger Hill. He and Billy did their best to stay in touch, though neither one is very good at writing letters.

Discharged from the service, he'd gone to SUNY Binghamton for a few months. The culture shock was so extreme he bounced from elation to despair several times a day. The braless girls, the running paths through the woods, along the Susquehanna and Chenango rivers, a halfway decent track coach, teammates who knew enough to just shut up and run.

On good days he ran right into a rhythm of forgetting, found a girl not quite so dedicated to her antiwar stance she'd forgo sleeping with a vet, and then drank enough to numb his nightmares. On bad days he was rendered speechless by fury and confusion. He grew his hair long. Learned never to talk about the war.

Dropping out of Binghamton, he took over his father's garage, freeing his dad to concentrate on his side business in gravel and sand. A business that will boom and bust in short order with the Route 5 & 20 connector. Progress and decline all rolled into one highway that allows the world to bypass their hometown.

He and Billy will breathe some life into the place.

When Nell gets home from school, Rosie's car is in the driveway and she can hear Connor and Collin playing in the side yard. It sounds like they're scalping each other.

Rosie and Marion are in the kitchen making dinner, deep in conversation. Nell greets them both, but it's clear she's interrupting. What's Rosie doing here on a school night anyway?

She heads up to her room with a stack of science journals and recent reports from the United States Fish and Wildlife Service for her independent research project. Nell is reading about mercury levels in fish, water, and wildlife. The amount of data is overwhelming, the spread of mercury increasing. United States Fish and Wildlife Service began reporting on mercury in the 1950s. Rachel Carson blew the whistle in 1962, but more chemicals are being introduced and approved each year. Chemical companies tweak an existing product, and the research begins all over again. Proof of harm is the standard, but the burden of proof is on the consumer or the government. How can the research possibly keep up? And why is the legislation skewed in favor of business rather than public health and safety?

She hears her mother's raised voice. Walks halfway down the stairs, sits, and listens.

Marion busies herself with the tomato sauce to give Rosie

time to collect herself. She rummages in the overhead cabinet, hoping there will be enough spaghetti to feed this crowd. Jack is not a big fan of spaghetti, but he'll live.

"No one has the right to harm one single hair on your head," Marion says.

"How do you know I'm not the one at fault?"

"You're the one wearing the bruise."

"Do you think I don't know how to provoke him?" Rosie asks. "To push and push until . . . "

Marion manages to keep her mouth shut for a minute or more.

"And please don't tell Dad. Or Billy. Okay?"

"I'm not going to stand by while this happens to you. I will pull you out of there."

"It was just one terrible moment in a good marriage."

"Are you sure?" Marion asks.

"Yes."

"One hundred percent sure?"

"Nick is a wreck right now."

"If it ever happens again . . . "

"It won't."

"Just tell me what it's about."

"I don't like telling tales."

"I'm your mother, for heaven's sake."

Rosie weighs the desire to tell with her promise not to.

"Two kids so quick, another one on the way, and we're just getting started. I'm not sure he should have stayed on with his dad in the shop and now he feels stuck. And I'm part of that somehow."

"So get a job. You're the smartest one in the bunch, if you hadn't noticed."

"And who's going to take care of the kids?"

"Your mother-in-law."

"Please."

"What about a babysitter?" Marion asks.

"So I should go to work to pay a sitter?"

"Or you could work part-time. When Nick is off."

"And never see him?"

"And carry part of the burden so he doesn't feel so stuck."

"He won't see it like that," Rosie says.

"Help him see it."

"He'll see it like salt in a wound."

"So because he's stuck, you should be too? And helpless to take action to change the situation?"

Rosie massages the small of her back, crosses to the window.

"Mom, you're right, but you're wrong. Right about what I could do, wrong about what that feels like to both Nick and me."

"Then go to work and save to buy him his own shop. In a town that's not dying, where you've got a chance."

"He can't leave his father."

"You're supposed to leave your family, Rosie. That's what it's all about."

"You don't . . . "

"Live your lives. Make your own mistakes. What happened to the girl who wanted to go to California, who wanted to write for a newspaper?"

"I grew up."

"That's not an answer."

"I got pregnant."

"Millions of women have children and work."

"Not in Nick Bliss's world."

"Talk to him. That's all I'm saying."

"It's not that easy."

"There's work for you girls. And it's not all secretaries and teachers and nurses anymore. You could go back to school, you could . . . "

Rosie turns from the window, brings Marion's hand to her belly.

"She's moving all the time."

"She?"

"I really want a girl this time."

Marion smiles to see the delight on Rosie's face.

Rosie holds her breath, waiting to feel movement again.

"Don't bury your dreams in your children," Marion says. "They won't thank you."

They look out at the roughhousing boys. Marion opens the back door: "Get out of my flower beds! That's your last warning. Am I understood?"

"Yes, Grandma," Connor says, cuffing Collin across the back of the head, sending him headfirst into the swing set. A good hard bonk, but no bloody nose.

Nell goes out to see what all the ruckus is about, comforts Collin, who stands with his back to his brother, shaking with the effort not to cry. Black-haired, bossy Connor taunts: "Crybaby! Crybaby!"

She gets them playing Red Light, Green Light. The three of them run and holler with abandon in the deepening dusk as swallows and then bats appear and disappear in the massive ivy-covered oak.

Jack wakes from a deep sleep, a rush of adrenaline pounding through him, instantly drenched with sweat. Every time he gets lulled into thinking he's through with the nightmares, they ambush him again.

And then he hears Billy: a haunted, choking cry.

He opens the door to Billy's room to find Nell standing at the foot of his bed.

"It's all right . . . Go to sleep . . . It's all right, Billy."

It looks like he's convulsing.

As Nell begins to sing to him, Billy quiets. Her voice follows Jack down the stairs.

He stands at the kitchen window, looking down to the lake. Mist floats above the water, a wash of moonlight. He hears pines soughing in the wind, feels a kindred sound rising inside. Turns the light on over the stove, finds the bottle of Scotch, two glasses.

"Will you join me?" he asks when Nell comes into the kitchen.

"I thought I'd make some cocoa."

"I recommend the Scotch," he says, pouring.

She tastes it, makes a face.

"We need to celebrate your good news. Cornell . . . We're so proud of you."

She pulls her hands inside the sleeves of her sweatshirt.

"Look, Dad, I know we can't . . . "

"We'll work it out."

"I can delay a year."

"No."

"Or maybe I could board with Esme," Nell says. "Earn my keep. Clean her house, learn how to cook a few things."

"I'm looking into working at the VA hospital two or three shifts a week. That should about cover it."

"You can't work twenty-four hours a day."

"It'd be temporary."

"I can help. You have to let me help," Nell says.

"You need to concentrate on your studies. The first year is so rigorous . . . "

"I'm not some hothouse flower. I can work, Dad."

"Your classes will be filled with students like you who were top in their school. It's gonna be tougher."

"I can handle it."

"I know you can handle it. This is something we want to give you—the chance to explore, to stay late in the lab . . . "

"It's not forever. Things are gonna get better, right? Let me talk to Esme," Nell insists.

"Just talk."

"For now."

He looks at her white throat, chapped lips, the sheen of her dark hair. "Billy's nightmares . . . "

"I had to learn not to touch him," she says. "Those bruises a few weeks ago? It wasn't a fall."

"He hit you?"

"Not on purpose. If you touch him he wakes instantly, scared and fighting."

"Does he tell you about them?"

"Sometimes."

"Tell me."

"He dreams Frank Buckles is sitting in the chair across from his bed."

"Buckles?"

"His copilot."

Jack looks into his glass.

"Did you have nightmares, Dad?"

"Still do."

The minutes tick long.

"You can't leave it. You just end up carrying it." He takes another swallow of Scotch. "I don't know how to help him," he admits, shamed to hear the words out loud.

"Just love him."

He looks at his daughter again, wishes it were enough, wishes he didn't know the limits of love and hope, how little, really, can be covered over, hidden away, made whole.

Saturday morning, Nell sits in the old canoe waiting for Billy. They always go out as early in April as possible. She'd scraped and caulked the bottom the previous week.

It's breezy and cold on the lake. Nell hopes the mild April

sunshine will do more than just promise some warmth. She has a thermos of hot coffee and cheese sandwiches.

She's been planning this outing for weeks. They'll paddle to their old sit spot south of Dodson's Point. Just an hour, maybe, listening and watching as they used to. It's a start.

Billy grunted at her when she knocked on his door, but there's still no sign of him.

Half an hour later, just as she's about to give up, Billy wanders down the path, a beer bottle in his left hand, Flanagan trailing him, all wag and shake. He fondles her ears. She circles his legs, comes back for more.

"Go get a jacket."

"What for?"

"I'm taking you to Dodson's Point."

"What makes you think I can manage a paddle?"

"If you can't, I'll get us there."

"In this old tub?"

He takes a long pull from his beer, looks at her like she's stupid. Billy was never mean. Sharp. Direct. Tactless, even, but never mean. He laughs once, a harsh sound deep in his throat; then walks up the path, not looking back.

She pulls the boat onto the landing, thinking of when Jack bought the canoe from Bobby Bascomb, a colleague down the lake, a gift to ease the ache of Brendan going off to college.

Jack brought both kids along to pick up the canoe. Billy begged to paddle it home with Nell. Bascomb encouraged Jack to let them go.

"How long?" Jack asked.

"You or me? An hour. The kid? Maybe two," Bascomb said.

"I can do it, Dad," Billy said.

"It's already 5 o'clock."

"We've got hours until sunset."

"You good to go, Nell?" Jack asked.

"We can do it, Daddy."

They were doing fine until the weather changed. Gray clouds massed north of the lake and the wind picked up, strong enough to create chop. Billy hugged the shore to stay out of the wind, but it was hard work and Bascomb's estimate of two hours had just gone out the window.

The canoe leaked, of course. Nell used Billy's baseball hat to bail. She worked like a little engine, not saying much. She didn't complain, Nell almost never complained. She'd learned that little piece of Flynn code early, and she would never admit she was scared.

Billy was getting tired. It was a heavy old broad-bottomed canoe. Probably safe as houses, but a lot of boat for fourteen-year-old arms.

"Hey, Nell, quit bailing for awhile and paddle, will ya?"

"What about all the water?"

"We'll put you on a paddle for five minutes and then bailing for five minutes. We'll make better progress."

She took the paddle and leaned into her strokes, like he'd taught her.

"That's good," he said. "You're doing a good job."

She was getting a taste of just how heavy the boat was.

"You cold?" he asked.

"Not too bad."

"Paddling will warm you up."

She nodded.

"We've passed Bishop's Landing; we're about halfway there. We'll be able to see the lights from town to guide us in when it gets dark," he continued. "What time is it?"

"Six fifteen."

"It's the clouds making it so dark."

"Should I bail again?"

"Another few minutes. You're really helping."

More clouds boiled up from the west, fluffy and white, lit by the lowering sun. They were alone on the lake as far as they could see.

"Did you hear that?" Billy asked.

"Screech owl?" Nell ventured.

"Good guess."

"They kind of whinny like a horse."

"Yes, they do."

"Was that a bobolink?" she asked.

"Bobolink, catbird, Baltimore oriole."

"I'll never be as good as you."

"It's just practice," he said. "Got any new jokes?"

"Nope."

"We could sing."

And they did. All the campfire songs, the songs they sang in the car on the way to visit Uncle Joe and Aunt Betty Lou in Old Forge, the ones with endless verses coming around mountains and stacking beer on walls. Nell came up with one of the Irish airs their father loved: *Isle of Innisfree*. Between the two of them they remembered verse after verse.

Nell alternated bailing and paddling until her head started to droop she was so tired.

"Close your eyes for five minutes," Billy told her. "A quick rest and you'll get some strength back."

"I don't want to leave it all to you."

"I'll be fine."

"Billy . . . "

"Just close your eyes."

"Wake me if I fall asleep."

"I will."

She lay across the seat resting her head on the gunwale. She was asleep in seconds.

Nell woke with a start when the wind dropped and the

storm clouds moved off to the east. The sunset was magnificent: bands of gray lifting as the sun descended in a show of red and pink and near purple. She bailed with a vengeance as if to make up for lost minutes and then picked up her paddle again.

Billy pointed out a male wood duck in breeding flight, the unearthly blue at the tip of its wings. They could hear the female, but couldn't see her, her high-pitched, rising call lingering in the air. Further on they passed a pair of northern shovelers migrating north; some would fly as far as Alaska.

"Is that our dock?" Nell asked.

"Where?"

Nell pointed. "Halloooo," she called, her voice fluting in the dark.

It felt like they were skimming over the water, not much feeling left in their hands, their arms exhausted. The lake took on a silvery cast and suddenly seemed a foreign place they'd never visited before.

They paddled up to the dock giddy with their success. Jack, on his knees, helped them from the boat and pulled both of them into his arms with a fierceness they were unaccustomed to.

"Good boy," he said to Billy. And, "You're a trouper, Nell, a real trouper."

Now, as she walks up the hill, Nell wants that circle back: her father's arms around both of them, united with Billy in their adventure, a homecoming that pulls them together instead of tearing them apart.

When she enters the kitchen, Billy is at the stove making a mess with milk and cocoa. His beer has been dumped out in the sink.

He fills two cups, spilling half of it. Hands her one.

"Thanks." She takes a sip. "You forgot the sugar!" She dumps in sugar, stirs. "That's a little better. Not as good as the stuff you made when we were kids, though."

They walk outside, sit on the porch steps; hear phoebes, waxwings, and the rumble of Asa's ailing tractor drifting down from the fields. The wind comes up, flattening the grass, smelling of the lake and freshly turned earth. Flanagan snuffles after a chipmunk. Rabbit, maybe. She senses their attention, circles back to Billy; then goes back to work.

"Listen, Nell . . . "

She isn't sure he'll continue.

"The drinking. I need to try . . . "

She waits.

"It gets a hold of you. Like it's some kind of answer. Even though you know it isn't."

"I wish you could talk to me," she says.

He stares at his hands, sees Megan suddenly, a hand on her throat, terror in her eyes. Shakes it off, whatever it is: vision, nightmare. He looks at Nell, puts an arm around her.

"Cornell, huh?"

"I can't quite believe it."

"When were you gonna tell me?"

"The day the letter arrived . . . I saw you burning your drawings and paintings. I couldn't . . . It just feels like it's not fair, like I'm taking your place."

"It's great news, Nell."

"I want you to come with me. We could get an apartment together. You could start with a course or two. Work for Esme."

"You don't want me tagging along after you."

"I do."

"I don't even think Cornell is what I want anymore."

"Billy, your whole life; the ornithology lab, the . . . "

"If I can get this hand and arm to function, if I can be patient and put in my time with work and therapy, maybe even find another surgeon, then I want to get my commercial pilot's license."

Flanagan barks, having treed something. Raccoon, probably.

"If that doesn't work out," he continues, "I'll think about college. Make Mom happy."

"That's what you really want."

"It's what I've always wanted."

Billy slips into the confessional at 5:30. Father O'Rourke groans. Billy tries to stifle a laugh.

"Billy Flynn," O'Rourke says.

"Yes, sir."

"You always had a wicked sense of humor."

"A little cockeyed."

"And you like to keep me from my Saturday libation."

"It takes me all week to get here, Father."

"I understand the difficulty."

A pause. The priest sighs.

"Bless me, Father, for I have sinned."

They hear one of the church ladies flipping up the kneelers as she dusts. Humming.

"What burden are you carrying? This is the place to put it down."

"I want to come to church, Father."

"Nothing stopping you."

"And take communion."

"The sacraments have the power to heal."

The woman. Still humming.

"It has been two years since my last confession."

"The Marriage of Figaro."

"What?"

"She's humming the Count's plea to the Countess. Note for note. That's amazing. *Contessa, perdono.* And her answer: *I am more mild than you* . . . Am I interrupting you now, son?"

"No, sir."

"If there's beauty in the world, if there's forgiveness, that's what it sounds like. The end of the opera is a hymn of peace. I wish you could hear it."

"I've never . . . "

"All the operas, Billy, all the Seneca and Iroquois legends you love so much are about sin and forgiveness and redemption."

"And raising the dead."

"Ah."

"Raising the dead, Father."

"Let's talk about the dead."

"I can't."

"Tell me what happened."

"I can't."

"Tell someone."

"It's too . . . "

"You won't tarnish their memory by telling their story."

"Why was I the only one to make it out alive, Father?"

"You can say you should have died with your men. That may be the easy way out."

"Are you kidding?"

"It relieves you of the burden—the responsibility—to carry them with you as you live, Billy. As you live."

"My gunners were eighteen years old. My copilot had two kids. My ship was full of wounded. The medic on board was six days from the end of his tour."

"How many other helicopters went down that day?"

"All but one."

"All but one."

"Yes, sir."

"Your penance is three Hail Marys, four Our Fathers, and a walk in the woods. Go in peace."

Harlow pulls into the drive, slams on the brakes as he turns sharply past the trashcans, sending a spray of gravel onto the back porch. The sound of his arrival is unmistakable, and, Nell realizes, has not been heard in almost two years.

He's shouting for Billy before he even reaches the porch: Get your boots, get your jacket; get your ass in gear.

Nell meets him at the back door, embarrassed, shy beyond reason, aching to know how to interpret his actions and non-actions alike. Harlow checks his speed to avoid knocking her over, and then the room is filled with Marion hugging him, Jack shaking his hand, Billy pulling on a sweatshirt. Nell tries to fade into the background but Harlow pulls her into a bear hug, squeezing the breath out of her, whispering in her ear: *I like a girl who can't hide her feelings.* She tries to keep her head down while also trying to gauge whether he's teasing or serious.

Billy catches Harlow's eye, raises an eyebrow. "She's a little young."

"Shut up!" Nell snaps.

Harlow takes her chin in his hand, tilts her face up. "I heard you got into Cornell." He kisses her on both cheeks. "Congratulations."

She manages to choke out a thank you.

"You want to come with us?" Harlow asks.

"No, she doesn't," Billy says.

"Where are you going?" Nell asks.

"Surprise. You'll like it," Harlow says.

She looks at her brother. He shrugs.

Flanagan whines to come along. Billy pushes her back inside.

They drive through town and head south down East Lake Road. Nell is squashed between them, not complaining, as they pass a flask back and forth in front of her. Harlow swings onto

Searsburg Road, which runs over the high escarpment between Seneca and Cayuga lakes. They pass a few hunting camps, little tin-roofed shacks made of doors and other castoffs, but no real houses.

Before the war she had tagged along with Billy and Harlow when they went tracking. She could be trusted to be quiet, not be a nuisance, and keep up. She learned how a trapper had to notice things: the nearly invisible paths pressed into fallen leaves, scratches on trees, turned-up earth, scat. She became increasingly aware that the knowledge Harlow and Billy shared, something between informed observation and instinct, was a rare thing, a remnant of an older world.

When the road becomes dirt, Harlow flips off the headlamps and makes his way slowly using his running lights. Finds the turnoff and carefully eases the truck through a narrow gap that opens up to a meadow bordered by white pines. Kills the engine, reaches out the window, connects two wires. He's rigged an infrared light on the roof of the cab so they can see what animals are out at night.

They sit in the dark, waiting. Nell hears the mewing whistle of a female snowy owl, turns to see if Billy heard it too. He is listening intently, staring into the dark, but not hearing. Impossible, she tells herself, alarmed. When the owl whistles again, much closer this time, he looks at her and smiles.

They don't have to wait long.

The colors reflecting back from the mirrorlike eyes in the dark allow them to identify the animals even before their bodies emerge into the halo of light. Deer: green. Raccoons: orange. Fox: red.

They never see the animals they came for, though they watch and wait for more than an hour. The night is rich with the scent of pine. Stars glitter overhead in the cold, clear air. The full April moon known as the Wildcat has not yet risen.

Harlow and Billy have always been fascinated by coyotes

and wolves as if they, too, know what it means to be an opportunist, to live on anything; to be subtle enough to disappear. Nell finds herself wondering whether Harlow had been a tracker in Vietnam, whether it had saved his life, the lives of his squad, if she will ever be able to ask him about it.

When Harlow disconnects the light and flips on his headlamps they see a gray wolf skirting the edge of the clearing. It disappears into the pines.

"Well, I'll be damned," Harlow says, turning on the heater. "When I think of all the hours we've spent tracking them . . . "

Nell listens as Billy and Harlow talk around her on the drive home, as though the dark makes her invisible. They are relaxed and profane and funny. When Harlow puts his arm around her she's shocked. She sits straighter, imagining Billy's response, and then decides so what, who cares; she can lean into him.

The smell of him. The rise and fall of his chest. The way she fits under his arm. What is she supposed to do with her hands? His leg is taut alongside hers, shifting to brake or accelerate. The rumble of the motor vibrating through the floorboards; like the left hand playing the rhythm while her body plays the melody.

If Billy weren't here . . . Well, it isn't likely Harlow would have rigged this up for her alone. But if he had . . . She indulges this line of thinking, wishing, perhaps for the first time in her life, to be free of her brother. He has always been free of her: the age difference, the freedoms all boys have. She has never felt free of him, even in his absence.

He casts a long shadow. Maybe it's time to move outside of it.

She dares to rest her hand on Harlow's thigh. Muscle, heat, the rough cotton of his jeans. Suddenly there are questions she'd give anything to ask Megan. There's no one else to ask. Not her mother, or her sisters, or Billy, God forbid.

Harlow puts both hands on the wheel when they get to East Lake Road and its streetlights. Nell looks at him, looks down at her hands, thinks of how he'd pulled her up into the apple tree beside him so many years ago.

No one understands children and their desires. No one.

On Tuesday, after working at the grocery, Nell is surprised to find Detective Johnson and Dale Pope sitting in the living room. Marion, concerned they'll upset Nell again, has already given them a piece of her mind.

"Again? We don't have enough to deal with, gentlemen?"

Nell sits down across from the detective. Dale Pope stands by the door, his arms crossed over his expanding girth.

Johnson consults his notes. He has very fine fingers, she notices, tobacco-stained.

"Janet Sims told us she overheard an argument between you and Megan the day before she disappeared. What were you fighting about?"

"Her boyfriend."

"Rob Chandler?"

"You haven't found another one, have you?"

He returns to his notes, waits.

"She'd dropped her old friends to be with her new friends."

"Meaning you."

"I missed her, I guess. I didn't like what I was seeing . . . "

"Which was . . . ?"

"Megan couldn't, or wouldn't, stand up to Rob. It almost seemed as if she liked how controlling he was."

"Controlling how?"

"He told her who she could be friends with. Where she could go. What she should wear. She thought it was romantic. I thought it was creepy."

"Had there been problems between the two of you before this?"

"We weren't as close as we used to be."

"And the reason for that?"

"Where's Rob Chandler now?" Nell asks. "I haven't seen him in a few days."

"You'd have to ask his family."

"Why don't you ask me about how he threatened me at school after you questioned me the first time? Or the time he stopped to offer me a ride home, but there were three other guys with him, and it wasn't really an invitation, more like if I was ever dumb enough to get into that car . . . "

"What do you mean?"

"Rob Chandler never said more than five words to me in four years of high school. And suddenly he's at my locker, suddenly he knows where I live and he's on my street when I'm walking home . . . It doesn't make any sense."

"He's been cleared as a suspect."

"What?" Nell asks, unable to keep the shock out of her voice.

"He's a seventeen-year-old kid," Johnson says.

"With a rich father and . . . " Marion adds from the doorway.

"She would have done whatever he told her to do. Even something stupid," Nell says.

"Like what?"

"I don't know. But he scares me."

When the policemen leave, Nell hurries through her chores at the Alsops'. The farm looks shabbier than ever and the onset of mud season isn't helping.

The week before when Nell had found the ponies' feed barrel empty she'd begged her father to buy a few bags of grain at the feed store. He was adamantly opposed, not because of the money, but because of the insult to Asa. When she would not be dissuaded and then developed a plan to sneak the grain into the storeroom barrels while Asa was in town, he was her reluctant accomplice.

Nell is mucking out stalls when Maeve Alsop steers up the rutted drive, tires spinning in the mud. Nell watches from the barn as Mr. Alsop helps Evan load two suitcases and a few boxes into the trunk and wishes she were not here to witness this. Ten-year-old Evan is fighting tears, stuttering his goodbyes. The onset of Evan's stutter is why he supposedly needs to move into town with his mother. Closer to school and a speech therapist.

Had anyone given any thought to what it was like for Evan alone in that house? Megan gone, God knows where, her room empty, his father shattered, grieving, raging for all she knows. Ten years old, so thin you can see the wings of his shoulder blades through his T-shirt. Painfully shy. He'd come out to the barn one morning to tell her something. Couldn't get the words out.

Mrs. Alsop stays in the car, her window cracked open, cigarette smoke curling into the cold air. Asa stands by his son's side, his huge hands opening and closing. Dash, still confined to the house, is barking frantically and trying to push open the back door.

Nell grabs a currycomb in the tack room, sees Megan's green sweater hanging on a hook. Ducks into a stall to curry the ponies; ecstasy for them as they shed their winter coats. When she hears the car head down the drive and the farmhouse door close, she makes a break for it, jogging down the farm lane, not looking back, even when she hears Mr. Alsop call her name.

That night she tells her mother she has to quit; she's too spooked to keep going to the farm. When her mother asks for details, Nell doesn't know what to say.

He makes me uncomfortable, the farm is sad and lonely, I

can't stand the way it feels like he needs me; that he wants to reach out and hold on to me, to touch me.

"Nell, Asa Alsop would never . . . "

"It's not the same since Megan disappeared. And now Evan's gone. I just . . . "

"What?"

"I can't go back there."

"Did something happen?" Marion asks.

"It's just different. It feels different."

"Did you see something?"

She thinks for a moment. What's bothering her? "Megan's green sweater. It was hanging from a hook in the barn."

"So?"

"It wasn't there before."

"Are you sure?"

Nell hesitates. "Yes."

"Was she wearing it the day she disappeared?" Marion asks.

"I don't know. But she wouldn't have left it there."

"There are dozens of possible explanations."

"Like what?"

"That she forgot her sweater at the farm."

"Why is it in the barn?"

"Maybe it's a talisman," Marion says. "He keeps it near him."

"That's kind of strange."

"You wore Billy's hunting jacket for two years."

"I can't go back, Mom."

"You have to call him."

"But . . . "

"Could Billy manage your job?"

"Some of it."

"So tell him you'll talk to your brother, see if he can fill in."

On the phone Asa makes it easy for Nell. He tells her he

understands and that he's sold the ponies. It knocks the breath
out of her.

"Where are they going?"

"A family over in Clifton Springs. Could you be here, Nell,
when they're picked up on Wednesday? I'm not sure I can
stand to see them go."

"What time?"

"You tell me."

"3:30, after school."

"I'll arrange it," Asa says. "I'll take myself off to town."

"My brother might be able to help you out. Do you want
me to talk to him?"

"Tell him to stop by."

"Mr. Alsop, was that Megan's green sweater I saw in the
barn?"

"She forgot it in my truck the last time I drove her to
school."

"Why is it in the barn?"

"I don't know what to do with it. I should probably put it
away in her closet, but I like to see it. I know that doesn't make
any sense."

"I miss her, too."

"Don't be a stranger, Nell."

"I won't."

They both remain on the line for a moment. When Nell sets
the phone down, she feels sick. It doesn't seem possible that
Mr. Alsop can walk through his barn without those ponies, any
more than he can walk through his house without his children.
Nell is just one more person leaving him behind.

Pamela Moss's body is found less than a mile from her
home in Penfield. Buried just off the path that all the kids use

as their shortcut between the new mall and Panorama Trail. Steep gullies, wooded slopes; an island of wilderness surrounded by the backyards of the latest housing development.

Still no suspects, no one in custody. Is she part of the Alphabet Murders—Pamela from Penfield—or is this an isolated case? Kids as young as seven or eight use the path to visit friends and neighbors. Teenagers love it for the privacy it affords. Many firsts occur just off the trail: kisses, cigarettes, joints. Now it's a crime scene.

The papers mention Megan Alsop in passing. One enterprising reporter dug up Megan's middle name: Grace, suggesting that Megan Grace from Geneva could, in fact, fit this serial killer's profile.

Billy is late for his PT appointment in the pool. Eight weeks out from his last surgery, he has a new prescription for his therapist, given to him by his surgeon that morning: Strengthening. No limits.

His range of motion is improving, but his hand is still more like a paw. He can barely grip a glass, turn a key, or wring out a sponge. But little by little, the pain is lessening. They say it's all a question of the nerves.

He wants to see what Kyle will do with those three words: Strengthening. No limits. And he wants to race his brother Brendan in June. To win.

Kyle is all for swimming, but he never encourages Billy's racing fantasies. His job is to get that arm in motion again, the hand less of a liability.

"We'll start with gloves; they'll give your hands a little support. And the webbing will give you some resistance, good for strengthening your arms and back, some additional pull, some speed."

Billy's eyes light up.

"That's a maybe on the speed. Expect to be slow. Expect to be awkward, okay? Then you can feel great when you start to improve."

"Okay."

"Lower your expectations."

"Got it."

"After the gloves, a week or so, we'll see how you do, we can work with hand paddles."

"Like the real swimmers."

"Like the real swimmers."

"For now," Kyle hands him a kickboard, "fifty meters kick, fifty meters swim. That's the drill. Stop when you need to."

Kyle walks the pool deck, correcting and encouraging him.

"Who the hell invented the kickboard?" Billy asks.

"You want to beat your brother? Shut up and kick."

"Come on . . . "

"It's your power. You think it's all about your arms. It's not."

"Fuck you."

"You've got some deficits, Billy."

"I thought one of your jobs was cheerleader."

"Your legs can make up the difference. We'll start with fins next week."

Billy finishes the fifty, pulls on a pair of webbed gloves.

"Keep it simple. Any pain, we stop."

"If it's minor, can I work through it?"

"Let's see how it goes. Start with breaststroke."

"Jesus!" Billy can't keep the flare of anger out of his voice.

"We on the same page here?" Kyle asks. "I don't want to push you into last week. Or last month. We clear?"

Fifty meters of breaststroke, with an ineffectual kick, and one and a half arms, is endless. Who invented this? He feels ridiculous.

"Take a break. Full stop. One minute rest. Then we walk it out. Then we talk."

Billy squats in the shallow end, dizzy, trying to catch his breath. He should've had breakfast.

"You a smoker?" Kyle asks.

Billy nods.

"Drink much?"

"I'm trying to quit."

"Good idea. How's the arm?"

"Tired. But not sore."

"One hundred meters crawl and you're done."

"No way."

"We start slow. We progress. Let's go."

Four lengths and his muscles are burning and screaming from the effort. Jesus Christ.

"It's a start," Kyle says.

"It's for shit," Billy replies, his anger refueled by having to use the set of geriatric steps with a handrail just to get out of the frigging pool.

"Where were you?" Kyle asks.

"Where was I when you were smoking dope and protesting the war?"

"I'm a vet, you dumbass. Marines."

"Where? In the rear with the gear?"

"Siege of Khe Sanh good enough for you? I've got a good idea what you're going through."

Billy takes this in. "I was at Camp Holloway. Then Da Nang."

"You talking to anybody?"

"I'm talking to you."

"You know what I mean."

"You calling me crazy?"

"Of course not, but . . . "

"But what?"

"Your doctor thinks you're not being realistic."

"And you?"

"Nerve damage is complicated, it's . . . "

"Enough with the relentless bad news!"

"I told him you could work through a lot of pain, that you wanted it bad enough to work through just about anything."

"Anything that's possible, that is."

"That's right."

"Is it possible?"

"I don't have a crystal ball."

"Is it possible?"

"It's not likely."

Billy looks across the pool to the wall of glass blocks refracting sun and blue sky. "Odds?"

"Billy—"

"Thanks, man."

Late that afternoon, when Nell finally finds him at the Veterans' Club, cheapest beer in town, extracts him from the booth in the back corner, and walks him home, he's in rough shape. Crap beer with rotgut chasers and he smells like the toilet he's spent half the afternoon puking in. Beer, bourbon, rage, self-hatred: a lethal brew. And some asshole kept playing Richie Havens over and over on the jukebox. *Freedom, freedom, freedom*, with that insanely fast guitar lick. The irony enough to kick your teeth in.

"You're gross."

"Thanks."

"No, you really stink, Billy."

"That bathroom is not a nice place to be on your hands and knees."

She hands him a packet of saltines. His hands shake as he pulls off the cellophane, crams them into his mouth.

He stops outside Nelson's. "Can I borrow a few bucks? I need some cigarettes."

"I don't have any money with me."

"Liar."

She shrugs. "You eat anything today?"

"What are you, my mother?"

"Did you?" she asks.

"I don't remember."

"Ha!"

"Crap coffee, maybe a piece of lousy pie . . . "

"You're beating yourself up pretty bad, y'know?"

"This is nothing."

"Maybe you could quit it."

"I need a shower, I need a cigarette; I need to get laid."

"Billy!"

"You need to get laid."

"Stop it."

"C'mon, little miss priss."

"Why are you being like this?"

"Like what?"

"Like somebody I don't know."

"Don't know or don't like?"

"Maybe both."

They turn onto Highland and walk down the hill to East Lake Road. Highland is Nell's favorite street, still lined with American elms, though the blight is moving through these giants, too.

She stops, listens. "Oriole . . . cardinal . . . catbird . . . woodpecker."

Billy stops beside her.

"There's the cardinal again," she says.

He shakes his head, as if to clear it.

"And a jay, too." This is what he taught her. "Hey, you learn any new birdcalls in Vietnam?"

He shushes her with a gesture.

"Not one?"

"What are you hearing now?" he asks.

"Woodpecker, 4 o'clock. Robin, 8 o'clock. Blue jay . . . "

"Crow?"

"Screeching directly overhead."

"The crow and the blue jay. That's all I can hear."

"You're just out of practice. Cardinal."

"I can't hear it."

"You're kidding, right?"

The robin again, its loud liquid carol: *Cheerily, cheer-up, cheerio.* Surely he can hear that.

He shakes his head. She wants to reassure him, but stops as the gravity of what he's saying begins to sink in. If he can't hear properly . . . They'd spent their whole lives listening. And watching.

"What do your doctors say?" she asks.

"Give it time. It's a fucking mantra. They're worthless."

"But . . . "

"Drop it, Nell."

When they get home, Rosie's car is in the driveway and Connor and Collin are playing in the backyard. Rosie sits in the kitchen while Marion makes dinner.

Billy heads for the shower, promising to come down to say hello as soon as he's presentable.

"What's going on?" Nell asks.

"Nick's taken a lease on his own shop," Rosie says.

"Really? Where?"

"Just outside Rochester. The Twelve Corners in Pittsford, between a wine store and a shoe store. Great location, a well-to-do community, and look at this, Nell." Rosie unrolls the floor plan. Explains how they'll have room for Nick's butcher shop and for prepared foods, too. All the things they wanted to do that Nick's father had resisted or outright refused.

"There will be so many more possibilities for part-time work. Or I could help Nick in the shop."

Nell hasn't seen Rosie this excited in years.

"There are good schools for the boys. And it's closer to home."

"Where will you live?" Nell asks.

"We've put in a bid on an old farmhouse with six acres on the outskirts of town. It needs work, but it's solid. And we can almost afford it."

"I can help you move. I can babysit, whatever you need."

"I'm going to hold you to that."

"Nell," Marion says. "Set the table. They're staying for supper. We're celebrating."

Jack asks Billy to help him for a day or two at the Ag Station. Jack, in his small corner, is a contrarian, bringing samples of soil from surviving Seneca Indian trees to his colleague, Grant Walden, an ethnobotanist. What can they learn about the soils and the Seneca practices of complementary planting? Jack is leery of the promises made by chemical companies. Living alongside lakes and rivers has made him protective, and *Silent Spring* confirmed a lifetime's worth of intuition and observation.

Billy is dressed and ready to go that morning, a surprise given his late nights. But that's the point. Get him up and out as early as possible, into the warming April sun. Tire him out so much he'll have to rein in the booze and the bars.

A father can hope.

Billy hasn't slept much. The nights are endless, the nerve pain relentless, sleep a release he both dreads and longs for. He's clinging to the belief that swimming every day will make him so physically tired the nightmares will cease. That his hand can heal; will heal, whatever it takes. Building himself back up one penny at a time.

The ringing in his ears is maddening. At its worst it sounds like the high-pitched whine of an incoming mortar. At its best it's a stubborn drone.

His father turns on the radio. Wall to wall blather about the Apollo 13 emergency landing. Billy snaps it off, irritated, without explaining to Jack that tinnitus, plus the radio, plus a hangover, sends him around the bend.

At the Ag Station Jack grabs a pair of pruners and a small folding saw. Together they load dozens of comfrey seedlings into a wheelbarrow and a basket full of numbered and labeled scions.

Today Jack will graft the new cuttings he's taken from the remnants of the Seneca orchards. He'd found these trees with Billy and Nell, a handful having survived the wholesale destruction of Seneca lands and livelihood during the eighteenth century, followed by the neglect and cultural amnesia of the nineteenth and twentieth centuries. They are miracles in their way, and, Jack believes, eloquent voices from the past.

If you live on Seneca Lake, you live with the buried history of the Sullivan Expedition of 1779. The Seneca Indians had cultivated the rolling hills lining the banks of the lake for hundreds of years before George Washington sent General John Sullivan and one quarter of the Revolutionary Army to destroy the fabled Iroquois Confederacy.

Their stated intent: to punish the Seneca and Iroquois for their loyalty to the British. The underlying strategy: to lay claim to the Northwest Frontier, as the Finger Lakes Region was called, thus opening the West to expansion.

Expecting to find a primitive wilderness filled with savages, Sullivan and his men instead found open country, fields of corn, beans, squash, and vast orchards of apple, peach, and cherry. They called Geneva "Apple Town," and were astonished by its hidden beauty. Rich deposits of soil crowned the long low hills carved out by glaciers. The lake's deep waters tempered the climate and created the best fruit-growing land they had ever seen.

They described the longhouses they found as castles, a sense of awe in their journals. They filled these dwellings with the Indians' stores of food, including more than 200,000 bushels of corn, and burned them to the ground. They clear-cut the orchards, burning the trees as they fell.

The Seneca melted away in front of the army's advance hoping to return when the invaders had gone. They retreated to the British fort at Niagara where they perished by the thousands of hunger and cold.

Cornell's extensive land holdings, including the agricultural research station, is carved from Seneca land. The more Jack learns over the years, the more disturbed he feels. He knows that resurrecting apple trees and adapting Seneca practices will not restore their lands or make amends. Still, it's the work he can do.

Jack will graft while Billy plants comfrey seedlings around the base of each tree in the test orchard. Jack thinks this work can be done with one arm and an assist, but he's not sure. If planting seedlings is impossible, he'll do it himself and have Billy rake the composted wood chips around the trees for mulch.

Billy watches his father, tamping down the impatience that's already rising inside him. Jack's methodical way of working drives Billy up the wall. Every single scion that his father will graft today is taped, labeled, numbered, and carefully recorded.

God help me, Billy thinks.

"So where do you want this stuff planted?"

"Rows two, four, and six. Four plants per tree."

Billy stows a trowel in his back pocket, grabs a shovel, and moves to the end of the row where his father won't be able to see him.

He can make a cut into the soil with the blade of the shovel, loosen the dirt, but he can't lift it out of the ground. He tries making the cut, then dragging the shovel out of the hole, but loses most of the dirt on the way and *still* can't turn the shovel over. He has very little strength in his right hand, arm, and wrist. Turning, gripping, lifting are beyond him; the pain acute.

He throws the shovel aside and gets down on his knees with the trowel. He can't believe how difficult it is to use the trowel left-handed. This is not skilled work, but five minutes of ineffectual digging yields a hole hardly large enough for one comfrey seedling.

When his father shouts for him to come and take a break his shirt is soaked through and he's shaking from exhaustion. Three months in a hospital can just about destroy a man.

Jack offers Billy hot tea and an orange, already peeled, and breaks open a chocolate bar.

"Maybe that's enough for your first day."

"Am I working here or not?"

"I'm just saying . . . "

"Shut up, Dad. Just shut up."

Billy pushes past his father to return to the awkward trowel and two hundred seedlings and his dogged pursuit of an impossible task.

Fifteen minutes later, he stands, shakes his arms out, then kneads his muscles, willing them back to life. And it suddenly occurs to him to ask not just if his doctors have been lying to him, but how much. He'd looked at those X-rays, listened to those specialists, all of it filtered through the disorientation of pain and youthful arrogance. Sure, I'm hurt, but I can get better. Sure, I've been badly burned; took shrapnel to my arm, wrist, hand, shoulder. But bones and tendons and ligaments and nerves can heal, scar tissue can be lived with. Right?

He looks at his hands. Will he ever pick up a pencil again; pilot a plane? He tries to grab the trowel in his right hand, but his grip is still not strong enough. He had imagined snatching the trowel, shoving it into the ground, the searing clarity of pain. But he can't even do that.

He hears the wheelbarrow squeaking on its wheel and glances up to see Jack lumbering toward him with a load of mulch. Billy massages his arm while Jack takes in the discarded shovel and trowel, the piss-poor plantings.

"Can't use that arm much?"

"Everybody's in denial," Billy says. "Including me, it seems."

"How about I dig and you plant?"

In minutes Jack digs planting holes, evenly spaced. Billy finds he can kneel and plant the seedlings with one hand, using his right to assist as he covers the plants with soil. He can even keep up.

They make steady progress down the row. The job that had been impossible an hour ago is getting done.

"I've been working with Arne Briggs," Jack says.

"The chemist? I thought you two didn't exactly see eye to eye."

"We're doing a project together."

"You're kidding."

"This is it. We amend the soil, mulch to correct imbalances, and work with complementary plantings. Arne's got a test orchard on the south side of the lake that's all chemicals all the time. Fungicides, insecticides, miticides sprayed eight to fourteen times a season. Just like every other major apple grower in the nation."

"Jesus."

"Not many people are looking at the whole cycle. The runoff from chemical use, the water and soil contamination. Those are the things we can attempt to measure and test. But we can't test the chemicals' impact on the public. Because we are just spraying the hell out of apples. And grapes. And strawberries. The chemical companies tell us it's safe. But I don't believe them."

"Neither do I."

"They told us DDT was safe," Jack says, "denied the research, the evidence. Think of the birth defects, the infertility; the near extinction of the bald eagle. And those are just the canaries in the coal mine."

Billy doesn't want to think about the millions of tons of chemicals they are using in Vietnam, with their rainbow monikers, Agent Blue, White, Pink, Yellow, Orange, as if candy is raining down from the sky. He doesn't want to think about the cancers he's hearing about, babies born without limbs or worse, his own loss of taste and smell and hearing.

He tries to shakes it off. He's home, he's outdoors with his father, the sun on his back; the world on the edge of spring. He grabs four more seedlings; moves to the next tree. Jack keeps ahead of him, digging holes. The work warms them. The clouds of the morning disperse and the day grows bright. They have found their rhythm.

Walking up the hill to the Alsops' the following Wednesday, Nell wants to turn around and go home. Twice she stops to look back over the lake. A strong April wind is gusting across the water, toppling clouds, the same wind that's making her eyes tear up. She wipes her nose on her sleeve and keeps climbing.

She finds the ponies in their stalls, halters on, saddles and bridles in a neat pile by the door, cleaned and oiled. She enters

Lucky's stall, currycomb in hand; leans into him, her face against his neck. Lindy kicks against the stall door, wanting in on the attention.

She and Megan used to give them strawberry ice cream cones every Fourth of July. Where'd they dream that one up and who knew ponies liked ice cream? Every Christmas they decorated one of the pine trees in the pasture with peppermints and carrots and apples. Watching Lucky's velvety muzzle peel back over his teeth when he got hold of a peppermint always made them laugh. Summers they rode bareback to the lake and swam with the ponies. There was nothing like that first moment when the ponies were floating, their legs driving hard in the water, grabbing their manes with both hands, gripping with their knees. The girls napped in the sun, lying on the ponies' broad backs, tickled and sometimes lashed by their tails.

Asa used to talk about finding a two-pony sleigh, or making one. That would never happen now. She should have put up a fight, tried to buy the ponies herself, or come up with a scheme to teach lessons so Asa could keep them. If Megan were here this would never have happened.

Maybe Megan's disappearance has knocked the stuffing out of all of them. With Evan gone to his mother's, Dash still recovering, and the ponies sold, the real life of the farm seems to be disappearing. You just can't get that worked up over chickens and goats.

Nell greets Mr. Walsh and his daughters. She opens Lindy's stall door, clips a lead rope to her halter.

"Lindy's easy to load. And Lucky will follow her."

Lindy walks up to the truck, stops, head high, looking around. Nell puts her hand on the pony's neck and waits. Lucky neighs at her, kicking his stall door.

Nell strokes Lindy, gets her voice under control.

"C'mon, girl."

Lindy looks Nell square in the eye, sighs, and walks into the trailer. Nell ties the lead to the hook in the wall and returns to the barn. Lucky doesn't pause to take one last look around, but trots into the trailer, neck arched, inspecting Lindy as soon as he's beside her again.

The girls load the saddles and bridles into the cab of the pickup and Mr. Walsh hands Nell an envelope.

"Would you be sure Mr. Alsop gets this?"

"Be gentle," Nell says. "They're used to . . . "

"They'll have a good home with us."

As they drive away the ponies neigh, haunting sounds that hang in the air. Those cries cut something out of Nell, carving up her childhood, Megan's childhood. To distract herself, she looks inside the envelope. Fifteen crisp fifty-dollar bills.

She heads into the house intending to put the envelope on the kitchen table and leave but instead finds herself drawn upstairs. She pushes open the door to Megan's room.

The bed is neatly made, the curtains pulled back, but the room is all wrong. It doesn't even smell the same. The things Megan loved are gone, taken to her mother's when she moved. The things she's outgrown, like Nell herself, are here. Dolls and trolls and Marguerite Henry books; discarded bits of junk that had once been treasured.

There's a copy of the picture Nell found in Billy's wallet stuck in a corner of the mirror. The four of them: boxes full of apples at their feet, the ladders behind them reaching into the trees. Sunburned, lit by the raking October light. Billy's hand, Nell notices now, twined in Megan's red hair.

Taped next to Megan's bed is Nell's favorite snapshot. She pulls it off the wall, peels the tape away.

Billy, ten years old, stands on the roof of the shed, wearing a pair of homemade wings. A hawk sails above him, tipping her wings in what looks to be invitation.

How they had wanted to ride the thermals coming off the

water, drift in the currents, creatures of the air. These were the visions that filled their dreams, waking and sleeping. Aloft without the encumbrance of harness and armature, a bird with a boy's body and sight and consciousness, a girl with the skill to dive through the air, skim the surface of the lake, rise with a single wing beat, roll, and play in the sweet pine scent lifting off the trees.

She slips the picture inside her shirt, takes Trevor's yellow cup out of her pocket, sets it on the dresser. She doesn't have the guts to give it to Asa directly, or leave it on the drain board with the other one. Maybe he'll find it here among Megan's things.

She runs down the stairs to find Asa sitting at the kitchen table. She hadn't heard his truck, hadn't heard the back door open and close.

"You shouldn't have done that," he says.

"Done what?"

"Gone into Megan's room."

"I didn't know . . . "

"Did you look inside? How much did you take?"

"What are you talking about?"

"The money."

"I didn't take the money. I put it on the table."

"There's fifty dollars missing."

"I didn't take your money."

"Where is it, then?"

"Where were you? Why didn't I hear you drive up?"

She moves toward the door. His chair scrapes back, blocking her way.

"Get out of my way, Mr. Alsop. I have to go home."

His hands are shaking; she can see that now. And he smells of whiskey.

"You want to join us for supper tonight?" Nell asks, trying to steady her voice. "My mother's making pork chops. You'd be welcome."

He stands. Pushes his chair in. Runs a hand through his hair, looking down at the worn linoleum.

"I'm making cornbread," Nell says. "My grandma's recipe. It's good with honey."

He can't look at her.

"You tell your mother thank you. Some other time."

He heads out the door to the barn.

Nell watches him go, sweat running cold down the small of her back.

What Asa Alsop couldn't bring himself to tell Nell Flynn was that the police had called. A girl had turned up near Tupper Lake. He drove three hours northeast to identify the body. The girl had been stripped and dragged through a stubbled cornfield, her neck broken.

It was not Megan.

Megan's disappearance gets folded into the story of that winter and spring with the war dragging on, escalating student and civic violence, and, in Geneva itself, the closing of not one but two factories and the Army Depot. Geneva Cutlery shutters their building, following Sampson's Wallpaper and Paste Company south to the Carolinas and cheaper wages. Burned-out street lamps go unrepaired, storefronts empty, their windows boarded shut.

In late April the investigation goes quiet. The police are no longer a presence in and around the high school. The flyers the Alsops put up all over town are torn and faded, or wrecked by wind and rain and snow.

Rob Chandler is sent to private school in Vermont. His parents put their house on the market and move to Syracuse.

There are still no suspects; no one has been taken into custody. Even the rumors have quieted down. Three weeks earlier, a kid found Megan's schoolbooks when the last of the snow-banks melted on Hamilton Street, her usual route home, too ruined to provide clues.

Evan Alsop meets with a speech therapist twice a week. His stutter has grown worse. He avoids speaking as much as possible, hates his mother's apartment in town; hates her for taking him away from the farm and his father and his dog. Lives for Friday nights when he can go home.

Maeve Alsop dresses for work each morning, packs a lunch for Evan, walks him to the bus stop, before heading to work at the bank. She is frozen, sleepwalking through her days. She no longer answers the door when Father O'Rourke comes to call.

Asa Alsop continues to hope for his daughter's return, continues to leave offerings for Maeve and Evan, saves egg money to buy Evan a baseball mitt for his eleventh birthday. He turns his back on his church, on God, but keeps faith with his inner conviction that Megan has run away and one day will return.

Asa grew up during the Depression; the War almost knocked him flat, and farm work is a daily struggle. He managed to hang on through Maeve leaving him, but without Megan and Evan under his roof, he's dredging up reserves he didn't know he had. He knows he's a fool to wait for Maeve to come to her senses, but patience seems to be the last thing he has left.

He avoids town. A furious energy spills around him wherever he goes. He works well past twilight every night, like a man possessed, plowing his fields with a feeling of sick dread. Hawks circle overhead, diving and feeding on the mice and moles and rabbits the plow makes homeless.

In a month of Sundays, he clears four more fields for hay and timothy. He has dairymen who will buy all the fodder he can grow. He will prove to Maeve that he can change with the times; he will save his father's farm.

Nell rides her bike to the garage first thing Saturday morning when she knows Billy won't be there. Finds Harlow sitting at his desk drinking coffee, reading the sports section. She sits across from him, says no thanks when he offers coffee, trying to gauge his reaction to seeing her. Calm. Neutral. Not like the mess inside her stomach.

She has her answer. But the way he looks . . . Shit. Just business today, she reminds herself. You're nobody special.

"What's up?"

"Billy's nightmares are getting worse."

He folds the paper, waits.

"I don't know what to do," she says.

"Stay with him, when you can."

"It's most nights."

"Yeah. I figured."

"Do you have nightmares?"

"Nah."

"Don't protect me."

"Why not?"

"God, Harlow, how do I talk to you about this if you're trying to keep me safe every minute?"

"I'm supposed to know the answer to that?"

"I don't know where to begin, how to ask you—or Billy—and it feels damn strange to act like it never happened. I know it changed you. I know it about wrecked my father. And now Billy. I'm not blind."

He's quiet for so long she wonders if he's angry, if she has crossed the line into unforgivable territory. If so, too bad, she needs to know.

"I've worked hard not to drag Vietnam home with me. You see that weight on Billy? Maybe I got off easy."

"But . . ."

"I'm not gonna unpack that bag for you, Nell. Not for anybody."

"How will I ever understand it then?"

"You won't."

"Not now, or not ever?"

"Never."

"Then it will always be there between us?"

"Let it go, Nell."

"I can't."

"Look. I have to swim against that current every day of my life. Or it will carry me away."

"Billy, too?"

"All of us."

Shrapnel keeps making its way to the surface, bursting through the skin, interior knives waiting to ambush his sleep. Billy wakes, massages his arm. Feels the nausea rising and the pain moving through his hand, arm, and shoulder, up his neck into his head, lodging behind his eyes. Piling images into him with each flicker of an eyelid, jumbled, out of sequence, but no less horrifying.

He presses the heels of his hands over his eyes, concentrates on his breathing. Waits. Breaks into a cold sweat as the nausea recedes. It's almost an hour before he can get up. He takes a long hot shower, dresses in jeans and an old flannel shirt. Feels almost human again.

Flanagan follows him up the rutted road to the Alsops' farm. It's steeper than he remembers. He stops halfway, the ringing in his ears amplified by his ragged breathing. The VA doctors tell him this is a typical complaint of returning soldiers. It might get better. It might not. Some days are almost tolerable, other days the internal buzz and hiss takes on a life of their own. The worst is when an intense spell of tinnitus overlaps with a headache, constricting his world to a tight, sick circle.

He fantasizes about being deaf, imagines a blessed silence.

Then he hears an ovenbird, its middle notes at least. *Tea-cher, Tea-cher, Tea-cher.* The high notes can't penetrate the ringing in his ears. The low notes, shit, he's starting to think the low notes might be gone forever. He lets the sound wash over him. Waits for more. The trill of a towhee: *Drink your teeee . . .*

Maybe it's getting better. If he can just be patient. Not his strong suit. Still.

Asa waits for him by the barn, the tractor idling. A cloud of exhaust hangs heavy in the air. Without preamble, he leads Billy into the feed room, shows him the bins of grain for the chickens and the goats, the rakes and shovels; then outside to the water pump, the wheelbarrow, the manure pile. He uses his hands with as little regard as if they were old iron tools. Billy envies him.

"Straw and hay are in the loft. Can you manage that or should I throw them down?"

"We'll find out."

"I'll throw them down until you tell me different."

"Sounds good," Billy says.

"Can I count on you? Every morning?"

"Yes."

"You're no use to me if I can't count on you."

"I'll be here. Juniper still the big boss?"

"He's getting old."

"How many kids this year?"

"Six. Two sets of twins. Can you drive the eggs into town? Schuyler wants them Tuesdays and Thursdays. You can take the truck."

"I'm a one-handed driver at the moment."

"I can't pay you much."

"I'm not worth much."

"Don't say that."

"Only a friend would hire a one-armed man."

"You've still got both arms, far as I can see. Luckier than some."

"Some days I don't feel so lucky. But I take your point."

"Your mother did some worrying over you."

"I'm sorry about Megan."

"Not a subject I can talk about."

"Understood."

"I'll leave you to it."

Asa swings up onto the tractor and drives up the hill, the harrow rattling behind him.

Walking past the stalls, Billy sees Megan's green sweater hanging on a hook in the tack room. Reaches for it. Brings it to his face. Inhales. No trace of her. It's like a kick in the gut.

He knows he's a fool holding that sweater in his hands, wishing things could be different, wishing, really, for anything at all.

By week's end, Billy has started to solve the puzzle of how to use tools one-handed. He asks for Asa's help with the wheelbarrow. He brings two sets of straps to attach to the handles: one to go over his neck, the other around his waist. They set it up only to discover it's impossible to balance a wheelbarrow with one hand.

His frustration erupts in combinations of profanity Asa has never heard before.

"You bring that one back from Vietnam?"

"Sorry."

"Don't be. I get a kick out of it."

The next morning Billy drags a beat-up toboggan up the hill. He figures if he can't push a wheelbarrow, he can pull a sled with a simple chest harness. Asa helps him rig the straps.

"Well, I'll be damned," Asa says when it works.

Using his good hand to brace a snow shovel against his hip, Billy pushes dirty straw and bedding onto the sled, which he then pulls out to the manure pile. It's not a perfect system, but if he makes a mess the chickens don't care.

He takes a child's pleasure in finding eggs, warm in their nesting boxes. More than once he falls asleep in the loft. Punch-drunk with exhaustion, he surrenders to the warm sweet hay. The kids climb the ramp and nibble his fingers as if each one were a milk-filled teat. They cry at him, pure as woodwinds. He starts to name them. The littlest one, Lucy, will come when he calls.

He finds a Carolina wren's nest in an old wooden box nailed inside the barn door. The box had been used by one of Asa's broody hens and is full of straw. In one corner, the wren has made a cavity to receive her nest, built with grasses, feathers, moss, and pieces of dried snakeskin. Her eggs are whitish, marked with spots and speckles of reddish brown.

The animals calm him, the work itself. This world that harbors good earth and apples and bees and birds. The sweep of the fields up to the woods, Asa's hay and timothy greening, the cultivated and the untamed side by side.

He sits against the haymow, sheltered from the wind, the strengthening sun promising warmth. Looks down the long sweep of the hill to the lake. Clouds like elephants are reflected in the water, a piercing blue.

Flanagan barks furiously; she's treed something in the woods behind him. Overhead a flock of geese appears, landing on the far side of the lake.

He thinks of Megan, remembers waking up in the loft to find her beside him. How fearless they were.

He has to shut his mind to her or risk a rage he knows he can't contain.

After helping Asa in the early mornings, Billy hitchhikes into town to pump gas at Harlow Murphy's station.

Hiring Billy frees Harlow to spend his afternoons in the garage, which, if he's not outside tracking, trapping, or hunting, is where he likes to be. He understands the insides of cars the way some men understand women. He has an ear for hearing what ails an engine, and a fine-fingered touch.

Harlow's boyish good looks have hardened but haven't disappeared. With Billy on board, even their workmen's coveralls can't hide their appeal. High school and college girls find them, their friends, and friends of friends.

He installs a soda machine to take advantage, get them to hang around long enough to buy a Coke and a pack of smokes. The girls pull in, one after another, driving daddy's car, a couple bucks in their pocket, drawn by the allure of good-looking men, the staying power of hurting boys.

It's almost too easy to be interesting.

Harlow thought he was doing Billy a favor by taking him on. Now that his gas business has doubled, he's grateful. He knows enough to leave Billy alone as he learns to do his job one-handed.

Billy struggles with the work, but after two weeks it no longer takes him twice as long to do every single thing: popping hoods, checking oil, washing windows, unscrewing the always too tight gas caps, making change. He allowed himself to drink away his first week's pay. Now he gives his paycheck to his mother. A drop in the bucket for his hospital bills.

Biking downtown one day, Nell sees Billy standing alone against the plate-glass window, smoking a cigarette, his hurt hand shoved deep in the pocket of his filthy coveralls. The scars along his jaw and neck are still vivid and angry looking. Joe Cocker blares from the transistor radio in the office. *With a little help, with a little help, with a little help from my . . .*

She stops at the far corner, in shadow. He looks trapped and miserable, enduring the asphalt, the stink of oil and gasoline. Two college girls drive up in a flashy Camaro. Billy grinds out his cigarette and walks over to the driver's side. He puts both hands on the roof of the car, leans in the window, flirting.

Playing a part.

The girls wear ragged denim and gauzy peasant blouses you can see through. Marion would say you have to have a lot of money to dress like that.

Harlow walks out of the garage, wiping his hands on a greasy rag. He feeds quarters into the soda machine for two bottles of Coke, hands one to Billy.

Billy finishes with the Camaro, the college girls suddenly invisible, and leans against the plate glass, talking with Harlow. And laughing.

Something lifts in Nell, hearing her brother laugh like that.

She looks at Harlow's hands. They're square and strong; the Coke bottle almost disappears in them. Thinks of picking apples in the Alsop orchard. The boys thought ladders were for sissies. Determined to keep up with them, she tried to find a handhold and a foothold to get into the tree. Harlow reached down, grabbed her forearm, and pulled her up beside him.

That sudden wash of closeness as she found her footing and her balance. The smell of his skin, touching him. The sun low in the sky, the trees heavy with fruit. Hidden from the others. Light-headed. Vibrating with a feeling she didn't know how to describe. Twelve years old. How she had wanted to kiss him.

Still does. But it doesn't look like that's ever gonna happen again.

The Methodist church bells chime the hour: four o'clock. Damn, she's late for work. She turns up Hamilton Street, hightailing it to Bob and Dave's. As she passes Maeve Alsop's apartment, tucked over the garage behind a larger house, Asa's truck pulls out, heading north. She stops, curious. The forsythia by Maeve's front door is in full bloom. A basket of eggs and the yellow cups from the farmhouse sit on the porch.

How often does Asa stop here, she wonders, leaving offerings for Maeve and Evan, maybe glancing in the windows to see what their lives look like without him.

Billy leaves the garage, needing to clear his head. He keeps trying to come to terms with Megan being gone, accept it somehow, believe it. His resistance to the facts is wearing thin. Every glimpse of red hair is her, suddenly her. He turns, follows, heart banging, hope fizzing, until he gets closer and sees that this girl toes out, not in as Megan does, or she is taller, shorter, older, younger, nothing like her really, nothing at all like Megan, and the vertigo of the word "missing" swamps him again and again.

He takes the jog on Exchange to follow Castle Street into the center of town, the head of the lake just beyond. Passes Saint Joe's. Father O'Rourke and half a dozen men and women stand on the sidewalk in front of the church holding peace signs, passing out pamphlets to indifferent shoppers walking by. He knows he should join them.

Coming into town as a kid for a Saturday afternoon movie was a big deal when Billy was a boy. Jack Flynn met his brother Trevor at the Empire for a drink, dropped Marion at the library. The big girls, Sheila and Rosie, loped off to the shops, when Geneva still had some nice shops. His brother Brendan off on a team bus somewhere, to the green, rock-free playing fields of wealthier towns.

Summers Marion bought Nell and Billy hot dogs on the pier before heading home. They watched the boats, the people fishing. Jack crossing the road to meet them, a hand on Trevor's shoulder, that bright spot of color in his cheeks when he'd had a few.

Billy feels the wind on his face, the lake smell in his head, faint but recognizable. He's a boy again, or wishes it. Wishes for another chance, another go. Wishes for Megan.

A flock of ducks lands near the shore, in the lee of the pier. And then another and another, until there are hundreds of them: mallards, mergansers, buffleheads, blacks. He wades into the water, his boots instantly sinking into the soft mud of the lake bottom, barely registering the cold, knee-deep, thigh, hip, chest. The birds eddy around him, groups form and re-form, moving in concert like schools of fish. But they do not startle or fly away. He trails his fingers through the water, his hands. And he is among them, as close as he has ever been. Green-capped heads, black bills, the bold blue patch on the mallards' wings, the red-billed, white-bodied mergansers. He wants to scoop them up in his hands, hug them to his chest, fly with them.

He sinks beneath the surface, hangs weightless, eyes open, looking up through the green water to the blue dome of the sky, sculls slowly with both hands. If only he had gills, he'd stay forever.

MAY

May breaks open in Geneva with a string of perfect days. The scent of apple blossom carries impossible distances, mixing with the smell of ploughed earth. Spent blooms litter the ground; the air is loud with bees and birds. The fields on East Lake Road take on their spring colors: pale green oats, bright yellow timothy.

Nixon, after promising to draw down troops in Vietnam, stuns the nation by announcing the invasion of Cambodia. When he loses his place halfway through his televised speech, his eyes darting down the pages, viewers think: He's made a mistake. He'll reverse what he's said. Others realize: He's lost, and so are we.

The war's escalation ignites a cascade of sit-ins, marches, and demonstrations. Nixon labels students "bums blowing up campuses" and calls out the National Guard.

The shootings and shocking deaths at Kent State in Ohio and Jackson State in Mississippi erupt in nationwide protests and the closing of more than five hundred campuses across the country. For some people, struggling to find work and feed their families, the rallies are a distant problem. Long-haired college students shutting down campuses are spoiled kids grabbing a few more weeks of vacation.

When students bomb the ROTC center at Hobart, the protests come home to Geneva. Even then, the pristine world of the college is as distant as the moon to most people living in town.

First Rosie, then Sheila and Brendan call home to check up on Billy. Marion reassures them: We're fine, Billy's fine; he's getting better. When pressed, she will admit that he's struggling, says to each one: Come home, see for yourself.

Sleep is over. Billy shifts, can find no comfortable position, his arm on fire. He's been pushing it at the Y. Upping the number of laps. The ringing in his ears is silenced in the water. There are moments when he almost feels whole again.

Flanagan follows him out to the sleeping porch. He sits down on the cot next to Nell's.

"I want you to read to me," he hands her a flashlight.

She looks at her watch. "It's 2:30!"

"I thought maybe if you read to me, I could fall asleep." He hands her a battered paperback. "I found this under your bed."

"*Valley of the Dolls*? You have to be kidding."

"Where'd you get it?" he asks.

"One of your nurses."

"That little Lizzie girl was reading *Valley of the Dolls*?"

"Looks like they all read it. It's crap."

"Titillating, page-turning crap."

"Too embarrassing to read out loud."

"Well, *The French Lieutenant's Woman* is too highbrow for me," he says

"How about *The Godfather*?"

"Gore versus soap opera? No contest."

"How about a comic like Brendan read to us when we were little?"

"You're stalling."

"Mom brought us all those Newberry Medal winners from the library and Brendan read us the comics instead. The three of us crowded into the hammock. You always teased me about my underpants. I was three maybe, so you must've been six. Brendan rigged up a string so you could make the hammock swing back and forth and you got us going so high I fell out and split my lip. You have to remember that. There was blood everywhere. Mom and Dad were down by the lake and the two of you tried to take care of me by yourselves. We all thought if you could get the bleeding to stop and I could quit crying, then no one would know."

"I remember getting whacked for that one."

"No. Brendan said it was his fault."

"You actually believe Brendan would take the fall for me?"

"He did."

"You're nuts."

"I remember because I had to keep the secret, the first time you trusted me," she says.

"Or coerced you."

"It wasn't like that."

"Everybody knows Brendan is not the fuckup. So even if Brendan said he did it, they all knew it was me. And Brendan being so honorable only made him look better and me look worse. As usual."

Billy stretches out on the cot; the springs protest.

"If you have kids, Nell, don't hit them."

"Dad hit you?"

"Are you kidding me?"

"He never hit me."

"He hated it. Probably why I worked so hard to provoke him. He about wore out his belt the year I wouldn't quit stealing."

"I can still see Mom marching you into Munroe's Variety."

"And the five and dime. And Nelson's."

"Why'd you stop?"

"It wasn't fun anymore. You gonna have kids?"

"How should I know? I'm seventeen!"

"Almost eighteen."

"I'm not thinking about kids. I'm worrying about college and if I can measure up."

"You're gonna do fine."

"You're my brother. You have to say that."

"Read."

She angles the flashlight, opens the book.

Several days without drinking and his hands are shaking and he can't quit thinking about Megan so he can't sleep and he's reduced to almost crawling into bed with his kid sister. It's always worse in the middle of the night. He feels thick, heavy, as though grief has a weight. He avoids looking at his body, wasting, he knows, the burned flesh, the looping, line-drawn, angry scars, the bubbles beneath the skin where shrapnel lies in wait. His fingers tease these bumps, pressing, pressing to the point of pain, sharp release, blood.

Of course he remembers when she split her lip, and skinned both knees, but she seems to have forgotten about her knees. She has a scar on her upper lip, very faint now, the scar a slightly different texture than the rest of her crooked smile.

He watches her read. She's dubious. And embarrassed.

She glances over at him. He's still awake.

"Keep reading," he says.

Billy's breathing changes as he finally falls asleep. A struggle to surrender. Like the dark is a dangerous place. Nell marks the page and slides the book under the bed. Glances at her watch: 3:45. The birds are waking up even though there's no hint, yet, of light in the sky.

She hears the ringing metallic trill of a junco, the high-pitched whistle of a tufted titmouse. Looks up to the ceiling to see the wings Billy made for her turning slowly.

She wishes she could say: Tell me about a day, a night, your tent, or your hooch or whatever you call it. How do you start a conversation about Vietnam with this wary, chain-smoking, boy? Man. He's a man. She knows that. He doesn't even smell the same anymore.

Asleep, you can almost see the kid in Billy again: his knees drawn up under the quilt, those long eyelashes his sisters envy. The bones in his face look sharp. Not like the bones of a boy who's growing so fast his body can't keep up, more like the bones of an old man, too prominent, the flesh burned away.

Why is she thinking like this? In the three months he's been home, has there been one night without nightmares, one day without too much to drink? She's not sure how much longer he can tough it out at the gas station.

So many things they can't talk about, don't talk about. The future a minefield. Everything he's dreamed of, worked for: drawing, flying, Megan. Gone.

Two years alone with her sad, quiet parents. The last kid. Her siblings envy her: all that attention, not so strict anymore. They have no idea how the old house echoed, the air thick with worry, how the six o'clock news beat them bloody every night.

She knows it's useless to try to sleep. She works through a few math problems in her head. Mental gymnastics, Mr. Ware calls them. Like crossword puzzles. Math is Nell's secret pleasure, the subject she found her way to all on her own. Everything she's learned: shape in geometry, operations and their applications in algebra, infinitesimal change in calculus, adds to her sense of the invisible, mysterious, beautiful world.

Tuesday, on his way into town, Billy pulls Asa's truck over to the side of the road at the crest of the hill on Route 16. Flanagan stretches across his lap, pokes her head out the window.

He loves this view of the lake. High enough to be eye level with the hawks riding the thermals, wheeling in slow sun-warmed circles. As a kid, he imagined running to the edge and throwing himself off to join the birds in their flight. This is where he and Nell rode their bikes and hatched their plans to build wings and fly.

An older woman pegs laundry to the line next to her trailer. The stiff May breeze slaps her hair around like a flag. Her small garden is fenced against the deer. Asparagus and foxglove push up out of the soil.

Maybe she knew the old man across the road who lived in a shack made of cast-off doors. Walter kept a mean-looking mongrel chained to a tree in the yard. Some unlucky devil must have had to put that dog down after Walter died. Billy hopes it hadn't been Harlow.

There are fox in the sumacs nearby, and once he'd seen a stag, hidden at the edge of the forest. Walter told them that big white stag was the legend buck; he'd hit it three different times with his bow and every time it walked away.

It's rare to be alone and in a vehicle. He can go anywhere, he realizes with a start. He follows the flight of a great blue heron, its extraordinary wingspan, feathers flashing silver in the sun.

He's so tired. Even his bones are tired. Where is he headed; where is he supposed to be? When did he get so slow and vague?

Deliver eggs to Schuyler's, swing over to PT, then to Harlow's, then to the Y to swim; that's it. Chores and work, not dreams. He's been making progress at the Y: he'd managed a solid three-quarter mile the day before. His muscles tired, a good tired.

He picks up his notebook, rolls down the windows, shoves the seat back, and finishes the worksheets Cindy gave him. Steely Cindy, the hand therapist, promises him he will write and draw left-handed. Like a pro. Doubtful, he thinks, as he traces letters. How about like an artist? Or a draftsman, at least. Competent. Can he settle for competent?

And a right hand that functions.

Two wrens bathe in the dust of the trailer's rutted driveway. He itches to sketch them, a few lines to capture their boisterous energy. Cindy has been badgering him to take a figure drawing class at the high school. Starting tonight. Maybe the models will be naked. And young.

Nell tags along with Billy. It's the last session of adult ed classes offered for the year. The half-lit hallways smell of dust and chalk. Nell walks with Billy to the art room door and then crosses the hall to an open classroom where she can finish working on her cell diagram.

She's detailing the workings of cell metabolism at the molecular level, down to the very last pathway. Drawing this helps her see and sense this information in a deeper way than simply reading about it or memorizing a chart. Nell's colorful rendering looks like several big-city subway maps blended into one.

She wonders what the disruptions of DDT and mercury look like at the cellular level. Is there an illustration somewhere? Surely someone has already done that. Miss Rosenthal or Esme will know. She's grateful for having learned to draw at Billy's elbow, all those years keeping field journals. The concepts she is learning come alive when she can imagine them in physical form, drawing the chamber of a heart, for instance. She thinks of the structure of a hand, the articulation of bones, the sheath of muscle fibers, the intricate nerve system. Wishes for the magic of regeneration for her brother, like a starfish or a salamander.

Billy introduces himself to Anna Barnes, the instructor.

She shows him to an easel. There are a dozen students, all ages, from a boy who looks to be about fourteen to a woman in her seventies with a long white braid down her back.

The easels are ranged around a riser with a chair on it. The model emerges from behind a curtain wearing a robe, steps onto the riser, hands the robe to Miss Barnes, and stands with his back to them.

"Quick sketches," she says. "The model will change his pose every three minutes."

Everyone sets to work. Billy is surprised at how little the man's self matters. His body is a puzzle to solve, form and shape to capture.

Billy has never taken a life drawing class before. Art classes in school, sure, but that was half horsing around and they never had models. Though he remembers Mrs. Higgins's patience and all he learned from her about watercolor and the serendipity of mistakes.

Here Miss Barnes moves among the students, making corrections, offering suggestions. In faded jeans, a paint-spattered man's shirt, and work boots, she is understated and matter-of-fact. Her dark hair is loosely twisted and pinned off her neck. She touches her students, stands with a hand on a back or a shoulder, changes the grip on a pencil; tells one student, a high school girl, to get up and walk the corridor, shake her hands and arms to loosen up.

When she sees Billy struggling, she brings him a thick piece of charcoal and suggests he use shading rather than line. After working left-handed through three poses, he tries it right-handed.

Confronting the evidence of his failures strewn on the floor at his feet, he wants a drink. And the door. He's promised himself, yet again, to quit drinking. On weeknights at least.

Miss Barnes puts her hand on his shoulder. "Can you stay after class? I'd like to talk to you."

She waits until the other students have left, her gaze frankly appraising him, unflinching as she takes in the burns on his face and neck. She had been unafraid to touch his crabbed hand, he realizes. Not even his mother has touched that hand.

"What's your story?" she asks.

"I used to be . . . "

"Really skilled. What happened?"

"Helicopter crash. Burns. Breaks. Shrapnel."

"Nerve damage?"

"Shredded."

"Therapy?"

"Three days a week."

"And you're here because . . . "

"They want me to learn to draw left-handed."

"What do you want?"

"I want my life back. All of it," he says, surprised to hear the words out loud.

"As far as drawing?"

"Is it possible to make the switch? Or are they bullshitting me?"

"Some people can do it," she says. "It's hard work. It takes time."

"How much time?"

"Not only are you learning a new skill, you're rewiring your brain."

"Can you help me?"

"Some. It's really up to you."

"What do you do?" he asks.

"I teach at the community college. Studio art. Art history."

"And this?"

"I love these classes. All ages. No pretensions. What about collage? Or big canvases, big brushes?"

"I want what I had," he says. "Maybe that sounds crazy. But it's all connected to birds for me."

"Bring me some of your work."

"The paintings are gone."

"What do you mean?"

"Bonfire." He sees the shock register. "My sister saved my field journals."

"I've seen field journals so exquisite the pages seem to breathe."

"They're not that good."

"There may be more than one way back. Remove the old expectations. Let your left hand develop; strengthen your right hand. You could surprise yourself."

"So maybe I'm in the wrong class."

"For now."

"Do you teach collage?"

"Tuesdays and Thursdays, 9–12," she says. "It's too far into the semester for you to register for credit, but you could audit the class, just a private understanding between you and me."

"Why are you doing this?"

"Why not? They moved the art department downtown. We're in the old Smith Opera House. Third floor. Come if you want. No pressure."

Harlow closes the garage on Saturday and goes fishing with Billy. It's May, God damn it. After a long, hard winter, it's finally fucking May. Fires up the runabout and speeds down to the Keuka Lake outlet before dawn. Cuts the motor. Drifts, drops a line, helps Billy bait his hook.

There's a deep pool beneath overhanging willows on the lee side of the outlet, enough current to keep the water running fresh. This spot has never failed them. Billy fights with his reel. Harlow lets him be. By the end of the morning he's more or less gotten the hang of it.

As the day warms, they tie the boat to a stump and walk the

stream to fish in the shade of birch and sycamore trees. They climb a series of cascades, high and loud in the spring runoff.

Harlow wonders if Billy ever thinks about flying any-more—is it off-limits, stuck in the freezer for later use and consideration—or does it haunt him and make him miserable every day?

They used to talk about running a plane for hunters and fishermen, making the rather large assumption that Harlow would be able to parlay his expertise with cars to airplanes. With some study, yes, maybe. If Billy can still fly. He'll need two fully functioning hands. And from what he's seen today, Billy's a long way from that. He's gotten good at hiding or min-imizing his deficits at the garage, but here, with a new task, the shortcomings are more glaring. He's clever and quick, devises compensations. Harlow's not sure any of that will hold water in a cockpit.

Returning to the boat and their beer, kept cold in the water, they eat lunch. Billy tips his face to the sky to follow the path of a kingfisher, rolls his shoulders to ease their stiffness, open-ing and closing his right hand. Testing, always testing.

They motor down to a small spit of land, leave the boat, and nap in the sun. Harlow promised himself to keep his mouth shut and let the lake take care of things. Time is what Billy needs. Time and the water. They have both in ample supply.

Billy slips inside Saint Joe's late that afternoon, sunburned and filthy. Father O'Rourke is escorting the elderly Mrs. Valenti to the door where her youngest daughter waits. He looks at Billy, taps his wrist. Billy stifles a laugh in deference to Mrs. Valenti and the recent death of her husband.

"You're late, Billy Flynn," O'Rourke says as they walk up the central aisle, taking in Billy's boots and pants, muddied to the knee. "Too late, today. And I'm sure your mother told you it's a good idea to clean up a bit before coming to the house of the Lord."

"I'm not here for confession, Father. I've brought you some trout."

"Son of a gun." The old man's eyes light up. "You have not."

"As I live and breathe." Billy hefts his canvas bag.

"Let's take those to Margaret right now." The priest walks quickly to the side door.

"I'll wait here for you." Billy hands him the bag. "Tell Margaret I'm sorry I couldn't clean them for her."

"She'll manage. I'll be right back."

Billy sits in a pew. He feels like an intermediary between the settled and the wild world. All day he's been thinking of the Seneca. As boys he and Harlow wanted to hunt as the Seneca did, to capture an animal, to outwit it with a trap or come close enough to catch it with their hands. To do this you have to know the animal intimately. And somewhere inside that knowing is the fact that you are an animal yourself.

He needs to get out of the church. The stone suddenly feels cold and oppressive. He takes the side door and finds half a dozen apple trees in bloom in the rectory's yard. The Seneca spoke of a Tree of Light whose branches held blossoming stars and whose fruit tasted of the sweetness of life. Billy imagines all of the apple trees bursting into flower on the hills and in the side yards of Geneva, with their white, starlike blossoms soon to fall like snow.

If, as the Seneca believe, the outer shell of a man crumbles into the soil after he dies and then passes into the roots of trees, then these trees, blossoms, apples contain the Seneca and the past itself.

Is Megan in the earth? A dark thought he tries to suppress. Or is she still breathing the air somewhere, waiting to be found? He keeps stubbornly fighting the thought: he will never see her again, hear her voice again, lift her into his arms, breathe her complicated scent.

She had refused to say goodbye, saying instead: Wherever you are you will think of me.

O'Rourke strides toward him.

"Margaret refuses to touch them until they can't look at her. I'm just going inside to hang up my cassock and lock up. Then I'll roll up my sleeves and clean some trout. She did offer you the casserole she already made to take home to your family."

"Please thank her, Father. But no."

"Will you stay, Billy? Have a drop with me while I gut the fish?"

"I'm gonna head home. I've been out all day."

"I still expect you to keep your promise and take me fishing."

"You tell me when you can do it."

"Soon."

"May I make a suggestion, Father? Give Margaret the night off. All you need is a frying pan, butter, a little cornmeal, and some salt and pepper. Margaret will just cook the life out of those poor trout."

"I'll take it under advisement."

"Wait. I almost forgot." Billy draws two broken eggshells from his pocket, a vivid blue. "Wilson's thrush. I found the nest in a moss-bottomed ravine." He places the shells in the priest's hand.

Father O'Rourke puts his palm on Billy's head, a quick blessing. "Billy . . . " He gathers his thoughts. "Curing and healing are not the same thing. To cure is to remove disease. To heal is to make whole. Wholeness can be yours again."

Just before dawn, Nell hikes into the woods above the Alsops' farm. She drapes a net between several trees and presses play on a portable cassette player. She waits, crouched on her haunches, hugging herself, conserving warmth. The trill of songbirds lures a wood thrush into her trap.

She gently disentangles the bird, slightly smaller than a robin, cups it in her hand, stretches out one brick-red wing, and counts down to the eleventh flight feather. Removes it with a quick tug, then, and this she likes even less, takes a sample of its blood. The large dark spots on its white chest are a beautiful surprise.

She releases the thrush. He flies to a nearby tree, settles his feathers. Briefly silent, then full-throated song. Protest perhaps. Or warning.

Cranky at first, *whit, whit, whit*, developing into an agitated series of *bup, bup, bup* notes, faster and faster. Now the loud whistled prelude, *ee-oh-lay*, and the softer fluting flourish that follows. He continues alternating one prelude with another in combination with a staggering variety of flourishes. Song after song, high in the trees, Nell's insult seemingly forgotten.

Nell is working with one of Esme's teams documenting mercury levels in songbirds. The toxin attacks the nervous system, making the birds act strangely. They have trouble sitting on their eggs long enough to hatch. They seem easily distracted and the impact on the rates of reproduction is alarming.

The birds exhibiting the most elevated levels of mercury are the wood thrush, Bicknell's thrush, rusty blackbird, red-winged blackbird, eastern wood-peewee, indigo bunting, Nelson's sparrow, yellow-throated vireo, and salt marsh sparrow.

Nell has proven to be the most adept with her nets. All those years with Billy, her knowledge of the woods and marshes, the stillness they cultivated in order to listen and observe. She'd like to bring Billy with her. Hasn't found a way to ask him yet.

She turns back to her work. Labels the specimen bag and bottle, checks the net; presses play again.

Billy is losing weight and Marion can't figure out why. He shows up for dinner and seems to eat, though the dog probably gets more benefit from her cooking than her son. On several occasions Marion has found Billy sniffing his food, looking skeptical.

Tonight she's made macaroni and cheese, a dish he used to love. But these days he smothers most of his food in Tabasco sauce. That little bottle has taken up residence on the dining room table.

Marion does not tolerate bottles and jars and cartons on the table.

"Put it in a dish," she tells her children, "or a pitcher or a glass." They don't listen. She can just imagine her own mother's response to that stuff slopped down on the table. God, it's hard work keeping up Mabel Morrissey's standards. All the way through raising five kids, how many meals would that add up to, to be felled at last by Billy, not hungry, not giving a damn.

Nell gets up and pours the milk into a pitcher.

"How was physical therapy?" Marion asks.

"Fine." Billy's chair scrapes back.

"Where are you going?" Marion asks.

"I don't know, Mom. Out."

"What? I'm suddenly some kind of lousy cook? You barely ate."

"I'm not hungry."

"You're never hungry."

Nell and Jack exchange a look.

Billy turns to the door, Flanagan following him.

"Come back here, please," Marion says with that tone.

Billy stops in the doorway, looks at his mother, that flat stare none of them can get used to.

"Can we talk about this later?"

"No."

It seems possible Billy will just ignore Marion and go. But some memory of family dinners, where each of them was sternly spoken to by their father, stops him.

"Well?" Marion presses.

"I can't smell much. And that means I can't taste much either."

"How long has this been going on?" Jack asks.

"A while."

"A week? A month?"

"Six months or more."

"I'm tired of either chasing you or tiptoeing around you. Sit down for five minutes," Marion says. "What about a specialist?"

"You want to fight with the VA to cover another specialist, be my guest."

"Yes, I do. Give me the number to call. What does your doctor say?"

"He says he's heard of it. It usually clears up on its own."

"And the cause?" Jack asks.

"You know the VA. Nothing's wrong until you and a thousand other soldiers can prove it."

"So what are you hearing?" Jack asks.

"There are plenty of vets who can't smell, or taste. Most everybody has hearing loss. And then there are the guys who just plain feel lousy, with low-grade fevers, constant fatigue, and vomiting. More and more cancers are showing up. The VA says they're slacking off, looking to stay on the dole. Nobody's getting any answers."

"What do you think it is?"

"We used a lot of chemicals, Dad."

"Jesus Christ!" Marion bursts out.

"Marion, please," Jack says.

"They deny the symptoms so the government isn't responsible for disability and medical payments. If you can't prove direct cause and effect . . . "

"Why can't you prove it?" Marion asks.

"Think about it. I say I've got hearing loss. They have experts who cite studies on hearing loss among eighteen-to-twenty-two-year old noncombatants due to loud music. Do I listen to music? Yes. Did I fly without proper audio protection? Yes, sir, I did, but—only they don't want to hear the explanation, the crap equipment, or good equipment that breaks down or malfunctions in combat conditions or jungle damp or forty days of rain and fog and mud."

"Did you personally handle chemicals?" Jack asks.

"You wouldn't believe what we did." Billy looks at his father. "Twelve million tons of Agent Orange, Dad. As if the Geneva Convention against chemical warfare did not exist. Think of what we've done, what we're leaving behind."

Flanagan whines, pushes against Billy.

"Can I skip the dishes, Mom?" Nell asks, getting up to follow him.

"What about your homework?" Marion asks.

"C'mon. She got into college already," Billy says.

"Can we take a walk?" Nell asks Billy.

"Or a drive?" He looks to Marion.

"You can't shift," Marion says.

"Sure I can. Left-handed."

"What? How do you hold the wheel?"

"Nell will do it."

"Billy . . . " Jack cautions.

"I steady the wheel with my right hand, reach under and shift with my left."

"That's so reassuring," Marion says.

"We'll stick to back roads. Or Nell will drive."

"Right. You're such a good passenger."

"Thanks, Mom."

Nell, Billy, and Flanagan burst out the back door.

"How much gas have we got?" Nell asks, as Billy awkwardly turns the key in the ignition with his left hand.

"A quarter-tank, looks like. You got any money?"

Nell pulls three dollars from her pocket, places them on the dash. "Where are we going?"

"Around the lake."

"All the way around? It's already 7:30."

"You afraid of the dark?"

"How about Sunset Ridge? I can't remember the last time I walked up there. With you, maybe, before you shipped out."

"You don't take your boyfriends up there?"

"Boyfriends. Right."

"C'mon. Not one boy? In two whole years?"

"I'm not talking about this with you," she says.

"Not one?"

Flanagan leans over the seat to put her head on Billy's shoulder, filling the front seat with dog breath. Nell cranks her window down.

"Did you at least manage to get yourself well and truly kissed?" he asks.

"You make it sound simple."

"It is."

"I have to like somebody first."

"At your age, don't you like just about everybody? Every boy, I mean."

"*No.*"

"So maybe you're a little too picky."

"I'm not."

"A little too shy."

"Okay, you were a fairly nice and relatively interesting high school boy. There aren't a lot of boys like that, trust me."

"I'm not talking about Prince Charming here, I'm talking

about some kid, some boy sort of person who'd be fun to kiss. There has to be one."

"Enough already."

"Did you at least get to go to your senior dance or prom or whatever they call it these days?"

"For all you know I have had a very intense affair with an older man who has completely spoiled me for boys my own age."

"You have not."

"How do you know? You've been gone."

"Let's grab a beer."

"I thought you quit."

"It's almost Friday."

"Jesus, Billy."

While Billy and Nell are out, Jack and Harlow Murphy tow home a broken-down 1960 Ford Falcon and stow it in the garage. The body's in rough shape, it's so riddled with rust you can't tell what color it is, and the engine needs a lot of work, but with some time and some tools, they might be able to get it back on the road.

A project. Billy needs a set of wheels.

Harlow promises used parts and assistance before getting into his truck and disappearing up the drive.

Marion will not be happy. They can't afford it, even though it came from a junk shop. Maybe she'll be so glad to get her own car back she'll forgive him. Still, Jack hesitates to go inside.

"Good lord, Jack. The insurance alone—"

"He needs his own car."

"You could have asked me."

"You would have said no."

"We should have talked about it."

"It seemed like a good opportunity."

"You're not listening to me!"

"Hey, hey . . . what's got you so worked up?"

"The VA will only pay for half of Billy's rehab. He has exceeded their customary number of visits. I can't cover the bills we've got and more keep coming in. The hand specialist is going to assess the nerve damage next week, make his recommendations. It just goes on and on. And I don't know how we're going to pay for it on top of everything else."

"Imagine what it's like for Billy."

"I do."

"No, we don't. Not really. We fret about money, the doctors' appointments. Billy's left to worry about whether his hand will ever work again."

"A car's not going to fix that."

"It'll help."

Billy pulls up in front of Riley's Tavern, the lone bar on this stretch of road. Riley's does especially well during the hunting and ice fishing seasons, and for drinkers who don't want to do their brawling and trawling for girls too close to home. The smell of stale beer has even permeated the asphalt of the parking lot. A "Jenny" sign blinks halfheartedly in the window. Billy is at the door when Nell calls out:

"You don't have any money."

He returns to the car and grabs the bills off the dash, both hands, Nell sees, shaking.

"That's for gas," she challenges him.

"The hell with you if you don't want to have fun."

"They won't serve me," she says to his retreating back.

"You don't have a fake ID? That is just plain dull, Nell. Grow up, for Christ's sake."

Before she can pry apart the contradictions, Billy is back, cradling two beers.

They switch places. He's halfway through the first bottle before Nell pulls out of the parking lot.

"You want any of this?" he asks.

"I don't really like beer."

"Suit yourself."

"We don't have enough gas to get all the way around the lake."

"Damn. I just wanted to drive these hills in the dark. Fast. Doesn't Mom keep change for parking meters in here somewhere?"

"She used to keep a few bucks in the glove box for summer ice-cream cones."

Billy jerks open the glove compartment and finds two dollar bills folded small and tucked under the registration.

"Gas? Beer?" He holds up each dollar in turn.

"Gas," she pulls into the Esso station on the outskirts of Dresden.

"Spoilsport," he says, as she hands the attendant their money.

"You get any change at the bar?"

He fishes the change from his pocket. Nell calls out:

"Make that $2.85 would you?"

The lanky attendant, no older than fifteen, pockets their bills, the stack of change, without bothering to count it, shakes out the filthy squeegee, and washes the windows, front and back.

"You want your oil checked?"

"What about him?" Billy asks.

"No thanks," Nell says to both of them.

As Nell turns onto Route 9, Billy throws the bottle out the window. She jumps at the crash it makes hitting a tree. Thinks back to Rob Chandler and his boys. So much unfinished business.

Billy opens the second beer, fiddles with the radio. "Can you still pick up Albany late at night?"

"Albany, Syracuse, sometimes the City."

"Cold winter nights."

"Not like tonight."

He pulls in a scratchy jazz show from Ithaca. Some white boy playing the blues.

"I keep seeing that picture of that little kid," he says, "what was her name, up in Penfield?"

"Pamela Moss."

"Wakes me up nights. And then I can't stop thinking about Megan and if it's somehow related." He doesn't tell her that he dreams of horses again and again; the same horse, he finally realizes, a gray-black Percheron. Nor does he tell her how often he goes up to the Homestead, dream-haunted, Megan-haunted, seeing that horse in the field, seeing their lives, all that might have been.

"There are crazy rumors floating around," Nell says.

"Like what?"

"Like someone supposedly saw her in Rochester. That she's pregnant and her family sent her away to have the baby." Nell glances at Billy, tries to assess his reaction. Had Megan ever told him?

"Even the police could have uncovered that by now."

"That she ran away."

"Where? And why?"

"Did you know that she . . . ?"

"What?"

"Forget it."

"What are you not telling me? Other boyfriends? She was sleeping with this Chandler asshole? Big deal."

She looks out the window. Thinks of that dark house, the long walk back to the bus station, Megan unable to talk the whole ride home.

Flanagan climbs into the front seat and winds herself around Billy's feet, her head on his knees. He strokes her absentmindedly.

Driving through the twilight hush, Nell feels that anything could happen. She gives up the wheel reluctantly and pushes Flanagan into the backseat. He can't be drunk on two beers, can he? She takes comfort in the fact that Flanagan is in the car and Billy would never let anything happen to her.

"Let's turn back."

"We're just getting to the good hills."

"It's another hour to get home."

"So what do you care? Plus, I don't poke along like you do. It's forty minutes, tops."

"C'mon, Billy, I've got school tomorrow."

He tromps on the gas. Marion's old Plymouth has crap acceleration, but if you're patient, it cruises all right once it gets to 60. Still too fast for these windy roads and a brother with one good hand.

He flirts with driving so fast she'll be scared into telling him the truth, a truth he probably already knows. Feels her fear then, takes his foot off the gas.

How stupid they were; believing nothing could touch them, catch them, destroy what they had. Willfully blind to the facts, to the birds and the bees, for godsakes. Charmed, meant to be, summer of love, ain't nothin' like the real thing, baby.

He looks at Nell, thinks of how he kept pushing Harlow away from her, but still took what he wanted with Megan. With everything. Grabbed what he wanted with both hands. Flying. The war. Intoxicated in the air. Every time he walked across the tarmac, climbed into the bird. All he'd ever wanted. More awake, more alert, more alive than anytime before or since.

"I think she's dead," he says finally.

Nell doesn't answer for a long time.

"Did you hear me?"

"Don't say that." Her voice quiet, strained. "Don't even think it."

"And they'll never find her."

"Billy, Christ . . . "

"Tell me what happened."

"There's nothing to tell," she says.

"Liar."

She turns away from him to look out the window.

"You're blushing," he says. "Telltale sign."

"Stop it."

"Who are you protecting?"

"I don't know anymore."

Nell's Friday night bus ride to Syracuse is hot, crowded, and noisy. She gets off the bus with a splitting headache and takes the shortcut to Sheila's apartment, even though she's promised not to walk through the parking lots and alleyways at night.

She runs up the stairs and makes a beeline to the medicine cabinet and some aspirin. Coming out of the bathroom, Nell realizes what's troubling her. The apartment is nearly empty.

"What's going on?"

"I've been giving a few things away."

Nell takes in the bare shelves, the lone chair with a lamp beside it. In the bedroom, Sheila's single mattress is on the floor. The dresser, mirror, and pictures are gone. Nell opens the closet: two pairs of shoes, two pairs of pants, skirts, shirts, sweaters.

"Nell, would you quit it?" Sheila says as Nell opens the silverware drawer in the kitchen: two sets of forks, knives, spoons. On the shelves: two plates, bowls, cups.

Sheila's beloved stand mixer is gone. She'd saved for two years to buy that thing. The wooden table they bought together at a yard sale has been replaced with a card table and two folding chairs.

Nell wonders if Sheila ever has company.

"Are you leaving?" she asks.

"I'll tell you while we bake. If you promise to let me tell Mom and Dad in my own way."

"What are we making?"

"Tollhouse cookies and that orange tea cake Billy likes. Will you cream the butter?"

Nell creams the butter, thinks about Billy's moods, the constant weight of Megan Alsop, adds brown sugar to the bowl.

"So what's going on? It's not some guy, is it?"

"I'm going to New York."

"You do that every summer."

"Full-time. I've given my notice at school."

"You're leaving your job to work at the Catholic Worker House?" Nell asks, adding eggs, vanilla.

"Changing one job for another."

"Do they pay you?"

"Room and board and a small stipend."

"But you're a nurse."

"Should be useful, then."

"Is this some kind of back-door approach to becoming a nun?"

Sheila adds baking soda, flour, takes over stirring. "I don't know yet."

"When will you tell Mom and Dad?" Nell asks.

"This weekend. You could grease the pans."

"When do you leave?"

"When school is done."

"You're leaving *now* . . . ?"

"I've needed to get out from under Marion's disapproval

for a long time. And I feel like I'll lose my soul if I don't do this work."

"That's a little dramatic."

Sheila smiles, eats a spoonful of dough. "Maybe. Maybe not."

Sheila's hair is pulled back; she has on a faded T-shirt and a skirt she made. She wears a five-dollar watch and sandals she's had since high school. Nell thinks of Sheila's apartment stripped bare; and looks at her sister's face, no trace of make-up. All the things Marion criticizes:

Would it kill you to wear lipstick?

I'll pay for a haircut, for God's sake.

A little bit of color won't compromise your principles, Sheila.

"I'm going to miss you."

"Come visit," Sheila smiles.

"I wouldn't want to get in your way."

"We'll put you to work."

"I feel like an idiot not knowing how important this is to you. Being caught up in my own little bubble."

"Marion likes to assign the starring roles."

"I should know better."

"No, Nell, Mom should know better."

"You're different."

"You know how Dad always says *not* making a decision is making a decision?"

"Yeah."

"This feels right."

Tuesday morning after working at the farm, Billy rides to the Ag Station with Jack and then walks down Castle Street into town. The sun is almost warm. Spring seems like less of a rumor and more of a possibility.

Across from the Smith Opera House, the old model and hobby store stands empty, faded flyers with Megan's picture pasted to the windows. The Strand movie theatre is shuttered, but the Roxie is still holding on. They're changing the marquee as Billy walks by, bringing back *The Wild Bunch*. Maybe Nell would like to go.

He climbs the stairs to the third floor, questioning why he's doing this. Taking time off from work at the garage to mess around. Just because a good-looking woman told him to. Likely to be another sucker punch; the classic one-two of hope and failure.

The art room stretches across the front of the building. Tall arched windows flood the room with light. There are eight large tables. Art books stacked on a beat-up desk. A bank of storage drawers and cabinets lines one wall.

Jazz is playing, sounds like Coltrane, and students are already gathering materials. Anna Barnes greets him, introduces him to the class, and leads him to a table where a boy named Ben is working. They will share a workstation. Ben looks too young to be in high school, let alone college. Billy wonders what number he drew in the draft. It's a curse, this way of measuring people. What's the age difference? Two years? Yet there it is, the fucking generational divide. He watches as Ben takes in his scars, his wrecked hand, meets his eye, then looks away.

Anna shows him where the supplies are, tells him he can bring his own things if he wants. She talks without pushing, a rarity. Some of the things he will remember:

Everyone's work is different.

There's no right or wrong here.

Begin anywhere.

He surveys the room. The projects range from miniature to enormous, and the variety of materials and approaches surprises him. It all surprises him. He'd been expecting glue and tissue paper. Instead there's a lengthy wall mural of a riverbank, both painted and collaged. Constructions. Boxes. Boxes within boxes. One girl tears images from magazines which she cuts in pieces and reassembles in startling ways. A man with a bird's head, a wheelbarrow with a woman's bare arms for handles. The kid named Simon is working with sand and paint; his tablemate uses found images and text to create antiwar posters.

"What do you want to say, or express?" Anna asks. "A mood, a feeling, a place, an experience."

She opens drawer after drawer as she talks to him. Paper of all kinds, colors, fabric, string in every texture and heft, thread, beads, feathers, seedpods, paints, pencils, crayons, newsprint.

"Pick up whatever you feel drawn to and play with it."

She hands him a piece of poster board.

"Assemble something. Don't overanalyze it."

"They all seem to know what they're doing," he says.

"They're each working on a project that grew out of this process. Trust me. Get your hands busy. Turn your mind off."

He lets his hands sift through seedpods, thinks of Megan: Where is she?

Snub nose, bony knees. She had a sly sense of humor and laughed so much when she slept over that Marion was always threatening to send her home when she and Nell were still horsing around at one and two in the morning.

They worked and played together all their lives, cutting hay, picking apples, mucking out the barn, swimming, rowing, fishing, hiking, though the one thing Megan refused to do was sit around in the woods listening to birds.

The summer she turned twelve they'd fallen asleep in the hayloft after haying all day. He woke to find her leaning over him. That first kiss tasted of sun and green grass. He pulled her against him, then rolled on top of her before he came fully awake and realized what he was doing. They'd crossed a line with the kiss; when he touched her they entered a new world.

He withdrew from her then, and for the next two years

ignored her, rebuffed her, kept his distance if they did have to be in the same place at the same time. Got himself a girlfriend to drive the point home, a loud, brash town girl, not his type at all.

Megan bided her time, wise—or cunning—beyond her years. She let him know she was waiting for him, revealing much in her steadfast patience. And even though he told himself she was too young, that he shouldn't, they shouldn't, it grew more difficult to stay away from her. His thoughts turned to protecting her, giving her time to grow up. Maybe next year, or the next.

Two years after that first kiss, during the apple harvest, Megan climbed into the tree where he was working. He lifted his head and suddenly she was before him, the late fall day so crisp it snapped against his skin.

The sounds of birds and human chatter from neighboring trees fell away as she came close to him. She filled every one of his senses: the rank tang of her sweaty T-shirt, the sweet girl smell of her bare arms, the tomboy scent of her worn-out sneakers and dirty neck. Her breath, ripe with apples, her skin hot and dry, lips chapped, hair littered with bits of leaves.

He noted that she did not smile in triumph. She was not playacting. She waited, not knowing how he would react.

She was daring him, he realized. Choosing her moment. Daring him to make a move.

He gathers paper and paints. A brush wide enough you could paint a house with it. He wishes he had dirt to apply to this board; he imagines cornfields, the ground softening in spring rains, a sense of motion, escape.

He crushes charcoal, stirs it into thick paint. Picks up the brush in his left hand. And begins.

After the other students leave, Anna joins Billy at a table by the window to look at some of his field journals. She pages through them slowly.

"These are so alive."

He turns away, suddenly agitated, on the verge of anger. He wants to slap those books shut and get the hell out of here.

He looks up to find her watching him.

"Can you pick up a pencil like this?" She shows him a four-fingered hold, then three. He has to decide if he will play this game or not.

He crosses to the window, watches as Maeve Alsop leaves the bank across the street, stopping to tie a scarf over her hair. She looks thin and almost girlish in her red coat and heels. Until you see how grief hunches her shoulders, lines her face. She seems fragile and terribly alone.

"Billy . . ."

He takes the pencil, can almost manage to hold it, but can't use it.

"But the other night you could hold the charcoal and use it some," she says.

"I could push it across the paper, or pull it, but there was no freedom, no . . ."

"Line," she finishes for him. "Has there been improvement?"

"Some. It's slow."

"Could you spend a year exploring other media?"

"A year?"

"How long since your last surgery?"

"Two months."

"That's not long."

"First surgery was in December," he says. "Feels like forever."

"It must have been pretty bad."

"Like I said, for me it's about . . ."

"A hyper-identification with the natural world."

"I don't feel the same anyplace else," he says. "Except when I'm flying. And being cut off like this . . ."

"I can't fix it. But I can give you space to explore. Here, if you want. If you're interested in sculpture, I'll get in touch with my friend Ron Crosby."

"How long will it take to gain some skill left-handed?"

"That depends on how determined you are. And you have to let yourself draw like a five-year-old again."

"That's a tall order."

"Without judgment."

"Right."

"It's not failure," she says. "It's learning. It's progress."

"I wish I didn't need it so much. Or miss it so much."

"Come and draw with us. Or paint. Just get your hands moving. For a few hours a day. Be patient. See what happens."

Jack has been sitting at the kitchen table since 3 A.M., having given up on sleep. His wife and daughter sleep in the rooms above him; his son has still not come home. A glass of water sits on the table next to his tattered prayer book. Propped against the butter dish is a postcard from his brother Trevor. Finally. He's found work on the docks in Savannah, Georgia. No phone number. No return address.

Here in the dark, in the presence of the coal stove, the whisper of pines outside the window, Jack Flynn is struggling back to prayer. The distance he needs to travel seems insurmountable to him, from rejection of God or any idea of God, to a profound hunger for God. But hunger and desire are not faith. Anger is not the way, either, though he is so full of anger some days it scares him.

What a crime, that another war should erupt in time to give his sons their own war, and take his sons from him, one teetering on the edge of living and he, their father for God's sake, unable to protect his own children in any real way. The shame of his personal failures claws at him, the failures of his generation, his government, his church, and the price, again, in his own lifetime, of youth and valor, squandered in the mud and jungles. Dear God, erupts from his mouth on a daily basis, how can you ask this of us again?

He and Marion, he has to admit, were complicit in their sons' decisions to serve. He thinks of the endless conversations around the dinner table where they found themselves arguing against their own self-interest. Sure, there were deferments; yes, you could find a way to dodge your responsibility. But what about sacrifice, doing the right thing, even when it cost you something? If his sons did not do their part, someone else's sons would have to go in their place.

All you had to do was look down the street and see the boys who would end up going, who didn't have the option of college, or some of the other less honorable deferments.

Jack opens his prayer book, though he has no need to be reminded of the confiteor, the forgiveness of sins, and bows his head.

Billy gets dropped off at the top of the driveway by the college girl he's just dry humped in the back of her father's car. She's drunk and sloppy but not so drunk and sloppy she lets him get her pants off. He slips halfway down the driveway, falls to one knee, recovers, wishes he were drunker, maybe dead drunk, passed out, blacked-out drunk.

Girls soothe him, their soft bodies, glossy hair, the touch of their hands, the dance they dance between innocence and debauchery, between yes and no. It doesn't last. Alcohol is much more reliable.

He slips his shoes off on the porch and lets himself in the back door. Trips against the doorjamb, curses softly, and starts to cross through the kitchen before he realizes that his father is sitting in the dark.

"Dad . . . ?"

Jack swallows his first flash of anger; takes in the smell of a woman, of cigarettes and spilled beer.

"Come and sit with me for a minute."

Billy turns the light on over the stove and immediately wishes he hadn't.

"What are you doing up? Not waiting for me, I hope?"

"Couldn't sleep," Jack admits.

"Runs in the family."

"Not long until dawn anyway. You know me."

Flanagan comes in from the living room. Yawns, stretches, curls up on Billy's feet.

Billy sees his father's hand on his prayer book, a morning ritual, his thumb rubbing the worn leather, and is surprised when Jack reaches out and takes his hand.

He registers the unfamiliarity of his father's touch, his hands layered with calluses, the strength of them. They sit quietly until Billy remembers where his hands have been, cupping that girl's pearly round bottom, and pulls away; his chair scraping across the linoleum.

"You might lay off the sauce," Jack says.

"I know."

"It's not helping."

"I've been trying," Billy says. "Stopped drinking during the week—for the most part—and then I just hit it harder on the weekend. Some days it's all I'm good for."

"That's not true."

"Feels true. Did you ever . . . "

"I did. Until your mother threatened to leave me."

"She did not."

"I was a scary son of a bitch when I was drinking. And it didn't stop the nightmares. It made them worse."

Flanagan rolls over, begs to have her belly scratched.

"I know you're thinking about leaving us," Jack says.

Startled, Billy covers by getting up to get a cigarette.

"It's all right, you know. Your mother and I have been expecting it."

He sits again, antsy, his legs jittering under the table.

One of the trashcans tips over with a crash.

"Those damn raccoons!" Billy crosses to the back door; Flanagan follows him, pushing at the screen.

"Leave it 'til morning."

"It'll be all over the yard."

"Five minutes with a rake."

Jack joins Billy, puts his arm around him. Billy allows himself the comfort of his father's touch and strength and belief, wishes he could bottle it, sup at this table until he feels whole again. All that communion promises. Bless me, Father . . .

"Talk to me . . . "

"I wish I could."

"Forgive yourself, son. Whatever happened. Let it go."

Rosie's baby gets himself born two weeks early, following a labor so brief Rosie and Nick barely make it to the hospital. William Matthew Bliss has Rosie's long black eyelashes, Nick's cleft chin, and Billy's blue eyes.

Billy and Nell drive to the hospital in whatever car or truck they can get their hands on. They bring flowers, donuts, gum and mints and chocolate. Billy spends hours holding the baby, carefully cradling his nephew's head in his hands.

Nell watches her brother, so gentle with this baby in his arms. Can't stop herself: thinks of Megan, thinks of Dorset Street, all that might have been and is not. That baby would be almost two. Boy or girl, she wonders almost every day. Shakes it off when she sees that Billy is quiet in this room as he has not been since getting home. At rest, almost at peace.

Rosie teases him: "Since when do you like babies so much?"

"Why'd you name him after me?" he asks.

"Why do you think?"

"He'll be everybody's favorite," Nell says.

"Just like Billy," Rosie adds. "Mark my words."

When Jack gets home from the Ag Station Monday evening, Marion is at the kitchen table paying bills. He kisses her; she smiles and returns to the checkbook.

"Let me finish this."

He draws a glass of water from the tap, picks up the paper, steels himself for the bad news and body count, as if you can conduct a war by counting casualties. Four hundred and fifty civilians killed in Saigon during Viet Cong raids throughout the city, the highest weekly death toll to date. And a glimmer of good news: The Senate is poised to repeal the 1964 Gulf of Tonkin Resolution. About bloody time.

He looks out the kitchen window at the side yard, his vegetable garden just beginning to green. They've been so busy and pre-occupied, he barely remembers planting the garden.

Pushing open the back door, he sits on the porch steps, rolls his shoulders to ease the stiffness from the day's work. He's a man who likes the comfort of his routines, and there's been nothing routine about their lives since Billy got home.

The elms around the house are on the edge of failure. No matter how much he doctors those trees, spending money they don't have, and he's sure to hear more about that when Marion joins him, he's not going to be able to save them. He's just been prolonging the inevitable. But he's grateful every spring they leaf out, every summer he spends in their shade.

It's hard to sit on the porch without making a list of all that needs to get done. All of the usual chores and maintenance have been usurped by visits to the hospital, to rehab, and more recently, the weeks they've spent working on Billy's car. If the roof could last one more winter, if the fence could go unpainted one more spring. And look at that, the pear tree isn't just dying anymore, it's dead.

Marion sits beside him, the screen door slapping behind her.

"I spoke to the hospital. We've worked out a more realistic payment plan. We've got eighteen months now. Twenty-four if we need it. And I spoke to Jim Denny, the assistant principal at the high school. I can teach summer school for a little extra cash. American History, here we come."

"You don't have to do that."

"It won't kill me."

"You sure?"

"You'll have to buy me a fan, though. My own personal classroom fan."

"I'll pick one up this weekend," he says.

"You'll forget."

"I won't."

"There's one thing I want."

"What's that?"

"I want them all home for Nell's graduation. Like we did for the boys. Can you do that?"

"I'll try."

"Not good enough, Jack."

"I'll make it happen."

"Don't let that fast-talking Brendan off the hook."

"I won't."

"He's a slippery son of a gun."

"I know."

"If you could arrange for that girlfriend of his to be too busy to come, that would be all to the good."

"Not likely."

They're quiet for a moment.

"How are we going to manage Cornell?" he asks. "Nell's scholarship doesn't . . . "

"It covers tuition, but not fees or room and board. I sent in a deposit. Not the deposit they asked for. I'm hoping it will take them all summer to notice we're short."

"Short by how much?"

"Let's keep that worry at bay a little longer, okay?"

Asa Alsop calls. The police stopped by. A man in Penn Yan has confessed to kidnapping and killing Megan, burying her along the abandoned canal path. The police are there now. Asa asks Jack to come along. He can't face the trip to identify the body alone.

An hour later Jack calls from a pay phone. The man was delusional. The police unearthed the carcass of a dog.

Jack and Billy, with help from Harlow, get the car back on the road. Countless hours in the garage, the radio blaring, brash music Jack thought he disliked, but he finds himself glad for its insistent energy, pushing them to work another hour, and another, obviating the need for talk, or thought for that matter.

Maybe that's why Billy and Harlow like it. Mind-numbing music, tools in their hands, an engine spilling its guts and getting put back together. Santana, Led Zeppelin, Three Dog Night to push them past midnight.

Jack watches Billy work one-handed, using his right hand to assist, awkward but getting stronger, more confident as the weeks tick by.

They work nights, they work weekends; the parts they need cost more than they're supposed to. Harlow scavenges what he can. Jack keeps a folder in the garage with the receipts. Marion stops asking.

The car looks like crap, rusted and dented and desperately needing paint. The leatherette on the seats is cracked and discolored, ugly as sin. None of them gives a damn what the car looks like, if they can just get her to run.

The night they take their first ride, Harlow stuffed into the backseat, 1 o'clock in the morning, the muffler rattles so loud it sounds like it will fall off before they get out of the driveway. But it doesn't fall off and that engine runs without a hiccup, all down South Main Street, the only other car on the road the local cop.

They don't say much, don't need to, the shared pleasure of a job finished, resurrecting an engine, gears in sync, the bald tires; one good thing about the bald tires, so quiet on the road.

That first drive, Billy at the wheel, almost stately, he takes it so slow, like they're kings of the town surveying their domain.

They head out past the State Park to 5 and 20 and on the dark, empty highway; Billy opens her up, pushes the engine to see what she can do. Sixty nice and smooth, sixty-five she begins to rattle, seventy the shimmy's so bad, Jack reaches out to help steady the wheel. He can tell Billy wants to push it further, but he takes his foot off the gas and drops back to sixty.

"Not bad," Billy says, looking at his father, meeting Harlow's eyes in the rearview mirror. "Not bad at all."

Asa Alsop surprises Marion by appearing at the back door just as she slides a meatloaf into the oven.

He comes into the kitchen carrying a basket of eggs and a jar of honey. Marion puts the percolator on even after he says no thanks to coffee, offers him a kitchen chair. He sits, his long legs stretched out in front of him, his overalls patched, his hands rough but clean. She dries her hands on her apron and picks up the jar of honey.

"The labels look good," Marion says.

"Schuyler's wants every jar I've got."

"These will sell fast."

"That's what he tells me."

"Let's have some." Marion slices bread, sets out the crock of butter.

"Spoil our dinner," Asa warns.

"I won't tell if you won't."

She pours coffee, sits beside him, butters bread, spoons honey from the jar. They both take a bite. Fragrant and sweet. Asa sips his coffee, smiles his slow smile.

"How's Billy doing for you?" Marion asks.

"Steady. What I need."

"Will you join us for supper tonight?"

"Thank you. Another time."

"When the school year's done, we'll all have a little more time. I'll send Nell or Billy up to fetch you."

She gets up to put potatoes in a pot of water. "Thank you for the eggs."

"The hens keep laying like nothing's happened. Be nice to be like that."

"Do you miss the ponies?"

"Every damn day."

"How's Evan doing over at Maeve's place?"

"As well as can be expected. He misses the farm."

"Any news?"

"The detective came by today to tell me they've suspended their investigation."

"Why?"

"They have no suspects, no evidence, no body."

"I don't understand how that's possible."

"Neither do I." He finishes his coffee.

"People do not just disappear."

"There was some talk of dragging the lake . . . "

"It's too deep, isn't it?"

"And they have no reason to believe she drowned."

The late afternoon sun flares across the water. Marion waits.

"They've downgraded the investigation to a missing persons case. Which will remain open, but, as far as I can tell, inactive."

"Oh, Asa."

"She's not dead. I'd feel it. I'd know."

Marion reaches out to him.

"But maybe there's something worse than dead . . . that's what keeps me up nights. Somebody got away with something, didn't they? Maybe somebody right here, somebody we know."

"A clue will turn up. They'll find her."

"I don't know how to live with this. She's just a kid. Hardly big enough to reach the pedals to drive the tractor. Some days I'd like to kill someone."

A Baltimore oriole flies through the open window into the art studio at the Smith Opera House. Anna asks the other students to leave the room while Billy imitates its call, a series of flutelike whistled notes, which calms the bird. Using his shirt he's able to capture and release it. After the other students leave for the day, he and Anna tape strips of paper to the large windows, each strip a hand's width apart. The pattern renders the glass opaque, making it impossible for birds to see their reflection in the glass.

"About a billion birds a year fly into windows. Mostly migrating songbirds," Billy says.

"A billion? That's a big number."

"It's true, though."

"Can you whistle other birdcalls?"

"A few."

"More than a few, I bet."

"I'm out of practice."

Anna starts to clean up. Billy tosses the collage he started in the trash.

"You hate this, don't you?" Anna asks.

"I don't know what I'm doing."

"Can you give it a little more time?"

"You've got this idea I'm an artist."

"I've seen your drawings."

"It was never about the drawing . . . It was about the birds. The pencil, the pen . . . I don't know how to say this . . . "

She waits.

"It's a doorway, a bridge, the space between us . . . Jesus . . . " He falls silent. "It's how I lived in the world."

She sets a large pad of newsprint on an easel, picks up a pencil.

"I'll hold the pencil. You direct my hand."

"That won't work."

"Who knows? Let's draw a branch."

"What kind of branch?" he asks. "Walnut? Willow?"

"Surprise me."

He covers her hand with his own, then steps away from her.

"You don't draw with your hand or your fingers; you draw with your eyes, with your body," he says.

"Just see what happens."

"I'm going to lean into you."

"Okay."

He takes her hand again. "I can't do this."

Without turning to look at him, she says, "Draw a line. One line."

Their first attempt: the pencil stammers across the page.

"This is pointless," he says.

"Let's try a brush."

She takes a watercolor brush, dips it in water and pigment.

The paint drips while she waits. Then he takes her hand and sweeps it across the paper, pushing too hard, too fast. She discards the sheet of newsprint. Dips the brush again.

She can feel his body move against her. She lets him have

her hand, her arm, her shoulder. The lines sweep across the page, uneven, lacking control. But the impulse is there. He drops her hand. She turns and looks at him then, sees the hope and disappointment in his eyes.

"Come home with me."

He looks at her for a long moment. He has wanted nothing but oblivion for a long time. That's not what she's offering. She wants him to wake up.

It terrifies him.

They drive her beat-up Chevy pickup out to her cottage.

Anna lived in Rochester with her lawyer husband until their divorce a year ago. She left the large Victorian on East Avenue, the house that was to have been home to the children she was unable to provide. Walked out of her husband's life and into her own. Winnowed her expenses and expectations to what she could afford as a teacher, leaving her time to paint.

Entering the one-room cottage, Billy can see all of it, and all of Anna's life in a glance. There are two tortoiseshell hair clips lying in the middle of the unmade bed, and sheer white curtains blowing in the open windows.

Her work on the walls, pastel, gouache, watercolor, landscapes, *this* landscape, the lake in every season, some so bold they're almost abstract.

He reaches for her.

She makes him slow down. She draws him out, asks for something—he can't quite say what, yet—maybe it's her way of not asking. There is none of the hurry up, now, now, now urgency of the town girls he'd known in high school, none of the yes, no, maybe dance required by the girls up at the college.

Her one luxury is an outdoor shower. Spacious, plenty of hot water. If you can stand the cold moments between leaving the cottage and entering the water's warmth.

Making love in the shower, the hot water pelting them, the cold air like a curtain around them, the views to the lake, Anna avid and adventurous, eyes open, fully present to her own pleasure. Kissing her throat, her thigh, the thrum of her pulse beneath his lips, the sky above them breaking into dawn or closing into night, worlds away from the blind, obliterating sex he has craved.

He licks the rime of sex and salt from her skin, wishes for a beer to chase it. Laughs.

Esme Tinker pulls into the gas station early Monday morning. Billy and Harlow sit at the old metal desk in the office drinking coffee and reading the newspaper. Harlow heads off to change the oil in a Rambler.

"There's something I think you'll be interested in," Esme says. "One of my students—Danny, the kid who recorded the dawn chorus—is working with sound engineers to create listening centers at Sapsucker Pond. Microphones will be placed in key spots throughout the marsh and two or three blinds will be equipped with headphones.

"We've got funding for this phase and I'm writing a grant for ongoing research.

"Danny has the technical side covered and wants to get going as soon as possible. I want to bring you in on the project."

"It sounds great," Billy says.

"Is that a yes? I really want that to be a yes."

"Listen, Esme . . . "

"Danny knows you're still healing, might need some time. He's a good kid. You'll like him."

A car pulls up to the gas pumps, the light bouncing off the chrome slicing into his head like he has no skin.

"I have to get to work," he says.

"If you can't give me an answer today, can you call me next week?"

"I'll call you," he promises. "Thank you."

"And think about coming to work with me as my TA for the fall, okay?"

"You couldn't stand to have me around that much," he says, stubbing out his cigarette.

"Try me."

He turns away, turns back.

"Look, my parents have spent everything they've got—and more—including whatever they saved for Nell's college—on hospital bills. I need to work for a while, get my head on straight. And what I really want, once my hand improves—is to get my commercial pilot's license. I know that's not what we talked about."

"It's all right, Billy."

"I feel like I've wrecked Nell's chances. Can you help her? She could be your TA."

"I'll see what I can do."

"I know you want it to be me."

"You take your time."

"And she needs someplace to live. The dorms are too expensive."

"I know someone who rents rooms to students. I'll call her." She puts the car into gear. "If you can fly, Billy, you should fly."

After working late, Billy and Harlow are rerouted around the campus on their drive home. They park the truck and walk up to the quad to a huge bonfire. Students burn Nixon in effigy, call for his impeachment. Boys burn draft cards in a barrel. Music. Dancing. The intoxicating idea that Nixon could be brought down, the war and the draft ended.

Billy and Harlow say nothing as they stand side by side. Billy understands their protests, or thinks he does, but despises the students for all they are ignorant of: the tens of thousands of young men doing a job, fighting a war that no one wants, fulfilling their duty to their country, to each other.

The honor in their service. They are not—we are not, he thinks—all baby killers and monsters.

He looks up above the fire. In the dark pitch of night the stars are blooming. He hears a nighthawk, unusually close. Imagines its invisible trail, etched against the sky.

"I'm gonna do some real damage if we don't get out of here," Harlow says, turning to leave.

"I wouldn't mind."

"It's not worth it. Let's go."

Tuesday, after swimming at the Y, Billy pulls over at the head of the lake, dark closing down the valley, the soft clatter of rain on the roof.

Too much is falling away from him. He feels less and less alive. Come back; just come back, he thinks again and again, let me keep my promises to you, the farm, the horses, I want to buy you a horse, sit with you on the porch as the sun melts into the lake and bats dance in the trees. Imagines turning to find her waiting on the dock, asleep in the loft, naked on his bed, walking through the door of the old farmhouse, the boards loud under her feet, framed in the doorway, the sun spilling over her like water, like benediction, like the future in all its blinding hopefulness.

He keeps trying to make sense of this, of being home, of Megan missing, of whether he should let whatever is happening with Anna continue to happen, whether it's a betrayal of Megan somehow, until the buzz in his ears crescendos, making all thought impossible. He flips on the radio, trying to shut his mind against the flak in his own head. Is tempted to smash his skull against the steering wheel.

Cars flick by on the road behind him. People going home. Families waiting. Children, dinner, homework, music practice. He thinks of letting himself be pulled into that orbit, remembers lying on the floor when they were kids, listening to Nell practice piano, the music playing on its own frequency inside him.

Exhausted, he turns the car toward home. Where they keep taking him in, in spite of his foul moods, bursts of temper, and the coldness he retreats behind. As if it could save him. Or protect them.

Billy goes to bed without eating. Falls asleep instantly. Doesn't wake until Flanagan complains to be fed, the sun already up, not a cloud in the sky, the wind testing the pines. Late for Asa's. Late for Harlow's. Late for everything.

Everyone has an opinion about the crash whether they know Billy or not. He must have been drunk. Or asleep at the wheel. Or both, to have survived. He must be one tough son of a bitch. He should never have been driving. They should revoke his license. Lucky no one else was hurt. What was he doing out on County House Road at three o'clock in the morning? Did that bucket of bolts pass inspection? We need stricter laws, better enforcement.

People were loud with these opinions, some of them even showed up as letters to the editor of the Geneva *Star*. The whispers were saved for the uneasy speculation that one of our own boys had deliberately run his car off the road. Some people may have connected it to Vietnam.

Billy was found by Bob Munson, a county policeman, wandering dazed and bloody along the side of the road. The blood

206 · LAURA HARRINGTON

was from a superficial head wound, but there was a lot of it. Otherwise he was shaken and bruised, but not seriously hurt.

The Ford was two hundred feet off the road, flipped on its roof.

Munson brought Billy to the local hospital. They stitched up a two-inch gash over his left ear and marveled, like everyone else, that he had walked away from the crash.

He asked them to wait until six before calling his father, no need to disturb his rest.

They left Billy in an examination bay, the curtain pulled around him, where he promptly fell asleep.

Driving Billy home, Jack doesn't say much. He believes that his kids' mistakes are punishment enough. And he knows not to jump to conclusions, to wait for Billy to tell him his side of the story.

He makes oatmeal while Billy showers. Jack had been skeptical that he could go to work, but Billy is adamant.

Coming into the kitchen Billy refuses to eat until Jack insists. Jack adds raisins and walnuts and brown sugar to the bowl. He pours coffee, puts sugar and cream within reach, makes himself a second piece of toast.

"Nell took care of your jobs up at Asa's this morning."

Billy picks up his spoon, sets it down again. Doctors his coffee, drinks.

"Try to eat, son."

"My stomach . . . "

"It'll get even worse if you don't eat."

The circles under Billy's eyes are so dark they look like bruises.

The lake is a deep slash of blue. Through the open door, the smell of grass, pine, basswood. The jays and juncos are loud as they feed and sing in the sun. There's nothing to say or too much to say; in either case it silences both of them.

"I could have slept forever on that gurney," Billy says and instantly regrets it for how strange it sounds.

He sets down his coffee cup, picks up the spoon again, the oatmeal congealing in the bowl.

"I'll make you a sandwich." Jack pulls bread, cheese, ham, and lettuce from the fridge.

"Just the cheese, Dad."

"Okay."

"You got cheddar?"

"I know how you like it."

"Nance's?"

"Like I said."

Billy pushes the morning paper aside. Kent State, Jackson State, SNCC demands: immediate withdrawal from Southeast Asia, release of all victims of political repression in the United States including the Black Panthers, the impeachment of President Nixon, and the end to war-related activities at universities.

Good luck with that, he thinks.

His head is throbbing; both shoulders ache and his knees seem to have taken a beating. He wishes he'd asked the doctor for painkillers. Not like anyone would write him another prescription after that fiasco.

"Where were you headed?" Jack asks from the counter.

"Nowhere."

Jack wraps the sandwich, packs a few of the ginger cookies Nell made the night before.

"When you got back from the war, did you ever . . . " Billy asks.

"It won't last."

"You never talked about it "

"You were too young."

"I'm not too young now."

"I never wanted to burden my children."

"Dad . . . "

"It took me ten years to come home from that war, leave it all behind me. Look at the pictures: I looked like a ghost. Just like you. That's why it was so hard to see you both enlist."

Billy brings his dishes to the sink.

Jack's natural reticence is choking him.

It's clear that Billy is in pain as he climbs awkwardly into the passenger seat and reaches across to pull the heavy door closed. The wound over his ear is bleeding through the gauze bandage.

Driving past the old army depot, Jack slows when he sees the herd of white deer appear out of the forest. They run past, flowing along the wire mesh fence, unearthly.

"When we were kids we thought the neutron bombs they stored in the ground had turned all the deer white," Billy said.

"Reasonable theory."

"For a twelve-year-old. They always scared Nell, but she loved riding our bikes over here at dawn. When you see them step out from the trees, they look like ghosts."

"Kids like to be scared."

Jack rolls his window down. The air is sweet with the scent of lilacs and newly turned earth.

"I'm sorry about the car, Dad."

"It's a pity. All our work."

"Yeah. I liked that car."

"Honestly, I'm amazed we got her to run."

"I'll pay you back."

"You don't need to worry about that right now."

Billy looks up at the sky where a flock of sparrows wheels over the cornfields spooling past.

"Was it an accident?" Jack asks.

Another long pause.

"I was going too fast, you know me, the wheel started to shimmy and then I hit a woodchuck, an opossum, I don't know what the hell it was—and I lost control. My right hand is fucking useless. The wheel was just spinning through my fingers. That's all I remember."

He takes a breath.

"Twelve weeks of rehab and I can't control a beat-up car. How am I ever . . . ? Shit."

Turning onto Exchange Street they pass an Army recruitment billboard: a soldier hanging from a parachute, drifting in a peaceful sky, and the most inane slogan ever devised: *The Army Wants to Join You.*

Jack looks over at Billy as he turns his head away, wipes the back of his hand across his mouth.

"You sure you're up to this? I could speak to Harlow . . . "

"Leave it alone, Dad."

Jack pulls into the station. Billy twists to open the door with his left hand, forgetting his lunch.

Jack calls out to him, the sack in his hand. "Eat something, will you?"

"You sound like Mom."

"I could come by later. Take you to Luke's. Quick. Say 1 o'clock. Blue plate special is corned beef hash on Tuesday."

"You just made me lunch."

"Tomorrow then."

"Maybe."

Jack puts the truck in gear.

"What's the blue plate special on Wednesday?" Billy asks.

"I have no idea. We always go on Tuesday."

"Looks like we're gonna find out."

Billy walks around the truck to his father's open window.

"Talk to me." He looks past his father, squinting in the sun.

"About what?"

"How you put yourself back together."

Jack flips the visor down.

"You saved me."

"Come on . . . don't rewrite history."

"When we finally brought you home from the hospital, I was the one to get up in the middle of the night, feed you, rock you to sleep."

"You did not."

"I was awake anyway. Drinking too much. Trying to numb the nightmares. Just like you."

"How long did the nightmares last?"

"You want the truth?" Jack asks.

"Yes."

"Years."

Jack wants to touch his son, lay a hand against his face. Knows better.

"There's nothing more peaceful than holding a sleeping infant. I held on to you for two solid years until you got too big and too busy. Even then, you'd fall asleep at night with your head on my chest. Marion kept telling me I was spoiling you and I'd better cut it out."

"I don't remember any of that," Billy says. And thinks of waking up on the hospital ship with the scent of his father in the bed beside him.

"I've always wondered how many men came home from the war and held on to their kids like I did."

"Maybe I should become a babysitter."

"Or you could spend some time with Rosie and Nick and the boys."

"Yeah."

"I'll pick you up after work. About 6 o'clock."

"I'll be here."

Harlow looks up as Billy limps into the station.

"Jesus! What happened to you? Oh, Christ, don't tell me. The car."

Billy looks at Harlow, that all too familiar blank *you can't touch me* stare.

"Totaled," Harlow says.

"Yeah."

"And you walked away."

"More or less."

"Can you work? You need a day off?"

"I'll be fine."

"Should I be worried?"

"About what?"

"Don't fuck around with me, Billy."

Billy reaches for his coveralls. Harlow grabs the front of his shirt. "Do we understand each other?"

Breaking away. "I don't know, do we?"

Harlow shoves him against the desk. Billy stumbles, winces. "You made it home, you stupid son of a bitch," Harlow says.

"I'm not asking . . . "

"I don't feel sorry for you and you are done feeling sorry for yourself. You hear me?" Shaking him. "You hear me?"

"Leave me alone."

"That's not how this works, you dumbass. Your job? You just hang on through the next weeks and months. And then you'll be through it, and out the other side."

Billy can't, or won't, meet his gaze.

"I know about the guilt phase, the pissed-off phase, the why-me phase, the pills and girls and alcohol phase. You can't change what happened. You have to find a way to live with it. I know you don't believe me. You don't have to believe me. You just have to hang on."

Billy slips out of his grasp and disappears into his own element, like a fish, coldness coming off him in waves. Harlow tries to shake it off, his hands clenching into fists, imagines beating Billy bloody. As if that would pull him back.

Jack turns on to North Main and then, instead of taking the

right onto Castle and driving up the hill to the Ag Station, he turns onto Center Street and pulls over in front of Saint Joe's. The big Catholic church is too sad and foreboding, so he heads west toward the college. He rarely drives through the campus of Hobart and William Smith. Not much reason to. It's like walking into a parallel world.

Today the quad overlooking the lake is host to another raucous demonstration. After the May Day firebombing of the ROTC office, he's surprised Hobart hasn't been shut down.

Jack parks in front of the school's chapel, an ornate wooden structure. This is the sanctuary Jack chooses when he wants a chance to think, free from the candles and the Stations of the Cross and the stink of death and incense in the Catholic church.

Save my son are the words that rise up in him as he bows his head.

No other words stir inside him as he sits in the plain wooden pew. Instead, there are images he can't shake, the car flipped on its roof, the blood seeping through the bandage over Billy's ear, the tremor in his son's hands.

The wan Protestant stillness does not bring him peace today. The tasteful abstract stained glass seems weak and watered down, without enough substance or fire to offer comfort or the complex embrace of faith.

Emerging into the May morning he stands looking out over the lake. The elation he usually feels in the presence of this landscape is tempered by a feeling of dread. A line of sailboats slides out from behind the trees at the foot of the hill.

A roar erupts from the demonstration behind him as the boats fan out on the lake. The students' chants float over the campus:

Hell, no! We won't go!

1, 2, 3, 4! We don't want your fucking war!

He turns back to the lake, lifts his face to the sun, to the

sweet promise of the lengthening days, and finds himself praying, finally, with a full heart: Let the summer save him as it
saves us all.

He looks at his watch, realizes he's missed a staff meeting;
shrugs it off. All he wants is to get outside into the orchards
with his trees, the buds bursting into flower.

Turning to his battered pickup, he finds a young couple
leaning against the fender, lost in a kiss. Their bodies' yearning
rushes through him. He feels envy, sharply aware he is not
nineteen anymore.

When he opens the driver's-side door, the couple pull apart.
They look dazed, a bit lost.

"Sorry, man," the boy offers.

Jack smiles at them, lifts a hand.

What a dream we had, to raise our children in peace.

Billy doesn't question why Anna shows up at 5 to pick him
up; he's too exhausted to resist Harlow's machinations. He
falls asleep with his head against the truck's window.

She wakes him when they arrive at her cottage and leads
him directly to the outdoor shower. She undresses him, the hot
water beating on them both. She bathes him, careful of the
new bruises and lacerations. The wound over his ear begins to
bleed again.

In the cottage she serves him hot soup. Sits with him, insists
that he eat. She ignores his anger, brings him to bed, lies beside
him as sunset pours through the windows gilding the sheets
and the floor. He startles and pulls away when she runs her fingers over his scars, tracing the path of the burns down his face
and neck, shoulder and arm, the rough overlapping edges of
newly healed flesh.

When she opens the window the smell of mossy green
water floats up to them along with the looping echoes of birdsong.

Billy waits for mercy, like a cool hand, to wipe away his memory, and the darkness he carries inside. Prays for it. Anna makes him hope for things, for the clean wash of water, of redemption, the possibility of forgiveness. He feels hollow.

He looks at the curve of her breast, wishes he could draw it. Closes his eyes.

Nell ignores the closed sign and walks through the office into the service bay. A Malibu up on the lift casts a fat shadow. Harlow wipes his hands with a dirty rag. He shaved that morning, she notices. He has the most beautiful skin, tawny and smooth.

The last time the four of them were together keeps coming back to her like an unfinished dream. It was freezing in Harlow's runabout, the June night unseasonably cold, tasting of snow almost, a cold wind streaming down from Canada. Harlow's last leave before shipping out to Vietnam, Billy on his way to Basic in less than twenty-four hours.

She sat next to Harlow as he steered them south toward Dresden, both of them trying not to watch Billy and Megan in the bow of the boat, their hands all over each other. He'd finally asked her to sit on the seat opposite, facing him, blocking his view. Blushing, glad for the dark, relief mixed up with being so close to him, the embarrassment of the display in front of them, her own hunger for touch, and knowing how soon both he and Billy would be gone.

The air was dense and alive; it felt like rain was on the way, even though the sky was clear and crowded with stars. She turned to look over her shoulder. Megan laughing as Billy got his hands under her jacket and then her sweater. Nell focused on her right sneaker, a hole in the toe, the laces broken and knotted. Harlow turned to check the gas line, gave the can a kick to determine its fullness and remind Billy and Megan they weren't alone.

Nell watched Harlow's hands, wanted to grab them, be grabbed. Closed her eyes. Only one step and she could be beside him. Nothing but air between them. She could kiss him. Nothing to stop her but shyness. She could touch his face, his neck, put her hand on his chest. Nothing to stop her; nothing but the terror of not being wanted.

Megan's laughter brought her back to herself, and, in that brimming moment, all that was not being said: fear, sadness, loss, every conflicting desire; stay, go, excitement, dread. She was too young to learn that nothing lasts; yet there it all was, slipping through their fingers.

She crosses to him now, skirting the patches of oil on the floor. She puts both hands on his chest, pushes him against the tool-cluttered workbench; reaches for his shoulders. He does not react, his hands still at his sides, still holding the dirty rag.

He watches her, waiting. She can hear him breathing.

She moves away, meets his gaze.

"You know how I feel about you," she says.

He grabs her belt, pulls her against him, his arms around her. All the air goes out of her. He puts one hand at the back of her neck, pulls her head against his chest. She wants to shake her head, no, no. He kisses the top of her head like she's a little kid, while she stands there, wanting to take her clothes off and climb into the backseat of that car. It might be funny if it weren't so humiliating.

"Look, you're gonna run through me like a knife through butter and I'm not sure I can take it," he says.

"What are you talking about?"

"Come September, you'll be gone."

"I live here. My family is here. Billy . . . "

"You won't be coming back."

"You don't know that."

"You're going places, girl."

"Well, I wasn't thinking about asking you to marry me."

"No?"

She looks down.

"So maybe you don't know how I feel," he says.

She looks at him, then, her whole body trembling, making it hard to think, or argue. The moment among the trees when he lifted her up rushes back at her. The apples, the bees, the russet leaves hiding them from the world. The clarity of that desire.

"I need . . . "

"C'mon," he moves out of reach. "I'll drive you home."

She stands her ground, stands in his way. He stops, tilts his head, watching her. That slow smile. She moves toward him as if she knows what she's doing. Kisses him, shocked at her own daring. *Yes or no*, she thinks, as he hesitates, *yes or no*.

JUNE

Well before dawn, Billy lights the gas under the percolator while Nell makes sandwiches.

"Heat the milk, okay?"

"More butter," he counters, pouring milk into a pan.

She butters bread, pulls ham from the fridge, the house quiet except for Flanagan scratching at the back door to go out.

In the dark, in the old broad-bottomed canoe, they paddle south to the Keuka Lake outlet through mist rising off the water. Billy is in front for the first time in their lives, still struggling to manage a paddle, but slowly regaining some strength and skill.

In fading starlight, they retrace the route of General Sullivan's 1779 expedition, hiking through wetland, then white pine and walnut forest, emerging into the remnants of Seneca fields and orchards.

Billy leads the way on an ancient trail, following a stream banked with Solomon's seal. Each spring they'd searched for the fire-blackened stumps of ancient apple trees with green shoots sprouting from them. The peach orchards, less hardy, were gone, but it was possible to imagine the long lines of their cultivation, to see, in the mind's eye, row upon row of trees white with bloom in the spring, heavy with fruit in the summer.

As children, they had paced off the dimensions of the longhouses that would have been here, pictured the plantings of the "three sisters": corn to shade the squash, squash to cool the roots of the corn, beans to climb the stalks. In their imaginings it was as if the Seneca had gone out among the hills one morning and would soon return. As if time could turn back on itself, brush aside the thin layer of grass and earth that separated Billy and Nell from those who had come before, and reunite them.

Billy lounges against a silver maple, nearly disappearing into his jacket. Head back, eyes half shut, his physical languor masks the intensity of his gaze. Nell sits beside him, leaning into his shoulder. She inhales the smell of loam rising from the woodland floor, the bright tang of dew.

In the near dark, the birds begin: a few individual notes, some call and response, then quartets, quintets, sextets, as the first hint of light appears.

"How much can you hear?"

"Enough."

A long, mournful wolflike wail rises from the lake, the howl used by separated loons to reestablish contact. And then the male loon's yodel, a repeating phrase of low and high notes.

"The Ojibwa say the loon inspired their flutes."

"Show-off," Nell laughs.

"And the Tsimshian tell of a loon restoring a blind man's sight. He rewarded her with a necklace of white feathers, adorning their necks to this day."

"Is that why you made me that necklace?"

"Maybe."

Color begins to light the hills. Geneva, at the north end of the lake, is still on the verge of day; then Saint Joseph's steeple catches the sun and flares like the beam of a lighthouse. The lake, as far south as they can see, shines like pewter.

The dawn chill loosens its grip as they begin their descent. They stop to watch the courting flight of a pair of eagles. The birds tumble over each other, right side up and upside down, until they take hold of each other's talons and, wings open, spiral toward the ground; letting go in time to right themselves and soar into the sky.

"They say there are only four hundred pair left in the whole country. DDT has made their eggs thin and brittle, too fragile . . . "

"I can't believe we saw them," Nell says.

"We'll have to come back. Find their nest."

Billy wades into the lake to push them into deep water, climbs into the front of the canoe soaked to the knees.

"You always have to get wet," Nell teases, picking up her paddle, turning them around.

He rocks the boat violently. "You could join me."

"Billy!"

"Come on, lazybones. Paddle."

Nell leans into her stroke, the way he'd taught her, as two green herons take to the air from their perch near the entrance to the creek. Their cries echo over the water, a commotion of wings across the bow.

The next day Billy unveils his plan to swim a mile every morning, Nell in the rowboat beside him, a stopwatch to time his progress. He'll borrow Asa's truck to drive her to school when they're done.

It creates a new pattern to their days, pulls them into tighter orbit, a circle as familiar as their names.

They stop at Delaney's for donuts and coffee, steal another half hour, squandering time like children. Nell is late to school each day, her hands blistered from rowing, the taste of cinnamon sugar in her mouth. Sliding into her desk for AP History, too late in the year to matter, too late to care.

Nell carries the lake, the rowboat, the morning's light and

rhythm through the day with her, buoyed by something new: hope.

First thing Saturday morning Marion manages to burn the oatmeal she left to soak all night on the back of the stove. No one, as far as she knows, has ever burned the oatmeal. It's idiotproof. In the morning, all you have to do is heat it through. The first cigarette and cup of coffee out on the porch have done nothing to dispel her mood or the smell of the scorched, ruined pan.

Her slacks are too tight and damn if that doesn't make them uncomfortable. God, she hates the thought of shopping almost worse than she hates the thought of turning into a fat old woman. Not that she's actually fat. Not yet.

After being too thin for most of her life, where is the justice in putting on weight now, just in time for her son's eyes to glance away from her every time she walks into a room, or parks her big butt in a plastic chair down by the lake.

She lights another cigarette. The one thing she and Billy still seem to have in common. She likes to borrow his Luckies. She makes a mental note to buy him a carton in town. No one likes a mooch.

Now that she thinks about it, what else do they have in common? She tries to remember trips to the library, or rainy afternoons when she might have driven him around for his paper route. Not a library kind of kid and not much coddling. Weather's weather; comes with the territory.

Maybe Billy will develop some interests as an adult they can share. Like what? Cars and booze and slutty girls are not pursuits you indulge with your mother. When is he going to take hold? He can't keep that lousy job at the gas station forever. Why is no one asking these questions? She's offered to pay for community college, whatever the government won't cover, although where she'll find the money is a mystery. He just looks at her like she's insulting him.

She pours herself another cup of coffee in the kitchen, hesitates with the bottle of cream in her hand, looks at the pan full of burned oatmeal in the sink, thinks what the hell, and tips in cream.

Upstairs Marion walks in on Billy shaving in the bathroom. Standing at the sink in those awful Army green boxer shorts. She hasn't seen him this undressed in years.

"Jesus Christ, Billy, you're skinnier than Nell!"

She sees the wreck of his flesh from jaw to hand; the bright trickle of blood at the corner of his lip. He slams the door in her face.

She knocks.

"Go away, Mom."

On the other side of the door, Billy leans against the sink, looking down into the floating bits of hair and shaving cream, the blood dripping from his face. He can hear the pulse inside his head, the unending buzz and ringing in his ears. His heartbeat is out of control.

He looks at the razor in his hand, the swirl of blood in the bowl. Walks out the door, leaving the grime in the sink; drops the bloody towel on the floor.

In his bedroom he pulls on jeans and a T-shirt and heads for the stairs, shouting:

"Marion! Where are you? Get in the kitchen, woman! I want food!"

Marion scrambles eggs and toasts thick slices of bread. She pulls out the homemade strawberry jam she's been saving. Warms his plate in the oven.

Billy sits at the table, makes a show of eating—too much, too fast—talking through a mouthful of eggs. She doesn't scold him, instead she sits across from him, steals a piece of his toast, slathers it with jam.

Billy pushes his plate away. The eggs and toast dissolve into dust in his mouth. He lights a cigarette, tips his chair back on two legs. Raises an eyebrow at her, waiting for the lecture—no smoking at the table, stop ruining my chairs—that doesn't come. Uses his plate as an ashtray, a further provocation.

He sips his coffee, waits.

"You've developed some nice manners," she says.

Silence.

"What am I going to do with you?" she asks.

"Kick me out on my ass."

"That's not what families are for."

When he does not reply, Marion asks: "Who's the girl?"

"None of your business."

"Be careful. Nell looks up to you."

"Don't you think she knows all about . . . "

"Don't wave it in our faces, that's all I'm saying."

How does she shame him so easily? Reproach turns rancid as his stomach clenches in protest at eggs and coffee and cigarettes.

He looks at his mother, her hair graying, her stomach going soft. The smile lines around her eyes he'd loved so as a child, etched more deeply now. The skin on her capable hands looks fragile as she reaches for her coffee cup.

It would be so easy to touch that soft hand. It's what she wants; it's not much, their old camaraderie full of jokes and shared stolen cigarettes, hidden from Jack, their shoulders touching as they dissolved in laughter, usually at someone else's expense. The yielding softness of her skin, the imploring softness of her need to be loved, the sharp sting of her tongue.

So easy to fall back into that if his mother's body didn't repulse him now. All bodies. His own body. Flesh and decay, the death inside every living thing.

Marion sees the disgust pass across his face, so potent it makes her flinch.

Give him time, Jack says to her, over and over. He'll come back to us.

Will he? she wonders.

Just like Jack, the hollow-eyed stare, the essential absence. Even when he was present, he was somewhere else. Even in bed, the need they both expressed, like a second honeymoon in its intensity, but lonely. How could you make love and feel so alone, sweat and strain after pleasure, new life, hoping for release, a moment of oblivion, how could this coupling, limb to limb, heart to heart, feel so full of air and emptiness? Like making love to a ghost, an illusion, the body but not the man himself.

She doesn't like to think about how they survived those years, how Jack somehow stitched himself back together, rebuilt the shell he had become. Don't talk to me about courage, Marion thinks, not until you've lived through that.

They had each other, they had three children and soon two more to pull them along, create enough velocity to pull Jack into their orbit.

What does Billy have to hold on to?

She sees him waver, soften, then harden against her again. Before she can stop herself she says:

"You could take a break from being such a selfish little shit."

Billy stands up too fast; his chair scrapes back and falls over behind him. He can't hear it hit the floor but feels the vibration of its impact in his feet and knees. There is a roaring inside his head. He holds one hand inside the other, the words *can't you see?* screaming to get out. He sees his scars split open, his bloody hands fusing to Frank Buckles's flak jacket.

He can't pull him free. His head lolls on his neck, blood soaks the collar of his jacket; blood, tissue, bits of bone. He smells flesh burning.

Another blast blows him clear of the wreck. Flames burst into the sky.

Can he get to Frank, can he . . . ?

He has kids, Frank has kids.

Can't you see? Can't you see?

Marion's mouth is open but he can't hear her.

She is shouting his name.

"Billy!"

He slams out the back door. He wants to beat his hands against the side of the house, the sharp corners of the porch railing.

"Billy!!"

He holds his hands in front of him to keep her away. She keeps coming toward him, puts her arms around him; tries to cover the flame of his rage. Holds him: It's okay . . . It's okay.

Her touch scalds him.

He wishes it would rain.

He wishes it would snow.

Two days later Billy wakes from a dreamless pit of sleep. Where is he? The curtains blowing into the room tell him it's not his hooch. Home, he realizes, as he watches clouds scudding over the moon. Flanagan stirs, stretches; settles again at the foot of the bed.

He sees grazes and bruises on his hands and arms as he drags on pants and a T-shirt. Who brought him home last night? Regulars at O'Donovan's have grown wary of him; the limited kindness they had for a returning vet has been spent. Who was he fighting with? He can't remember.

Drinking with a vengeance. Another broken promise.

He'd started the night at Saint Joe's, intending to invite Father O'Rourke to come fishing. But the church was locked up tight. When he knocked on the rectory door Margaret told him the priest was in Rochester. He was being called on the carpet for his antiwar work again.

"He's been ordered to keep silent. And threatened with a transfer." Margaret was nearly in tears. "He's an old man, Billy. This is his home. And he won't stop. I know him. He won't stop."

Billy is unexpectedly gutted by this news and wonders at the old priest's nerve and resilience.

Now he remembers. His appointment with the new hand specialist in Syracuse. There's nothing more they can do. Full stop.

He will never fly again.

Must have been his father who got into his truck at 2 A.M. to come get him. Soft-spoken Jack, who never reprimands his son, who seems shattered in some terrible way Billy can't begin to understand, and sure as hell doesn't want to be responsible for, whose reactions to his screaming nightmares are so intense, Billy wonders if his father is having his own flashbacks.

His throat feels chapped; he's so thirsty. He heads downstairs to the kitchen for a glass of water. Turning the tap in the bluestone sink, he thinks of Brendan, the two of them stuck washing and drying the dinner dishes, the Fiestaware and the iron kettles, singing some dumb camp song, Nell thumping out the tunes at the old upright in the living room, his father at the kitchen table with a beer, singing along, his mother in the living room or out on the porch with a cigarette and a book. Every moment she could grab for herself there was a book in her hand, her best escape from the noise and chaos of five kids.

He should call Brendan. He should call Rosie. And Sheila. He misses Sheila. Spend some time. He should do a lot of things.

He walks onto the back porch to take a piss, swiveling at the last minute to avoid the Plymouth. Four sets of eyes blink at him from the overturned trash barrels: the fucking raccoons. The rocks he'd piled on the lids had done nothing to deter them.

Does he want another drink? There's no whiskey in the house; he knows that, his mother cleared it out. Not even a pint of scotch or gin for their usual late afternoon cocktail. As if their abstinence could slow him down. Now it's lemonade and iced tea while the coleslaw chills and they start a fire in the grill for the burgers or chops. There'd be a roast chicken with mashed potatoes and gravy for Sunday lunch. Still the big midday meal even without the usual visit to church.

Does he still believe? He remembers learning the catechism for his first communion, his father patiently coaching him. Who made the world? Who is God? Why did God make you? What must we do to save our souls?

What did he know of the communion of souls at thirteen? And his mother, trying to stick it out in the church of her childhood, trying to hold on, or let herself be held onto, because of Jack and his stubborn faith or his stubborn certitude that going through the motions, regardless of how you felt about it personally, was what you had to do for your children.

He can see his father kneeling in the pew, long after the rest of them sit down, kneeling through all of communion. His father's prayers are not soft things. His back tenses, his shoulders hunch, the cords in his neck stand out. There is an edge to his prayers, a simmer of anger and impatience: Why are you testing me?

His parents don't even keep the form much anymore, only attending church together on the holidays, though Jack still goes to Mass every week. What's it like for Nell, the way so much seems to be disappearing from their lives? All the siblings gone now, the last high school graduation, the last high school dance, church an afterthought.

We needed an entire pew. Rosie and Sheila in their dresses and pigtails, then he and Brendan, so alike even though they were four years apart and Nell, the baby, passed along from

Mom to Rosie who was so much better at keeping her quiet. The boys in short pants, hand-me-down white shirts, narrow black ties. Their faces scrubbed by Sheila, shoes polished the night before on newspapers laid out on the kitchen floor.

Our Father who art in heaven . . .

We were the Flynns, by God; we were the Flynns.

"Why am I all alone in the goddamned kitchen?" Marion shouts from the ancient stone sink where she is peeling potatoes. She crosses to the porch as Nell makes her escape, disappearing beneath the canopy of trees, reappearing on the grassy stretch down to the lake.

Brendan pulls Nell onto his lap, tickling her as Sheila gets her transistor radio to work, pulling in the not-too-distant Binghamton station. Rosie is instantly on her feet, grabbing Nick, winding her arms around his neck. Connor and Collin run circles around them while the baby sleeps in the shade. And look at that: Sheila, the one who thinks she wants to be a nun for God's sake, shaking her hips and shimmying in what probably passes as dancing, though in Marion's book it looks more like having some kind of fit. The boys join in, reluctantly at first, teasing wild-woman Sheila, but soon they are all laughing and shouting out the lyrics they somehow know by heart even though they sound like gibberish to Marion.

And Nell. Good lord that girl can move her hips. She stands behind Billy and Brendan, imitating every step; where in the world did those boys learn to dance like that?

"Hey! Turn it down! Are you trying to wake the dead?" she shouts down to them.

Nell laughs up at her mother, still shaking her bottom like something Marion would rather not put in the same sentence as her youngest daughter.

A phrase bursts clear:

Paint it, paint it, paint it black!

"Did you hear me?"

"Let them be," Jack says, appearing beside her. "They're having fun."

"Nell was supposed to send Sheila up to help me in the kitchen."

"I'll help you."

"You will not."

"How many potatoes have I peeled in my life, Marion?"

"I don't know, Jack. How many?"

"As the youngest of nine . . . "

"This is beginning to sound like a comedy routine."

"Shanty Irish comedy routine."

"Lace curtain, if you please."

"Oh, the infinite ways of being poor and Irish and proud," he says, putting his arm around her.

Down by the rickety dock, Rosie dances, eyes closed, Percy Sledge crooning: *When a man loves a woman.* She reaches out to Nell, linking hands.

Brendan, best-loved Brendan, ticked off to be pulled away from his girlfriend for a night, for the "family only" graduation party for Nell. No friends, not even Harlow; no aunts and uncles, just the tight circle of Marion's brood. The circle always a bit too tight for Brendan.

"Sheila! Rosie!" Marion's voice drops down from the cabin. "I could use a hand!"

In the kitchen, Sheila and Rosie take over the potatoes and the coleslaw, freeing Jack to return to his sketchbook.

Jack sits at the picnic table on the front porch with his colored pencils and pens and the field journal he's been keeping for as long as he can remember. He pushes the newspaper aside, begins with where and when: Seneca Lake: June 24, 1970.

When he was a toddler, Billy used to climb onto his lap and scribble on scrap paper while Jack drew in his journal. A bit older, three and four, Billy would lie on his belly on the floor, drawing airplanes. By five he was coming with Jack into the field with his own journal. Billy quickly outstripped his father in his ability to both find and draw birds, especially birds in midair. It was as if he could glance into the sky, record shape and motion with his mind's eye, and then, with a few strokes, capture that flight and that freedom on paper. He made it look easy but Jack knows, from trying and failing and trying again, it is almost impossible.

He looks up to see the boys bombing off the end of the water-worn dock, followed by Nell. They are like seals, beautiful creatures. How is it possible these are his children and grandchildren, that somehow they will carry pieces of him into the future?

Jack thinks of teaching Billy how to swim on top of the water. By the time he was five and getting teased about swimming underwater like a fish, he learned the crawl. Then he started teaching himself to hold his breath for longer and longer. Jack would time him; make a game out of it. Brendan couldn't beat him; even Jack couldn't beat him. It got to be terrifying when Billy stayed underwater for forty-five seconds and then a minute and then more.

As the sun sets, Jack and Nick gather wood, Connor and Collin trailing them. They scrape the old grill rack and set it on stones over the fire. While Rosie feeds the baby, Marion, Sheila, and Nell carry down platters and plates, cups, cutlery.

There is too much food. When making her list Marion could only add, never subtract, and so they have hamburgers, red and white hots, potato salad, macaroni salad, coleslaw, baked beans, deviled eggs, radishes, and lettuce salad, lemonade, milk, and iced coffee. They can barely find room on the picnic tables Nell decorated with red gingham cloths and wild-flowers in jelly jars.

Packed away in a separate basket are Sheila's brownies and Rosie's cupcakes. These are the accompaniment to the main event: Marion's prized strawberry shortcake.

Brendan and Nick manage to eat two hamburgers apiece, though it looks like Billy has barely touched his food.

When it doesn't seem possible anyone could eat another mouthful, Marion carries the strawberry shortcake down the hill, piled high with whipped cream. The boys clamor for bowls of it, not just those dinky little dessert plates. Jack passes out the sparklers he drove into Canada to buy, dozens of them, more than they'd ever had for the Fourth of July. Connor and Collin run and twirl with the sparklers, streaks of light up and down the path, in and out of the trees.

There are graduation gifts. Nell is embarrassed by all the attention. Wearing the gown and crossing the stage was more than enough spotlight. Megan had not even been mentioned at the ceremony, although what could be said? The cruelty of not knowing silences them all. Her absence is like a stitch in Nell's side, a missing rib.

As Nell crossed the stage, she'd looked up to see Asa Alsop standing at the back of the auditorium. He'd raised a hand to her, a salute.

Who else thought of Megan that day, remembered her, turned to each other to ask: Did they ever find that girl? Reduced now to that girl, fading from view, mind, memory. Not for Billy, she knows. Not for her family.

Jack and Marion make toasts with lemonade until Brendan reveals the stash of beer. Even Sheila has a bottle.

Jack throws more wood on the fire. Sparks scatter into the sky.

"Give us a song, Sheila," Brendan asks.

"No, no way," she says.

"C'mon," Brendan insists.

Connor sits beside his grandfather. Collin claims Nick's lap. Sheila, embarrassed, clears her throat.

"Quit stalling," Brendan teases.

I've met some folks who say that I'm a dreamer
And I've no doubt there's truth in what they say . . .

Jack joins Sheila. Nell looks at him, surprised. It's so rare now, he's shy of his voice, though anyone would tell you it's a beautiful voice, high and sweet.

But sure a body's bound to be a dreamer
When all the things he loves are far away.

"Oh, for the old Ireland of freezing to death in front of a smoky peat fire and never enough to eat," Marion carps.

"Not our problem tonight," Brendan says. "I can hardly move I'm so full."

"Great shortcake, Mom," Rosie says.

Marion joins in on the chorus with Rosie and Brendan and Nick.

Billy leaves the table, walks out to the end of the dock, and lies down, Flanagan at his feet. Nell watches him go. She can see how spent he is, feel the undercurrent of agitation, how often he needs to shut down, withdraw.

Marion notices Billy leave as well, tries not to read too much into it.

Nell follows her brother, lies down next to him, her head on his shoulder.

"You okay?" she asks.

"Tired is all."

She waits for him to tell her more or the truth or anything at all. She looks across the lake, feeling the weight of Billy's sadness, the darkness that sometimes engulfs him. Thinks of Harlow's distance and wonders if the two are related.

"Will you sing to me, Nell?" he asks, turning to look at her.

"After those two . . . ?"

He nods, holding her gaze.

She's unsteady as she begins, her voice catching in her throat. She sings softly, hardly more than a whisper.

Oh, if I were a blackbird, could whistle and sing,
I'd follow the vessel my true love sails in
And in that dark rigging, I'd there build my nest
And flutter my wings o'er her lily-white breast.

Nell sings all the verses for Billy, while Sheila lights the candles, full dark falling down on them through the pine trees. Nell imagines soaring like a blackbird. From high above she would see the candles shining on the table, the smoke from the fire curling into the sky. Higher still and she would see the kitchen lights from the old camps and small cottages around the lake, a few blinking dock lights, the warm windows where families eat dinner, talk about the weather, plan tomorrows. Higher still and she would see all ten of the Finger Lakes, surrounded by thousands of acres of forest and farmland.

If she could see her family running down through time, into their future, what would she see? Can she guess their hopes and their fears; can she imagine Rosie's boys grown, Billy fully healed, all of them living out their days and their years?

Will they be so lucky?

Billy wakes her, as he does every morning, by walking onto

the sleeping porch and pulling the covers off her bed. She glances at her watch: 5:30, half an hour earlier than usual, and stretches, playing for time, trying to get a look at him. But he turns away before she can see his face.

Nell pulls on a sweatshirt, makes a quick dash to the bathroom and hurries down the stairs. Billy hands her a thermos of tea. She follows him down the steep path to the lake.

Cold clouds blanket the water as she climbs into the rowboat. She wishes she had boots on instead of bare feet. Flanagan barks and whines from the dock, weaving in and around Billy's legs as if she wants to push him back to shore.

"Today's the day."

"What?"

"No wind. We're going for it."

He pulls on his goggles and dives in.

Nell turns the boat around and catches up with him easily. His first strokes are choppy; he's wasting energy. And then she sees him settle. He is no longer a graceful swimmer, but he's gaining strength and his determination has surprised them both.

It's quiet on the lake at this hour, except for Billy's steady flutter kick, the rhythmic splash of his stroke, the oars grinding in the oarlocks. In the last few weeks she has gotten good at timing her strokes to stay abreast of him.

The mist on the water is eerie. Now that they're a few hundred yards out, she can no longer see the house in its shelter of trees and the dock is shrouded in shadow. Where's the sun and when will it burn through this haze?

Billy switches to backstroke and she tries to exchange a few words with him.

"I'm fine," is all he'll give her.

The breeze picks up, cold on the back of her neck, and the fog thickens opposite tiny Swan's Island. They used to talk about camping on Swan's when they were kids. They leave the island behind, and here, where the lake narrows a bit, she can see a few docks and boats. But no other early birds.

Visibility drops to near zero. She can't see the channel buoy. And she's managed to miss their halfway landmark. *This is insane*, she thinks, as the mist becomes so dense she can only see a small circle around the boat and her swimming brother.

She shouts at him to get his attention, but he ignores her. The loss of landmarks is disorienting; they could be going in circles. Billy plows on.

There's a momentary break in the weather; she can see the Harrises' cottage with the blue and yellow Sunfish pulled up on their landing. Is it the fog that makes the cottage seem so far away? Or have they drifted out of the center channel and closer to the western shore? She twists around to see if she can see the east side of the lake when the breeze drops and closes them off again.

For a moment she can't see him. The shot of adrenaline to her heart reminds her of waking to his screams last night. She stops rowing and listens. He's on her right instead of her left. How did that happen? She adjusts her course and pulls alongside him.

"You okay?"

He lifts his head and nods. A moment later he surprises her and turns to look at her.

"You're doing great," she says.

He holds her gaze, his dark hair plastered to his head, and smiles at her.

For the rest of her life she will wonder what he was thinking when he looked at her. Was he thinking at all, or was all the thinking and deciding already done?

When he slips beneath the surface, her first thought is: Quit messing around. Now I really can't see you!

She cranes her neck, calculating where he'll come up.

The goggles keep him from seeing much; he can't even see the pines that line the shore. When he looks back at his sister she is just a shape. Just as well. He hears nothing but the water. The sound of it has been in his ears all his life.

His crummy crawl stroke doesn't matter anymore. He is so tired. Tired of doctors, of drinking, tired of trying to talk or not talk, to tell stories, to lie, to know when to shut up.

He misses sleep like it's a country he can't go to anymore. The water feels like the promise of sleep. He can feel the giddy deep cold of the channel beneath him. Quiet and dark and mysterious.

There is nothing to stop him. No sergeant, no harness, no chopper door. No tent, no jungle, no father, years ago, grabbing the back of his pants at the edge of the dock before he could fall in.

What does he see in the water below him? His own face, his staring eyes, everything that hurts him and haunts him that doesn't have a name. All the words that can't be spoken, all the things he's done that can't be undone float around him.

Nell.

Megan.

In a few seconds he'll be free. In the water where the pain stops, the ringing in his ears is silenced.

He lets the dark take him.

Nell screams herself hoarse, calling his name, calling for help, every sound she makes swallowed by the fog.

She strips down to go into the water and hesitates. What's stopping her? The possibility she will lose the boat and her mother will have two children to grieve. The length of rope they use to tie up the boat lies coiled on the dock, useless to her now. She settles on diving directly below or beside the boat, shocked at the surge of panic that rises hot into her throat, of what she might find, of what she might not find, of all she is certain to fail to do.

The murk beneath her is impenetrable, the depth of the water unknowable, the current strong. How far is she drifting from the boat, from safety, how far out of reach has Billy already gone?

The thought of Billy lost to her, lost to all of them; a sob catches in her throat, involuntary, she breathes in water, chokes, suddenly fighting for the surface, disoriented.

But there. She goes still. Did she feel his touch? She tries to remain quiet enough to feel which way her body is moving and then kicks her way to the surface, breaking through the water, choking and gasping and retching up water and more.

She turns in a circle once, twice, her panic rising. The boat is gone.

Listen, she hears inside her head: Billy's voice. Stop your crying and listen.

She closes her eyes, tries to quiet her breath, loud and rasping in her ears. Nothing. More nothing. And then there it is: the faint lap of water against the hull, the creak of an oarlock.

She swims toward the sound. Stops to listen again. Corrects her course. Drags herself into the boat and lies in the bottom shaking. Pulling her clothes on, her fingers are almost useless; her hands so stiff from cold and shock she has trouble zipping her jeans. Even dressed she can't stop trembling.

The image of Billy's car floods her. So damaged from the crash and the rollover, she knows it's impossible anyone could have survived. How relieved they all were, all their talk of luck and mercy. Billy himself quiet and wary, not quite ready to return to the land of the living.

How easily the wind shifts, the world tips, slides out from underneath you. And she knows. She knew from the instant of that last look. He's gone.

There's nothing to do but wait, nothing to break the oppressive monotony of the fog around her. Could anyone have stopped him? Doesn't your body fight you; fight back? In the end, is it bliss or terror or sadness? Or simply relief. And release.

"You can't patch them up," Marion would say. "These boys cannot be healed."

Marion wakes with a start, breathless from a dream about her mother. She never dreams about her mother, but there she was, gray hair, always a dress, a dress with a belt, bought on sale, darned stockings. How skilled she was at "making do." Mabel Morrissey never owned a car or a house, worked a factory job until mandatory retirement at sixty-six, somehow managed to go to work through all but the very worst of her depressions.

She throws off the sheet, gets out of bed, and stands at the window looking down to the lake. The fog so thick she can't even see the dock. A glance at the clock: just seven. She hopes to God Billy and Nell aren't out in this.

She pads downstairs barefoot to find Jack sitting at the kitchen table, holding a cup of coffee, his prayer book open, staring out the window. She kisses him. He slips his hand under her nightgown, caresses her thigh. It's so rare to have a moment alone like this. She kisses him again.

The weather begins to lift as the wind kicks up from the north. Nell turns the boat slowly, scanning the water, forcing herself to take her time.

She has drifted farther than she would have thought possible, far beyond Tucker's dock, far beyond Wheeler's Point. She twists her head around, looking at each channel buoy, each piling her brother could be clinging to. Nothing.

She puts the oars in the oarlocks. It's going to be a long row home with that wind. She knows the news will be too much for her mother and father. She is the one they trusted. She is the one who was supposed to hold on to him. His shadow, his partner in crime and childhood. She is the one he chose.

Two hours later the sun burns through the fog, revealing a mocking blue sky, clear enough you can almost see tomorrow or, if your God is a cruel God, yesterday all over again, with everything you might have done differently.

The sheriff, Dale Pope, and two of the divers crowd into the kitchen. Sheila pours coffee. It's not a social call, Jack wants to holler at her, but holds his tongue.

"We can authorize the divers for one more day if the weather holds," Dale Pope offers.

"And that's it?" Jack asks.

"What about dragging the lake?" Marion asks.

"Can't be done," the sheriff says.

"Is it a question of money?" she presses, sounding angrier than she meant to.

"We can't do it. It's too deep."

"And if we can't find the body?" Jack asks.

"Let's cross that bridge when we come to it."

That first night, anybody who has a boat is out on the lake. No one organized it, as far as Jack knows, but when the divers and the police leave and darkness falls, one by one the boats appear. Neighbors, friends, people the Flynns know from living on the lake all their lives. Teachers and firemen and some of the chemists and apple men Jack works with from Cornell.

Most everyone figures out how to rig a light of some kind. There are heavy-duty flashlights, more like torches, the soft glow of kerosene lanterns, running lights on a few motorboats.

One kid loops strings of Christmas lights over the cabin of his dad's runabout.

Nell and Jack are in the old rowboat. She's wearing Billy's moss-green hunting jacket, the one Marion made him in high school, so soft from wear the sleeves are beginning to shred. Jack passes her his flask. She declines.

He watches her strength, rowing, and realizes what he's asked of her getting back into this boat. She's not crying, nothing as simple as that, nothing that might offer her a moment's release.

"Is there any chance we'll find him?" he asks.

She shakes her head.

He thinks, then, about when the kids were little and he and Marion would toss them out of the rowboat with life vests on to teach them to swim. How cavalier they were, how at home they were on this lake, in all its seasons.

There's a burst of laughter from a boat near Dobbin's Bay. And then another and another. Seems the harder people try not to, the more they laugh. It rises up in waves.

Nell rows to the center of the lake. People give them a wide berth, and in the dark, there's not much expectation of talk.

It's beautiful with all those boats. Beautiful in a way he'll never forget and may end up wishing he'd never seen. Funny the way Billy can pull all of them up into the light. Everything they're afraid of: death, drowning, all of it, so close. A layer of wood, a layer of cloth, a layer of skin, that's all that keeps them apart.

Nell looks out at the water. "It's not my fault," she whispers.

"Nell . . ."

"I didn't know."

"Honey . . ."

"I didn't help him."

"I know."

"I couldn't have stopped him even if I'd known what he was going to do."

A pause.

"There's no stopping Billy. You know that, Dad. You know that."

The boat rocks in the water. Jack is starting to feel the cold. He offers her the flask again and this time she takes it.

Marion is stuck at home with the other kids arriving one by one. Not that she wants to be out on the lake. Feigning exhaustion so she can just get away from everyone, their noise, their concern; their sympathy. The way they all look at her, prod and push. Just let me be, she wants to spit at them. Go home; just go home. You are crowding Billy right out of this house.

She goes up to the sleeping porch, to Billy's cot. That side of the cottage sticks out from under the white pines and you can see the sky. She lies down on the bed, the springs loud. The old Hudson Bay blanket, older than Marion, came with the cottage when they bought it, worn soft as a baby's blanket. She sinks into that bed the way Sheila is sinking into prayer downstairs, the way Jack and Nell are trying to sink into the night out on the lake.

Holding their breath, all of them, suspended between knowing and not knowing, as Billy is suspended between presumed dead and found dead. This must be one of the rings of hell, having a boy lost where she can see where he is, but not find him. Is every pain of motherhood a physical pain? Childbirth and letting them go and now this. Her ribs could burst.

Lying on the cot, looking at the black sky above the lake, the curtains of stars, she knows. He's left them, left the house, their lives, this world. The space where she expected to find him, some trace, a scent, is already empty, an emptiness that makes her shudder and climb under the blanket. The breeze that blows through the screens carries the lake on it, the last trace of her son.

The people who have no truck with boats, like Asa Alsop and Anna Barnes and Maeve and Evan Alsop, find their way down to the water. They come to stand on a neighbor's dock or the fish pier or along the shoreline at the state park. Harlow Murphy parks at the edge of the water, ignores the policeman who tells him to move along. Esme Tinker drives up from Ithaca, walks out on the town pier as far as she can go. People gather, drawn by the loss of one of their own; the haunting refrain of another kid gone missing. How many people think of Megan Alsop that night and wonder if she will ever be found. Recount their parents' and grandparents' stories of the lake and those who were lost to its depths. So cold, so cold, they say over and over, a body will never surface.

Sitting in the boat is turning into a kind of torture.

God, even the Fourth of July was never like this.

Nell breathes in. She's been afraid to breathe, afraid to exhale, afraid to let go.

And there it is. The softest breeze, so gentle; like a caress. She hears the boat rocking on the water, crickets, peepers, poplar leaves like coins.

Close your eyes and listen, Billy would tell her. You can distinguish the lake sounds from the marsh and the bay. The marina's easy, all that rigging making all that percussive sound. Listen for the willows in the marsh, the way sounds soften as the weather softens. Use your ears, Nell, pick them out, one by one.

Is Megan here, she wonders, drifting in the bottomless depths of Seneca Lake? She thinks of the "little water" the Seneca speak of, an ointment so precious and rare it's kept in a tiny hidden vial of obsidian or diamond. They believe that the little water can bring the dead back to life.

But first the dead, and the missing, will have to be found.

Nell ties up the boat and hurries up the path ahead of her father. She ducks around to the back of the house, pulls her bike out of the shed, and rides off. No lights. But there's no stopping her.

For Jack, every step gets heavier as he climbs the hill. He doesn't want to go inside, find and comfort Marion, answer questions for whoever else is there. He wants the dark quiet of the porch and solitude. Dragging up the hill with him is the word no one wants to say. If it was an accident, then Billy can be buried in consecrated ground, the prayers for the dead recited. If it was a suicide, he will be outside the church forever; outside the embrace of our Lord that is promised to every sinning one of us.

And if there is no body to bury, what then?

Marion sits in the dark, smoking a cigarette, a glass of Scotch in one hand. Jack climbs the porch steps, crosses the scuffed wooden floor, and sits beside her on the old glider. She exhales smoke, sets the glider in motion with one bare foot.

"I didn't expect to be so angry," she says.

She takes Jack's hand, brings it to her face.

"I'll be an old woman. Overnight. From tonight until tomorrow. I can feel it happening. It's like a blood transfusion, but instead of blood they are pumping old, old, old into me."

"You exaggerate."

"Nothing new there."

"Nell took off on her bike."

"She'll be back."

"She feels responsible."

"We all feel responsible."

He kneels down then, the hard wooden boards a shock under his knees. "You're praying," Marion says to the back of his head. Jack hears the ice clink as she takes another drink from the glass.

He wouldn't be surprised if she put a foot in the center of his back and kicked him over onto his face. Instead she gets up and leaves the porch, the glider swaying empty, Jack on his knees waiting for a miracle they all know will never come.

Anna Barnes stands on Geneva's crumbling stone pier looking at the boats on the lake, some far enough out they're no bigger than fireflies.

People will talk about this, talk about and remember it for years to come. It makes her sick to imagine Billy in that water, his family gathered and waiting.

When the boats start to scatter and head to shore, she climbs into her truck and drives home. Billy left her a package earlier in the week, told her not to open it until he gave her a sign. This, no doubt, is the sign.

She unwraps his field journal from 1962, opens to the first page, where he was mixing greens, then blues. Turns the page to a sketch of an American bittern, then a green heron, with its blue-capped head; the nest and eggs for each bird rendered to scale on the opposite page. Impossible to think that a fourteen-year-old boy created this.

Nell rides to Harlow's apartment. Drops her bike near the outside stairway leading up to his place, where it clangs against the garbage cans. She lifts her hand to knock, thinks she hears a woman's voice, and is about to leave when he opens the door. She tries to look around him.

"I thought I heard someone."

"Just me." He holds the door for her.

She is surprised at how neat it is. One large open room with a peaked roof, windows on all sides. Kitchen along the back wall, bathroom in an alcove, bed, couch, record player, bookshelves made of planks and cinder blocks.

"You want something to drink?"

"Just a glass of water."

"You riding your bike without a light?"

"I had to get out of there."

"Were you out on the lake?" he asks.

"Yeah. You?"

"I couldn't get in a boat tonight."

He hands her a glass of water. She drinks it down, knowing she should leave, not wanting to. She imagines him asleep in that bed. She wants to climb in under the blanket, lie against him, smell his skin, feel his chest rising and falling; take her time.

If he lets her into the shelter of his arms, she might never want to leave.

"Harlow," she says, and stops. Gathers her courage to ask: "What if Billy and Megan had waited?"

"Not like that was ever gonna happen."

"I swear he'd still be here if Megan . . . " She wipes her nose on her sleeve. "I'm tired of trying so hard. I thought with you I could just . . . stop."

She can hear him breathing, her own breath loud in her ears. She can hear the brush of his sleeve as he moves his arm, the rasp of his rough hands. Holding her breath now. She has waited so long.

She moves toward him. "I need . . . "

"Nell . . . "

She shivers, shy, blinded as she pulls her shirt over her head. For a moment she can't remember if her brother is alive. The word dead sinks into her, the impossible fact like a stone in her mouth. She remembers that strange kiss underwater before he left for Vietnam. Breath, she thinks, the breath of life, imposed or given or snatched away.

Harlow draws her to him. This kiss, when it comes, an invitation, a claiming, that jolt of desire, and knowledge. This is life, she thinks, living, her hands on his back pulling him against her, fierce now with need, with want, the wanting its own kind of nakedness.

His blunt hands are on her belly, back, breasts. She wraps her arms around him, legs shaking. She folds inside his arms, curls against the length of him. When he kisses her neck, she goes soft beneath his hands.

Eyes open, she pulls him down to her. She wants to see his face, his eyes, when he's touching her. Her nails dig into his arms and he is inside her. Body and blood, those words inside her, too; pain, then something else entirely radiating the length of her. Kissing him, moving with him. The shock and surrender of it.

She wishes they were outside, grass beneath them, sky above. This room is too small to hold all she is feeling, loss and yearning, living and dying, knowing and not knowing. Impossible to articulate or describe.

He holds her close, not talking, stroking her hair. She is drawn to that stillness in him. It's like communion: so ephemeral the rest of the world needs reminding every Sunday. Remembers drifting in Harlow's dinghy the night before he left for Basic. The town silent around them, streetlights blinking out along the shore, houses darkened beyond. Harlow let them float, playing out a hand line. She tucked herself into the bottom of the boat, his coat wrapped around her. She knew she was there on sufferance as Harlow and Billy passed a bottle back and forth over her head, but she felt unaccountably happy. And sad. For all they had and all they stood to lose. For a long time, an hour maybe, they didn't speak at all.

She closes her eyes now against sudden vertigo, against the black lake at their feet and all that it contains; *lift me up*, the prayer on her lips.

The search is called off after two days. Dale Pope comes to the house to inform them and has to endure Marion's sudden burst of fury. He stands in their living room like a small boy being scolded, apologizes again, and dares to lay a hand on her shoulder before he replaces his hat and lets himself out the door.

The authorities wait two more days for the body to surface. When it does not, the coroner rules the death accidental. With no body and no note, the ruling is a mercy, but does nothing to stop the wag of tongues in town.

They look everywhere for a note. All the obvious places, some less so. His desk, bedside table, beneath his pillow. Jack searches Billy's toolbox, combs every inch of the garage, taking the opportunity to throw out clutter and sweep the earthen floor.

Marion and Nell look through his clothes, empty each drawer. Finding nothing, they sit on the bed and fold every stitch, putting everything back, stacked and waiting.

In the middle of another sleepless night, Marion strips each bed on the sleeping porch, creates a storm of feathers as she removes every pillowcase. She pushes the beds this way and that, their iron legs scraping the soft pine. When no note falls to the floor, she upends the beds one by one so she can search their springs.

There are a dozen books on the floor under Billy's bed. Each one picked up in hope, discarded in anger. She pages through them.

Maybe he's slipped away, boarded a bus to Colorado. No, not Colorado, he'd need a lake or an ocean. San Francisco,

South Carolina, the coast of Maine. Maybe he just needs to get away for a while, get his bearings; get out from under his family and the weight of their worry.

She wouldn't put it past him to disappear for five or ten years, drift, heal, explore.

Maybe one day there will be a postcard in the mailbox.

Jack watches her from the doorway. When she senses his presence, she looks up at him, dry-eyed. She doesn't send him away, but goes back to turning pages. Even from the doorway, Jack can see the vibrant colors of Audubon's birds.

He crosses the sleeping porch, sits on the floor behind her. She shakes off his touch. He knows enough to wait, let the energy of her search wind down. Her unwarranted hope fuels her just as her anger fuels her. Neither can be sustained indefinitely.

When she finishes, he pulls her into his arms. They sit among their children's empty beds and wait for the dawn.

Brendan arrives on the dock as Harlow finishes loading the runabout: two canisters of gas, two old army blankets, rope, a torch, a thermos of coffee and a bag of sandwiches.

Harlow fires up the engine and heads south. Their plan: trace the perimeter of the lake, explore every inlet, outlet, and lay-by on the off chance the police missed something.

It's 5 o'clock in the morning; there's a faint blush of pink on the horizon. They huddle into their jackets as they make their slow way along the shore.

Shortly before noon, with the sun high and warm, they reach the marshy thickets south of Dresden and the Keuka Lake outlet. They're a mile or so south of where Nell reported she'd seen Billy last.

Harlow turns into the small cove and noses the boat carefully among the sunken branches and tall grasses. There are two new beaver dams. Twice he has to back out, turn, and take another approach. Nothing.

They leave the cove, a relief to be in clear water again. Harlow had felt all along that this might be where he would find Billy. His instinct for the strength of the current, his knowledge of where a body might get caught and held, has made him single out this cove and connector of one lake to another.

He guides the boat around another small promontory, past rocks and branches, winter's debris still evident. Here the trees come down tight to the shore. He cuts the motor and they sit in blessed silence. Brendan unpacks sandwiches, passes Harlow the thermos of coffee.

Harlow takes a sip, then starts the engine and turns back the way they came. Shouts to Brendan that he wants to take one more look.

Throttles down to enter the cove, past one beaver dam, and there, by the second dam, dark hair, looking so much like the shredded bark of the structure, the body facedown.

Neither Brendan nor Harlow is prepared for the shock of their discovery. Harlow steps into the water, slips on a submerged log, then finds his footing. It's deeper than he expected. He has to force himself to touch the body.

He tugs on a shoulder, the skin icy cold. One arm is caught beneath a branch. Harlow dives beneath the body to free it, the water brown and murky from the mud he's stirring up with his feet.

When he surfaces and turns the body over, Billy's eyes are open, the blue dulled, the light drained away. Harlow closes his own eyes when he puts his hand on Billy's face to close the lids.

It seems to take more strength than either man has to hoist Billy into the boat. They wrap him in a blanket, both noting, but not speaking about, the scars and burns running from his face to his fingers, so much more extensive than they had known.

Harlow thinks about the invisible circle Billy and Nell drew around them all their lives. Wonders how Nell will manage without that sanctuary. How it will mark her and change her. Like losing a twin.

They ride north to the Flynns' on the flat blue surface of the lake. Brendan scatters their sandwiches on the water for the birds and the fish.

Harlow guides the runabout alongside the dock, ties up. Flanagan, barking furiously, scrabbles to get into the boat. The dog's howls bring Nell down the hill as Harlow and Brendan lift the body from the boat. Flanagan noses the blanket aside; begins licking Billy's face, frantic. Her distress tears through the rest of them.

Brendan gathers Billy in his arms as one would lift a child and carries him up the hill.

In the kitchen, Marion sweeps everything off the long table. When Brendan lays Billy down, she pulls him into her arms, keening.

The sound drives them all from the room.

Nell sees her father and Brendan talking to Harlow before he leaves. The effortful composure, speaking in low voices, the veneer of calm, all cut to pieces by her mother's grief.

When Nell ventures inside, she finds Marion and Sheila with basins and clean cloths, working quietly, mirroring each other. She wants to run away, but forces herself to stay.

"Let me help," she says after several minutes, picking up a cloth, wringing it out.

So this is how we take care of the dead, she thinks. His cold limbs, heavy and wooden. Washing away the final vestiges of the lake, of his life on earth. To prepare him for the grave and beyond. If there is a beyond.

She looks to her mother hoping, perhaps, for some reassurance. Marion is unreachable, her head bowed. She pauses in her work, both palms flat on the burned flesh of her son's body.

Nell washes Billy's hands, wants to fold them. The slender, tapered fingers, uncommonly white after their time in the water, will not yield. She realizes they will never yield, never touch or be touched again.

Flanagan circles the table, settles, finally, near Billy's head.

Marion refuses to release Billy to the police. Dale Pope quietly argues the law, the necessity of the coroner's report. *If the coroner wants to examine him*, he can come here to do it.

She refuses an autopsy, refuses the Army's repeated offer to send an honor guard, refuses any and all government intervention: Leave us alone. You have no further claim on my son. Refuses the visit from the funeral parlor director, sample books in tow.

Nell knows that strings must have been pulled and guesses it was Father O'Rourke or Dale Pope himself who signed off on the legal documents.

The following morning, Jack, Brendan, and Harlow walk up the hill to the Alsops' farm, shovels and pickaxes over their shoulders. There's a level stretch of ground on a rise above the orchard, not far from Asa's bee yard, with wide views to the lake.

Asa joins them. The men dig in shifts: two on, two off. The topsoil is nearly two feet deep. Beneath that, the going gets tougher: a combination of clay loam, rocks, and sand.

Nell, furious to be left out, follows them up the hill, carrying a shovel of her own. The day is overcast and humid. When she crests the hill, Harlow and Brendan are waist-deep in the grave, their shirts discarded on the grass. Asa and Jack lean on their shovels, blowing hard. They are filthy, sweat drips through the dirt on their faces and necks, their undershirts stick to their backs.

Brendan clambers out and hands Harlow a pickaxe, a one-man job in that tight space. All of their activity has silenced the birds, though she can hear a low hum from the nearby hives between each swing of the axe.

She is struck, suddenly, by the fact that she is neither needed nor wanted. So full of her own conflicting desires, she hadn't thought to bring a jug of water, or a thermos of coffee or a pint of whiskey.

Nell walks down the hill to the farmhouse, finds mason jars in the kitchen, fills them at the tap, folds them into a kitchen towel so she can carry all four of them, and walks back up the hill, leaving her shovel behind.

The men take the jars, drink deep. They are exhausted. She stands looking into the grave. Harlow and Brendan don't bother to climb out even though she can see they've cut steps into the sod to make climbing in and out easier.

"How much longer?" she asks.

"Another two feet," Asa replies.

"How will you measure?"

"Harlow's our yardstick."

She walks up through the aspens to the white pines beyond. The low pine branches she cuts are fragrant, sticky with sap. She lashes them together and drags them back to the hollow where the men are almost finished.

Nell asks for help lining the grave. She does not, after all, want to climb into the open pit. Brendan stands in the bottom and places the boughs, overlapping them as instructed.

"Ample make this bed," Jack begins, and stops.

"Make this bed with awe . . . " he tries again but can't continue.

Brendan climbs out of the grave to stand beside his father.

"Be its mattress straight,

"Be its pillow round," Brendan says.

"Let no sunrise's yellow noise

"Interrupt this ground."

They gather their tools and their shirts; Nell collects the water jars. Harlow puts his arm around her, pulls her close. Together they walk down the hill through the orchard, the lake spread out below them a sullen gray.

When Jack and Marion leave their bedroom, he in his navy suit, she in a dark dress and shoes that pinch her feet, Jack has his hand on the small of her back. He waits while she puts on her hat and adjusts the veil.

Nell thinks, my God, they are smaller, and suddenly older. She sees her father draw himself up and square his shoulders, a soldier still. Marion leans into him briefly before Jack reaches out to take Nell's hand.

The Mass for the Dead at Saint Joseph's is a public ordeal, the crush of people before and after the service overwhelming. Then the family, with Father O'Rourke, Asa Alsop, and Harlow Murphy, drive to the Alsops' farm for a private burial.

Nell looks at the pale silver-green aspens, the white undersides of their leaves tipping up in the wind. How is it possible she will never hear her brother's voice again, or his laugh?

She had thought to sing but is unable to make a sound after the coffin is lowered into the ground. She sees her mother's knees buckle, sees Brendan and Jack move close to support her. Sheila runs her rosary beads through her fingers, praying silently. Rosie, holding the baby, leans against Nick. Connor and Collin hide behind her.

As the family heads toward home, Nell stays behind. The grave is covered with fresh pine boughs. She waits until she sees them cross the road and then, alone, sings for her brother.

At home, the church ladies have laid out the collation on folding tables borrowed from the vestry. Marion walks slowly up the stairs, her right hand gripping the banister. She goes up to change her clothes, but does not come down again.

Father O'Rourke carries a bottle of Jamesons out to the porch and sits down with Jack. Neither one seems to be getting much use from the bottle until Brendan joins them, tops off their glasses and his own. The whiskey is smooth and treacherous. Brendan pours again. They might make a dent in the bottle after all.

Esme Tinker stops by, and Anna Barnes shows up briefly. Asa Alsop, carrying his own loss, sits silently on the couch. Harlow joins the men on the porch.

Maeve and Evan Alsop come to the back door, knock quietly. Sheila welcomes them, pours Maeve a cup of tea, piles cookies on a plate for Evan. They sit on the couch next to Asa. Nell gets up to say hello. Maeve takes her hand.

"I'm so sorry, honey," she says, then, taking Asa's hand, "We're so sorry," her sudden emphasis a surprise to them all.

Rosie's boys are bored and restless. She finally lets them change into play clothes to go down to the lake, but makes them promise to stay out of the water. This is a promise they are unable to keep.

Jack follows his children up the stairs, so drained it's an effort to climb each step. He can hear Sheila and Rosie putting the sleeping porch to rights. The springs on each cot clang and vibrate as they're dragged into place, as they lift the mattresses from the floor and replace them on the bed frames.

Sheila unearths stacks of mismatched linens from the hall closet. Later they will launder the old sheets, and find several so worn they don't survive the washing machine intact.

Tonight, four Flynn children will sleep on the sleeping porch, or not sleep, as Jack Flynn cradles his wife in his arms in the room down the hall.

Collin begins to cry and climbs into bed with Rosie. Connor teases him until Rosie hushes them both. The baby is tucked into a cradle between Rosie and Nick. He will be known forever after as Matt because none of them can bear to call him Billy.

Nell chooses Billy's cot so she can see the sky, pushing the dog off the pillow. Sheila begins to pray. Is it the words or the repetition that is comforting, or the belief that someone is listening?

"Hail Mary, full of grace," floats on Sheila's voice.

"Shhh . . . Shhh . . . " Rosie says to Collin.

"Pray for us sinners . . .

"Now and at the hour of our death."

"Amen," they say together.

"Amen."

The house subsides into silence except for the rain falling steadily on the roof. The smell of the lake is strong on the sleeping porch, the air they breathe saturated with moisture. In the morning, their blankets will steam in the sun.

For now the house and its people settle beneath the heavy air, heavy enough to hold them to the earth, the rain washing their thoughts clear, allowing their minds to empty, the chorus of grief temporarily stilled.

Brendan is the first to leave after the funeral. His C.O. gives him one more day and then one more before hauling him back to Texas. Rosie and Nick return home to finish packing, their move to Rochester imminent.

Nell takes advantage of her parents' distraction and disappears with Harlow. Spends the night for the first time, though she is unable to sleep. She watches him as the moon rises, lighting his face. He wakes, curls around her, tells her the story of how the world was made, built upon a turtle's back. In the morning she cooks breakfast, learns to make coffee the way he likes it. They linger, late for work. Time suddenly means something. They grab all they can get.

Nell drifts through her days at the grocery, delays her fieldwork with Esme. Not quite ready to walk or work in the woods. Comes awake and alive each afternoon as she walks up Castle Street to the garage, a steak from the butcher bleeding into a paper bag, a few potatoes to bake in the fire.

She is afraid to need Harlow too much, to turn to him too often, to reveal the cracks and fissures that appear daily inside of her. But who else can understand what Billy's absence means, how it rewrites the past and puts her imagined future into question?

She keeps dreaming Billy alive, sees him sitting on the edge of his bed, packing a duffel, drawing, smoking, driving. Night after night she finds him in the water, they kick for the surface, laughter rising as their bodies rise; relief, release as they break the surface.

She wakes to the sun pouring carelessly down on the lake, now menacing and strange. They might as well be landlocked the way she turns her back on the water.

Maeve and Evan Alsop move back home to the farm. Maeve keeps her job and her car, lets the apartment go. Evan takes over Billy's chores and then joins his father in the orchards. Dash rarely leaves his side.

Nell gets time off from work to help Rosie and Nick with their move to Rochester. Leaves them with beds made, the boys' rooms unpacked, and the kitchen organized. She is grateful to have something else to think about, to do. Promises to return.

Jack and Nell drive Sheila to the bus station for her move to New York. In the car, the three of them are subdued; at the gate they're tongue-tied. Jack tries to tell a joke but can't finish.

He hugs Sheila fiercely, "If you change your mind . . . "

Nell cannot let Sheila go.

"Come see me," Sheila says, smiling. "Come work with me."

"Don't leave."

"We're meant to go," Sheila whispers in her ear. "And you, Nell, you'll fly furthest of all. You'll see. Billy always said: 'Nell's the one. Watch her.'"

Nell stands beside her father as Sheila boards the bus. They remain for several minutes as the station empties. Jack is waiting for the strength to return to his watery limbs so he can walk back to the car.

"Nell," he says, when he can speak. "I'm proud of Sheila. She's a brave girl. It took her years to stand up to Marion, to work up the courage to live her own life. That's what I want for all my children."

They watch Sheila's bus pull onto East Main.

"We're knocked off our feet right now. But don't you mix up that sadness with the ordinary sadness of saying goodbye."

The weather is hot and dry and still, day after day. The leaves grow dusty, the grass brittle, nights pass like a fever.

Rain threatens. Does not come. The air is heavy. It weighs

on Nell, humid, muggy, hard to breathe. Her chest hurts, her eyes, her head. Summer lightning teases; she feels it crack and boom inside her body.

She escapes to walk Turner's Ridge with Harlow, build forbidden fires; make love in the grass as dusk turns to dark.

She is embarrassed by how much she wants him until she sees how much it pleases him. Her awkwardness melts away. He is comfortable in his body, like no one she has ever known. He finds her beautiful, tells her so despite her protests. She revels in his irreverence; his ability to make her laugh and, for long minutes, forget.

They make plans almost daily to swim or take the boat out, but Nell cannot bring herself to get into the water.

Nell continues to look for a letter, a note, something Billy left behind. It's when she stops looking that she finds it, a folded piece of paper stuck into the inside pocket of his hunting jacket. The one piece of clothing he knew she would wear and wear again. This is where he always kept a small sketchbook.

And deeper in the pocket, his dog tags. She reads his name: William Edward Flynn, and slips the chain over her head, dropping the tags inside her shirt, the metal cold against her skin.

Now that she has his note in her hand, she hesitates, not sure she wants to read it. She unfolds the piece of paper. It's an old drawing, a study for the great blue heron. And on the back, scratched in faint pencil:

Nell.

Forgive me.

The title floats up inside her: *Some Call It Flying.*

The smell of Billy's jacket brings Flanagan to her side.

Together they walk down to the dock. Nell lies on the rough wood planks, the dog stretched out next to her.

The reckless scent of roses comes to her on the wind. She has the sense that Billy is somewhere in that freewheeling sky. She waits for the sky to open up and take her, or the lake to rise up and swallow her.

She tries to imagine stripping off her clothes and putting her body, her face inside this water ever again.

What else will the lake take in her life?

Billy.

His name echoes inside her.

She closes her eyes and catalogues what she hears: water over stones, the creaking wallow of the rowboat. A cardinal, now two. Finch, eastern phoebe, common yellowthroat. The poplar leaves are the most distinct to her ear, but she can sort out the great pines and the swaying hemlocks, too.

All that Billy taught her to see and hear washes over her. She waits to feel the release of his death; wonders if she will ever be able to let him go.

Flanagan lifts her head as an egret rises from the marsh. Nell turns to see its white breast faintly glowing in the raking afternoon light. The slow beat of its wings is barely audible, the sound of air moving over feathers so faint, hearing it feels like knowing one of God's secrets.

Nell falls asleep on the dock and wakes as the sun disappears behind the low hills opposite. Flanagan is still beside her, ears pricked as bats begin to flicker in and out of the beech tree.

She sits up when she hears Harlow's boat crossing the lake, the motor throttled down, a low growl. Hesitates, then strips off her clothes; slips into the water. It closes over her head then buoys her. The water, the water, she thinks, the beautiful, the treacherous water.

Stroke by stroke she finds her rhythm: prayer, blessing, benediction.

Billy.

Harlow flashes his light once, twice, his pale shirt glowing in the dusk.

When she reaches him, soon, soon, he will lean out, take her hands, and lift her up into the boat, out of the silver-skinned water, into the falling light.

ACKNOWLEDGMENTS

For being my first, last and best reader, always, thanks to David Rosen.

For their wisdom, patience and superb guidance, I'm indebted to Stephanie Cabot and Ellen Goodson Coughtrey.

For editorial insights and support, or the right idea at the right time, thanks to Charlotte Gordon, Lynne Hugo, Liza Rutherford, Kate Harrington-Rosen, Bill Britton, Liza Wiemer and Lynn Barclay.

For generously sharing their experience and expertise, thanks to Bob Vinson, Bill Britton, Matt Adrian, Rob Morrow, Nadia Rosenthal and Roseann Vidal.

For their patient attention to getting the book made, thanks to Emanuele Ragnisco and Eleanor Nussbaum.

My work could not have a finer editor than Kent Carroll.

The following works of nonfiction were invaluable while researching this book:

Silent Spring, Rachel Carson; *On a Farther Shore: The Life and Legacy of Rachel Carson*, William Souder; *Dispatches*, Michael Herr; *Shrapnel in the Heart: Letters and Remembrances from the Vietnam Veterans Memorial*, Laura Palmer; *Apologies to the Iroquois*, Edmund Wilson; *Wolves & Honey: A Hidden History of the Natural World*, Susan Brind Morrow; *What It Is Like to Go to War*, Karl Marlantes; *America's Other Audubon*, Joy M. Kiser; *The Singing Life of Birds*, Donald Kroodsma; *I Have Heard My Praises Sung in Screams*, Matt Adrian.

Laura Harrington has written dozens of plays, musicals, and operas, which have been produced in venues ranging from Off-Broadway to the Houston Grand Opera. Harrington has twice won both the Massachusetts Cultural Council Award in playwriting and the Clauder Competition for best new play in New England. Laura teaches playwriting at MIT where she was awarded the 2009 Levitan Prize. *Alice Bliss*, her first novel, won the 2012 Massachusetts Book Award in Fiction.